Steel Breeze

By
Douglas Wynne

JournalStone
San Francisco

JOURNALSTONE
YOUR LINK TO ARTISTIC TALENT

JournalStone books may be ordered through booksellers or by contacting:

JournalStone
www.journalstone.com
www.journal-store.com

ISBN: 978-1-936564-84-2   (sc)
ISBN: 978-1-936564-94-1   (ebook)

Library of Congress Control Number: 2013936498

Printed in the United States of America
JournalStone rev. date: July 19, 2013

Cover Design and Artwork   Jeff Miller

Edited By: Dr. Michael R. Collings

Endorsements

"Douglas Wynne's *Steel Breeze* is my kind of thriller, fast-paced, peppered with some well-handled guts and gore, and told by characters buried under crushing layers of paranoia and pain and fear. Douglas Wynne develops this terrifying and violent crime novel with the sure hand of a seasoned craftsman." –**Joe McKinney**, Bram Stoker Award-winning author of *Flesh Eaters* and *The Savage Dead*

"Steel Breeze is intense at almost every moment. It's unpredictable and well written and defies you to put the book down. I cannot recall a thriller in a long time that had me so captivated. Douglas Wynne is the real deal and I'm certain we will be enjoying his books for a long time to come." –**Benjamin Kane Ethridge,** *Bram Stoker Award Winning Author* of BLACK & ORANGE and BOTTLED ABYSS

For River

When you wield a sword, if you are conscious of wielding a sword, your offense will be unstable. When you are writing, if you are conscious of writing, your pen will be unsteady.

—Yagyū Munenori
The Book of Family Traditions on the Art of War

It is crucial to think of everything as an opportunity to kill.

—Miyamoto Musashi *The Book of Five Rings*

Best,

Douglas Wynne

Chapter 1

There were at least three good playgrounds within a short drive of the Ocean Road apartment, but on the day Desmond Carmichael lost his son for a terrifying ten minutes, he had chosen one farther away, the one they called the Castle Playground. It wasn't Lucas's favorite, but the days when the boy would argue for a favorite anything were behind them by then. Desmond figured that when a child loses his mother at the age of three, pretty much every other preference takes a back seat. He knew that *he* wasn't Lucas's favorite either.

Desmond parked the car in the jam-packed lot and at the last minute remembered to rub sunscreen into Lucas's cheeks and arms before popping the latch on the car-seat harness. It was best to get the lotion on while Lucas was restrained because once the straps were loose, he'd be off like a greyhound out of the gate, racing past the wooden castle toward the sandbox or the climbing tree. *Click.* And there he went, sliding down the seat and out of the SUV, then vanishing into the crosscurrents of running children while Desmond rubbed the excess lotion into his forearms.

It was a Thursday in July—one of the first really nice days of summer after all of the rain they'd had in June—and the good weather had drawn a bigger crowd than usual. He capped the sunblock, slung his laptop bag over his shoulder, and plucked Lucas's sweatshirt from the canvas bag where he also kept the wet wipes and snacks, just like Sandy used to. The sweatshirt had been an afterthought. Even though the park was inland and sheltered from the sea breeze, he knew from experience that if one of those majestic white clouds trailing tendrils of gray way up high in the blue drifted across the sun, the temperature was likely to drop ten degrees in an instant.

The Castle Playground was almost always bustling at mid-day, but Desmond didn't choose it for the children or the mothers; he chose it for the sandbox where he could count on Lucas staying put for a little while, and for the bench in the shade beside it where he could work from his laptop. It was the only playground they frequented where he felt comfortable focusing on work while Lucas played. There were so many extra eyes on the kids and even a wooden fence to keep them from straying out of bounds.

He knew that some of the other parents judged him for working when he should be watching his son—he'd caught the dirty looks. Let them judge. They didn't know what he was up against. At least he wasn't taking the kid to a bar. Sometimes he didn't know which was worse—the dirty looks or the whispers of the ones who pitied him. *Don't you know his wife was murdered? It was all over TV. Cut him some slack.* Whenever he heard one of these rare defenders, he tried to remind himself that it was some kind of credit to the town that not everyone thought he did it.

On a good day, a day without whispers, he could get some writing done while Lucas played. He had calculated the risk of divided attention and had decided it was minor. That was what he thought until the day of the ten minutes of terror, the day when the man in the indigo hoodie took Lucas on a nature walk.

Scanning the mayhem, Desmond saw that Lucas had reappeared at the front of the car, a serious look on his face. "My dump!" he said. "Daddy, get my dump."

"How do you ask for things?"

"*Please* get my dump."

"Okay, buddy."

Desmond reached over the back seat and retrieved the toy dump truck. He squatted to Lucas's height and set it down on the gravel. As Lucas bent to pick the toy up, Desmond brushed his son's longish brown hair aside and planted a kiss on his forehead before Lucas could spin and take off again. His knees crackled as he came up off of his haunches. He shielded his eyes from the sun with a saluting hand and followed the boy into the noisy scrum.

The cheerful cries and delighted shrieks, brazen shouts and dramatic sobs all clashed and rebounded in the warm air above the wooden castle like the raucous chatter of tropical birds in a rain forest. Such familiar sounds to a father. And that was the other thing that excused the laptop he now hugged under his elbow as he clicked the key fob and trotted toward the sandbox: even with eyes averted, a parent could hear the difference between these sounds and some vocalization truly worthy of alarm. Like the crying fit emanating from the eastern quadrant, over by the swings. It wasn't his own child, but Desmond knew the pedigree of that particular cry and that it wasn't the sound of authentic pain. He shot a glance in that direction and saw a mother in big sunglasses and white Capris holding a sobbing, squirming toddler to her breast while bouncing gently on her heels and offering a spurned sippy cup with her free hand.

Desmond sat down on the bench, took quick inventory of the toys that littered the tiny dunes in the sandbox, and did a rough calculation of the territorial politics currently in play. The box was crowded with three boys, besides Lucas, and a girl. Lucas was clinging to his dump truck for fear that someone else would touch it, the girl was piling scoop upon scoop of sand atop her own buried foot, and the oldest of the boys was flinging sand in the air with a plastic shovel. Desmond looked around to see if he could figure out which parents belonged to these kids, but to no avail. He thought of telling the boy with the shovel to stop throwing sand, but it wasn't being thrown *at* anyone for now, so he let it go and flipped his laptop open.

The Word file **Orpheus** was still open from the morning's predawn composition session. He reread the day's pages, fixing a few typos as he went but resisting the urge to rewrite. With the scene fresh in his mind, he closed his eyes for a moment and watched events move forward, then opened them and began to type. He'd only written a sentence and a half when he heard Lucas's voice rising above the din with the closest approximation a toddler could muster to a steely edge: "We have to *share*."

Desmond looked up and saw that Lucas was issuing this ethical commandment to one of the younger boys while dragging his dump truck away from the kid. Scanning the screen, he said, "Lucas, sharing means letting other kids play with your stuff too sometimes." He watched Lucas grudgingly release the toy. Desmond sighed and tried to bring the story back into focus. The playground was better for Lucas than being in front of the TV, but it was a compromise for Desmond. Here, the noise could really fuck with his mental Wi-Fi link to the land of Make-believe.

He heard the shouts of children, the murmur of mothers, the drone of passing cars and planes, and the crackle of the flag beside the baseball field. He tried to dial down the environmental noise and increase the brightness and contrast of the image in his mind's eye, but with eyes closed all of the other senses competed to fill the void. Now there was a scent to distract him—a strange perfume on the wind, smoky and sweet, like incense, and strangely familiar.

He opened his eyes and looked around for the source.

Maybe it *was* incense drifting from the open window of a nearby house. But why was this particular scent familiar? He'd never used the stuff, never gotten into yoga like some of his friends, and Sandy had been more of a Lemon Pledge kind of girl. Desmond's gaze lighted on an old Asian man sitting on the bench opposite, smoking a cigarette, and his breath froze in his chest.

The man looked like a statue, like one of those sculptures of a park bench complete with a bronze man reading a bronze newspaper. Desmond had seen something like that in a city one time. Had it been New York or Boston? The man was sitting perfectly still. Desmond's eyes fixed on the cigarette tucked between the man's fingers where they lightly touched the bench seat. A curling wave of smoke wafted up from those fingers for about nine luxurious, milky white inches before it was torn asunder on the breeze. The smoke and, he now noticed, the man's eyes were all that moved. Everything else about him was somehow still, but not rigid. Not like a bronze statue at all, he realized as he tuned in to the odd figure. There was a deep sense of relaxation about the man. It was an odd thought to have about a person, but when Desmond tried to articulate to himself what he was observing, his first unrefined shot at description was that the man looked as relaxed as a willow tree. Just perfectly balanced in the way that a thing rooted to the same spot for centuries would be. Unmovable, yet flexible, with limbs hanging down in perfect relaxation.

Desmond caught himself drifting into a reverie and snapped out of it. He wasn't getting any work done by musing on the old man. And he *was* old. Ancient wasn't far off. The man was dressed in khakis and a black polo shirt. His muscles were atrophying, and he had a bit of a paunch, but it was obvious that he had been strong in his youth. His hair, cut to a single length just short of his collar, was swept back, streaked gray, and possibly oiled. Desmond wasn't great at differentiating the features of Asian people. The man could have been Nepalese or Vietnamese. But no, he thought, those eyes must be Japanese, and a deep coldness coursed through his nerves when the man gazed at him and their eyes locked.

The man on the bench raised the cigarette to his mouth, the hand drifting up like a helium balloon. He took a drag, all the while watching Desmond, his expression unchanging. Then he turned his head toward the baseball field and exhaled a plume of smoke, and Desmond suddenly knew why the scent was familiar. It was a clove cigarette. He had once dated a girl who smoked them, and ever since they reminded him of warm summer nights in Boston. Before Sandy, before responsibility, before tragedy. He'd never liked to smoke them himself, had tried one and found it too pungent to take directly into his lungs, but on her lips the flavor had been sweet and exotic.

Long ago that had been. You seldom saw anyone smoking in public anymore. Even more rarely at a children's playground. Desmond scanned the grounds again, this time looking for an Asian child. The man had to be a grandfather.

There were too many kids in motion to make out their features at a glance, and no doubt many more who were presently obscured by the wooden castle walls and the plastic tunnel slides. If you were tracking your own kid's progress through the structure, it was never more than a few feet before a gap between the planks or a diamond-shaped window into the labyrinthine crawl spaces gave you a view of the interior, but to see all of the children at a glance? Impossible. After casting his gaze over the wider area, he settled it back on the sandbox.

Lucas was gone.

Desmond stood up and snapped the laptop shut. He had just taken stock of the entire playground and hadn't seen Lucas, but now he did it again, looking for brown pants and a green sweatshirt. The dump truck was lying on its side, a full load of sand trailing out of its bucket, the other boys ignoring it now that it was no longer the coveted possession of the boy who was no longer there, the boy who was gone.

Gone.

Desmond could have quizzed the kids, but he knew immediately that it wouldn't be worth the time it would take. All they would know was that Lucas went "that way" or something. And the direction would already be irrelevant in a sprawling layout like this one in which streams of running children crisscrossed like ocean currents, knocking small vessels off course or sweeping them along. There was no way of knowing what distraction had drawn Lucas away from the sandbox in the first place or what other diversions might have attracted him since. The best bet was to go for maximum coverage.

Desmond ducked under a wooden arch and trotted up a ramp to the castle's upper level. He had seen other dads occasionally climbing as acrobatically as their children—sliding down the fire pole, or jumping from low risers, finding footing in the gaps between planks. Younger men, thinner, too. This was his first time on top of the structure, and he felt like an oaf, but he discovered that the upper passageways were wide enough for him to get around on. He had to put his hands out once or twice to keep running kids from crashing into his legs, but most of them registered the desperation on his face and gave him a wide berth as he made his way to the highest point he could reasonably reach.

With a bird's eye view of the park, he rotated, shading his eyes with his hand, searching for Lucas.

He didn't call out, not yet. He looked at his watch and realized that he couldn't recall when he had last checked it, but it couldn't have been more than three or four minutes since he had last seen his son. How far could he have gotten? *But he's fast. Short legs but so very fast when something gets his attention.*

Desmond shuffled across a narrow bridge to another tier of the structure and peered through parapets at the woods. A few boys and girls with a young woman chaperone were gathering acorns and pinecones by the tree line, probably part of a school trip. He turned to face the opposite direction, where the parking lot lay, and found his blue SUV. Lucas wasn't near it. Where the hell was he then? Had to be down below in the passageways, obscured by the planking.

Backtracking to the ramp would eat up valuable time, so he grabbed hold of the fire pole and jumped to the ground. He was starting to pant as he circled the castle, sweat prickling under his arms, his spine hunched as he peered through the cracks. Calling Lucas's name from up top would have been an announcement to all of the other parents that, yes, he, the guy with the laptop, had lost his son, but down here on the ground with the kids, he started doing just that. The sound of his own scared, shaky voice made him more afraid than he already was.

There was no reply.

He knelt on the damp woodchips and poked his head into one of the openings the kids used to enter the castle. The white soles of a girl's sneakers blocked his view, and he heard giggling. He yelled into the tunnel, "Lucas!" The girl startled, then scampered around to face him. Was she Asian? Maybe. Whatever.

"Is there a little boy in there wearing a green sweatshirt?"

She shook her head.

Desmond backed out, stood up, and broke into a jog around the perimeter, dodging children, parents, and trees. He called his son's name in increasingly harried tones and felt the fear rising toward the pitch at which something fundamental would change.

It was rapidly turning into the kind of mounting dread that he knew should be reserved for nightmares.

A woman wearing a faded Red Sox baseball cap and carrying a rake in her hand appeared around a corner and stopped in her tracks when she saw him. He felt sweat running from his hairline to the corner of his left eye and rubbed it away. Residual sunscreen stung his eye from fingertips that had touched his son's face less than twenty minutes ago.

"Did you lose a kid?"

Desmond nodded and drew a ragged breath. He held the palm of his hand parallel to the ground at waist height, Lucas's height. He said, "Boy. Green sweatshirt, brown pants, brown hair." He felt the bulk of the laptop bag against his hip and wished he could have ditched it somewhere, but the work it held was irreplaceable.

The woman looked at the bag, looked at his eyes. Her features softened as she read the panic in them. "Jeez, that's practically camouflage in a place like this," she said, nodding at the stand of pine trees that sheltered the playground, and the increasingly dense woods beyond, which led by neglected trails to the reservoir. The trails on this side of the water were probably only used by the rare hiker who knew how they all connected and by teenagers who wanted privacy for petty indiscretions. Looking at the gray tangle of deadfall, he felt his heart sink. Would Lucas go in there without him? It wouldn't have been easy for him to reach the woods from the sandbox without walking all the way around the three-foot-high wooden corral fence to where it ended at the baseball field on the right and the woods on the left. But, Desmond remembered, he *had* picked Lucas up and set him down on the other side of that little fence on more than one occasion when the boy had needed to pee, and had accompanied him to the privacy of the litter-strewn trailhead. What if Lucas had felt the need and had gone to the same place on his own without announcing it?

Desmond trotted to the edge of the woods, scanning them for the half-concealed trail. It was back in the direction of the sandbox, but for a child who had to walk all the way around the fence rather than going over it, there were other paths he would come to first. And they might all look the same to him.

"Lucas!" he called.

No reply came from the woods. He walked up the first trail he came to, listening to the wind in the trees, the noise of the playground fading with every step. His stomach revolted against the idea that he was moving away from the playground, away from the zone in which he and Lucas had last been together.

The paths here at the edge of the woods were chaotic and neglected, blocked by fallen trees and choked with brambles. Heavy rain in the preceding weeks had left the ground swollen, spongy, and muddy. In places, the water had pooled into miniature ponds the length of a man, impossible to cross without boots or a willingness to get soaked. Desmond knew that these would have stopped Lucas from going forward in several places, and he was able to rule out certain paths. He saw no children's sneaker prints, but the grass was so thick and the mud so wet that he couldn't be sure the ground would have held an impression. The water was too shallow for drowning, he thought. Or at least, too shallow to conceal a body. He'd heard that a child could drown in mere inches of water. He couldn't believe he was having to consider such things and tried to remind himself that he was wired with an active imagination, a predisposition for chasing remote possibilities to vivid and devastating, yet unlikely conclusions.

As he neared the place where he had taken Lucas before, he came to a wooden plank that had been dragged across the path to make a bridge over one of the larger puddles. The wood was mud stained with child-sized sneaker treads. He couldn't be sure, but they could have been Lucas's. He ran across the board and searched the ground on the far side for more prints but found none.

His mind reeling, he turned, and *there*: a patch of dark blue about thirty feet up the trail, not the color of sky but a shade of fabric. Walking toward it, he could make out voices, low and conversational, one higher in pitch—*Lucas's* voice.

"Lucas!" he shouted and broke into a run.

As he approached the clearing, the blue swatch turned out to be a hoodie sweatshirt, actually more a shade of indigo, over black jeans, hood up. The person wearing it was shorter than Desmond, maybe five foot six or thereabout, back turned to him. The figure's hands were tucked into the pockets of the hoodie—a non-threatening pose, and yet something about the posture was iron straight, rooted to the ground and coiled to spring.

Lucas stood beside the stranger, their bodies not touching, looking at something on the ground. At the sound of his name, he turned toward Desmond, and his face lit up with a smile. "Daddy!" he cried. "Look, Daddy, a duckie!"

Desmond followed his son's pointing finger to a black puddle and saw a mallard bobbing on the glassy water. When he looked at Lucas again, the figure in the hoodie was gone.

How the hell was that even possible? The guy had been *right there* a second ago. Desmond swept Lucas up in his arms and held him tight to his heaving chest, spinning slowly on his heels and searching the woods. *There*—a flash of indigo between the trees, deeper in the forest, already twenty yards distant. With as much alpha dog as he could inject into his voice, Desmond hollered, "Hey! Wait! Come back here." But the figure only ran faster and vanished behind the branches.

Desmond set Lucas on the ground, squatted to his level, and examined him. Aside from the shy, concerned look that Desmond recognized as the face Lucas wore when trying to read if he was angry, he saw no signs of harm or distress. "Are you okay?" Desmond asked.

Lucas bobbed his head. "Did you see the duckie?"

"Yeah, buddy. But who was that man, and why did you go with him?"

Lucas shrugged.

"Did he tell you his name?"

"No, Daddy."

"Lucas, why did you go with someone you don't know?"

"I went to get acorns for my dump, and he asked me if I wanted to see a duckie."

"Listen to me. That's not okay. You can't just leave the playground and go with someone you don't know. Remember?"

"But you said it's okay to talk to grownups at the playground. Right, Daddy? You said it's okay."

It was true that every time some friendly mother tried to strike up a conversation with Lucas in a place like this, every time Lucas was being shy and silent, Desmond told him that it was okay to say hello, to answer a question about his name or age. And fuck if it didn't defy logic to tell a kid that it was okay to talk to strangers sometimes, but not others.

"That's only if I'm with you. No talking to strangers when I'm not with you, and definitely no following them. Understand?"

Lucas turned his eyes down toward the mud at his feet.

"Do you understand?"

Lucas nodded. When he looked up, he found his delight again, and brightening, he said, "Do you see the duckie?"

"Yeah, buddy, I see it. Come on. Let's go home."

They were approaching the parking lot hand in hand, passing the bench where the old Asian man still sat alone, passing the deserted sandbox, when Lucas broke free of Desmond's grasp and veered off to the side. Desmond turned to yell that they were going home now, that they were finished playing and he was losing his patience, when he saw what had caused the diversion. "Don't forget dump, Daddy!" Lucas yelled, and Desmond could practically see the exclamation point in the air. For a four-year-old boy, if a thing is worth saying, it's worth exclaiming, and if a place is worth going to, it's worth running to.

Lucas climbed over the sandbox wall, picked up the plastic truck, and threw it out of the box, freeing his hands for the climb back out. When the truck hit the ground, it rolled and something fell out of the dumper bucket. Desmond let out a short yelp at the sight—a naked Barbie doll, scratched and dirty from long neglect… headless.

Desmond felt his muscles go limp. He dropped his laptop bag to the ground beside the plastic abomination. He spun around looking for the indigo hoodie, but there was no sign of Lucas's trail guide unless he had ditched the sweatshirt. Black jeans on a fit young man? Couldn't find that either. Lucas picked up the truck, but ignored the broken doll. He looked up at his father with concern.

"Let's go," Desmond said. "Let's get out of here." He picked up the laptop and got a good look at the doll. For a second he considered taking it with him. It could be evidence. But evidence of what? There had been no crime committed here, and the doll didn't look as if it had been purchased and damaged for the express purpose of fucking with him. Parents donated old toys to the sandbox all the time, and kids surely lost things here as well. The doll looked dirty enough, old enough, to have been buried under the sand for at least a year, unearthed today by chance.

He resisted the urge to reach out and pick the thing up, and he tried to tell himself that this was rationality winning out, that he was avoiding the doll for Lucas's benefit, to sidestep the questions that his interest in it would raise. But he knew the real reason he didn't pick it up was the sickening fear that it triggered in the bottom of his belly.

Chapter 2

It was the dishes that haunted him in the months following Sandy's death. Dirty dishes. What a stupid thing to be arguing about before going to bed in cold silence. What a small thing to get defensive about. He should have just owned it and said okay. But no, he'd had to go and get all self-righteous about how he couldn't believe she was giving him shit for leaving dirty dishes in his study when the only reason he was eating in there in the first place was to grade papers while *she* was watching TV, even though he was the one who still had to read bedtime stories to Lucas at the end of a long day and couldn't she just do the damned dishes herself? It was a shitty final exchange to have had with the woman he loved just hours before finding her decapitated in the back yard.

The day after the scare at the playground Desmond woke before Lucas and, plodding groggy-eyed into the living room, caught sight of the little plate of crumbs left over from Lucas's grilled cheese dinner. How had he missed that? Well, he *had* been a bit distracted while they'd watched the *Dumbo* DVD for the umpteenth time. Lucas had a thing for his mother's Disney collection, and a few favorite titles were kept in steady rotation. *Dumbo* was the current favorite, even though Lucas always wanted to skip the thunderstorm scene because it scared him.

"Stay with me, Daddy. Watch this with me," Lucas would implore, and Desmond would focus his eyes on the big-eared elephant while letting his mind play with the novel in progress—a notepad tucked into the couch cushion. But last night his mind hadn't been on the book, it had been on the man in the indigo hoodie and the headless Barbie.

He heard the coffee maker go into its gurgle-and-sputter stage and decided not to wait for it to beep. He pulled the pot out and poured his first cup while the machine dripped all over itself. Time to get some work done before Lucas woke up. Time to shift his mind to that other world, that imaginary world where his wife had a different name and could still be saved from the monster.

He had lost his teaching job a few months after Sandy's death for experimenting with the efficacy of alcohol as a pain-numbing, memory-erasing agent. He knew now that the firing had pained Principal Rosenbaum. The man had barely been able to do it, but Desmond had given him no other choice. The kids came first. Now, almost a year later, the drinking was behind him. But he hadn't done the program, and maybe that was a little dangerous. He hadn't found God instead of the program, either. In fact, that was his whole problem with the program: you had to surrender to a higher power. And Desmond still spent many a sleepless night ruminating on just what kind of power a higher power might have if He didn't use it to prevent a loving mother from getting cut down by a crazy man.

The drinking had stopped because of Lucas. Desmond couldn't bear the thought of losing him to Sandy's parents. Phil and Karen Parsons had made no secret of the fact that they thought Desmond was a sorry piece of shit for getting himself fired with a young child to raise. And he didn't disagree with them on that score; he just wasn't going to lose Lucas over it. So he'd cleaned up his act and started writing again, and the book, when it emerged, did the rest. It took care of him better than the booze ever could. He knew he would have to find work again soon—royalties from his last book were down to a trickle now, and the advance for the current one would only carry them so far—but for now, writing was keeping him sane, and keeping them both fed.

Without a second income, they'd had to move to an apartment near the beach, and that wasn't so nice, but it wasn't exactly squalid either. Desmond knew he couldn't have lived in the old house anymore anyway. Too many memories. The apartment felt a little bit like a vacation, and the book felt even more like one, but he knew damned well that he wasn't on vacation from supporting

Lucas, and that meant making the word quota every morning. Two-thousand words per day allayed his fears of failing as a provider.

On the morning after the playground incident he didn't get any words down. He sat at his desk and flipped open his laptop with the **Orpheus** file still running. Words were waiting for him on the page, but they were not his own. Three lines of unfamiliar text blazed up at him, separated by a line break from the unfinished sentence he'd started writing at the playground.

Floating on dark water
The solitary drake dives
And seizes the worm

Desmond stared at the words. Whatever meaning they held eluded him. But the *meaning* of the little poem didn't matter, not yet anyway. What mattered was that it could be there at all, on his screen, in his home. And when the force of *that* meaning struck him, he stood up abruptly, knocking his chair over behind him and staggering back from the laptop as if he had opened it to discover a giant spider on the keyboard.

He looked around the room. The apartment was a split-level and his desk was in a corner of the living room on the ground floor. There were two windows, both facing the sand-drifted street in front of the building. He went to the windows and checked the latches. Both were still locked from the inside. The front door was also still locked, the chain still fastened.

He walked fast and light-footed to the kitchenette. There was a small window over the sink—too small for entry—and a couple of steps that led down to a little laundry alcove through which the back alley was accessible via the only other door to the outside.

It was unlocked.

Desmond ran up the stairs to Lucas's bedroom.

Lucas was tangled in the blankets, still sleeping. Desmond stood in the doorway catching his breath, waiting for his heart to slow down. He rested his elbow against the doorframe and whimpered into his forearm. Stepping lightly again, as if he hadn't just made all the noise of a wild boar crashing through the brush, he moved to the closet door where a poster announcing A DAY WITH THOMAS THE TRAIN covered a door that had been coated with white paint so many times that it could no longer be fully closed. He took a deep breath and threw the door open with a long step backward, half expecting a blade to arc out at him from the darkness, but the closet held only Lucas's clothes and puzzles.

Lucas stirred in the bed. He looked like a different boy when he was sleeping, his face somehow older. Desmond thought about the backdoor downstairs in the laundry alcove. Had he left it unlocked last night? He didn't think so, but could he rule that out with one-hundred-percent certainty? Yes, he thought he could. The locks on this place were kind of a joke, but he knew he used them vigilantly. He might have been a bit of a space case about that sort of thing before Sandy's death, wandering around half in a creative trance while taking out the trash at the old house, forgetting to lock a door, but not anymore. Not after the murder. *Right, Des?*

He went back downstairs to the laundry room and opened the door to the alley. The frame showed no signs of tampering, and it dawned on him that he shouldn't be touching the knob, that it should be dusted for fingerprints. There didn't appear to be any damage to the keyhole either, but he'd never examined it up close before, so he couldn't say if all of the scratches around the slot had been there already.

Fingerprinting. If he called Fournier about this they would probably want to check his laptop for prints too. And that would mean letting them look at the file. Desmond didn't care for that idea at all. He needed to think this through before he made any calls.

Desmond returned to his desk and glared at the text on the screen, stroking his beard. He had hovered over the machine from this standing position untold times over the years, pondering plot problems. Well, here was a good one. The lid on the computer hadn't been opened since yesterday on the park bench when he'd noticed that Lucas was missing. The unfinished sentence above the haiku was the one he'd been working on then. It *was* a haiku, wasn't it? He counted the syllables—eighteen. As a high school teacher, he had taught his students the seventeen-syllable (five-seven-five) form, but he also knew that that was just an English convention for a Japanese technique that didn't exactly correlate. Still, this was a haiku. Someone had invaded his personal computer, possibly even his home, and had left him a message somehow related to Sandy's murder.

He thought back to the playground. He'd kept the laptop with him the entire time. There had been no opportunity for someone to type the lines there. And after the playground, when Lucas was hungry and they stopped for pizza, the computer had been locked in the car the entire time. Upon returning home, he had set it down on the desk.

He read the poem again, and this time, knowing that Lucas was safe in his bed upstairs, he could focus on the words. He was pretty sure he knew what was being described, at least on the surface level, and he felt a deep unease crawling into his gut. Not wanting to touch the keyboard, he went to the coat rack by the front door and dug his smartphone out of his jacket pocket. He pulled up Google and typed: drake.

There were four meanings: The Elizabethan explorer, Francis Drake; some singer he was unfamiliar with; the term for a male duck; and a more obscure use—a name sometimes used to refer to a dragon. He vaguely recalled some reference Tolkien had made to "the fire drake."

A duck. A solitary duck, just like the one they had seen yesterday.

A dragon, like you might find decorating a kimono, or a samurai sword.

Desmond closed the browser window on his phone and typed in a number from memory.

Half an hour later Desmond sat at his kitchen table across from Detective Chuck Fournier. The laptop sat between them, along with two cups of coffee and an open metal case that housed a horsehair brush, a jar of dusting powder, clear tape, and blank cards. Fournier had checked both the computer and the door for prints. He had found only Desmond's on the computer and the outer doorknob, but had picked up another set from one of the windowpanes inside the door. It seemed likely that these would belong to the previous tenant or the landlord. If someone had indeed broken into the apartment to type the enigmatic haiku, then the intruder had worn gloves while handling the laptop and likely would have had them on the whole time. Fournier said he would run the prints through AFIS anyway.

Desmond rested his wrist on the table, his fingers curled loosely around the handle of his coffee mug, inches from the laptop. He tried to read Fournier's face—bushy moustache and eyebrows, flinty hazel eyes that belonged in a poker game. Desmond considered himself a pretty good observer of human behavior and facial expressions, but all he could read on Chuck Fournier was the plain fact that the detective was also reading him and making no bones about it. But that was nothing new. Fournier had been appraising Desmond with that same cold, calculating eye ever since Sandy had first introduced the two men.

Fournier swiped the heel of his hand across his nose to relieve an itch he couldn't scratch while handling the prints. He sniffed, and then speaking in a low voice—possibly because Lucas was still sleeping upstairs or possibly because Chuck Fournier always spoke in a low tone—said, "You wanted me here in an 'unofficial capacity,' you said. Like how they talk on TV. Why?"

"I wanted your opinion on this before I take any action…as a friend of the family."

"A friend with a fingerprint kit and a database. Look, Desmond, you can't have it both ways. And I don't really buy this line about my opinion. You're a guy claiming a break-in, right? So you think this a crime scene."

Desmond flinched at the use of that word from a year ago to describe the apartment. "I don't know. All I know is that the back door is unlocked, and I locked it last night. And I sure didn't type those lines."

"Do you know how it looks: you asking to meet with the lead investigator on your wife's murder case alone? You asking to see her ex-boyfriend alone for that matter?"

Desmond straightened his posture. "Chuck, I know you cared for Sandy, so I assume you care about her son. Lucas was too young to understand most of what was said back when there were cops all over us, but that would be different now, and my job is to protect him."

Fournier placed his fingertips on the laptop and watched Desmond uncurl his own from his mug handle. "I think what you're trying to protect is your privacy. What are you afraid of, Des?"

"I don't want Lucas finding out that I think someone broke into our apartment, okay? I don't want to scare him."

"And you're afraid of me reading what else is on this computer. Right?"

"It's my work. I need that to make a living."

"And you believe someone tampered with it just to fuck with you?"

"Someone may be stalking us. It's on a wireless network. Can you tell me if it's possible for someone to hack in and change my file while the computer's in sleep mode?"

"I don't know. I'd have to get a computer forensics guy in here to check out your security…or bag up all your gear and take it with me." Fournier said with a grin.

Desmond ran his hand through his hair and stared at the laptop.

"Listen, Des…this kind of thing—somebody playing a prank by typing a poem on your machine—it wouldn't get police resources if Sandy wasn't a murder victim. But you ought to know by now that when that happened, your family's privacy became a thing of the past. Tossed out in service to the truth. So are you asking me to be a cop and find out the truth about a cyber-breach, maybe even a break-in? Because if you're not, then my job here is to find out what you're playing at."

Desmond sighed and deflated into a slouch in the rickety vinyl-upholstered kitchen chair. "Alright, look: I make shit up for a living, but stuff from real life is grist for the mill. It's a personal process, and frankly I don't want you or some FBI profiler going through it, taking things out of context."

Fournier nodded. "I see...mining your family tragedy for literary gold is a very personal process."

Desmond looked at a spot on the table and shook his head. "I should know better. I shouldn't have called you."

"But you did. For Lucas's sake, help me understand before I make some choices here. Is there more to this than just a few lines on a computer that make no fucking sense whatsoever? I mean...it's not exactly an explicit threat."

"*Drake* is a word for duck. The lines describe a duck floating on the water and eating a worm. There are a couple of reasons why that alarmed me."

Fournier waved his pen over his pad as if he were stirring a pot, one bushy eyebrow cocked.

"A male duck alone could be a reference to me as a widower...but the word *drake,* is also an old word for dragon."

"And?"

"Dragons are prominent in Japanese art."

"Seems a little thin, Des. But you're the one with the symbolism college credits. What's the other thing?"

"Yesterday at the playground Lucas wandered off, and I found him with a guy in a hoodie, looking at a male duck floating in a puddle. The guy ran away when I came near. I didn't see his face."

"Shit, Desmond, you've been saving that for last?"

"It seems like the haiku is meant to tell me that the same guy who could have taken Lucas yesterday can also get into our house if he wants to."

Fournier whistled. "How the hell did a guy make off with your kid, anyway? Weren't you watching him?"

Desmond averted his gaze from the laptop.

"You were writing?"

"I was right next to the sandbox."

"Yeah, that helped. I should confiscate this thing just for that."

"The guy took off when I showed up. I think he's trying to get my attention, but I don't know why. I mean, wouldn't it be easier to hurt us without warning?"

"Yeah. Did you set the computer down when you were looking for Lucas? Was there an opportunity for someone—this hoodie guy, or an accomplice—to type on it at the park?"

"No, I had it on me the whole time."

"Because you wouldn't want to risk losing something so precious."

"Fuck you, Chuck. If you don't want to help, I think we're done."

"Too close to home? You more involved with your work than you are with your boy?"

"I didn't ask for your opinion on my parenting. Are you a cop or a social worker?"

"Thought you didn't want me here in an official role. Doesn't that make this a social call?"

Desmond did his best to glower at Fournier, but he couldn't hold the stare.

Fournier burped. "Alright, you keep the machine for now. I'll get a guy over here to check it for remote hacks, but if you want me to post a detail on your street, you are not only going to have to report this—Oh my God, look at 'im."

Desmond turned in his chair to follow Fournier's line of sight to the stairs. Lucas was sitting on the balding carpet runner, mid-flight, clutching one of his action figures, sleep clinging to his eyes. "Hey, little man," Fournier said. "You got big since the last time I saw you."

Desmond got up from the table and went to sit on one of the lower steps. He touched the unruly hair on the back of Lucas's head and kissed him on the temple. "Good morning, buddy. You want some water?"

Lucas shook his head almost imperceptibly. In a whisper, he asked, "Daddy, who is that?"

Fournier waved a meaty hand. "I'm Chuck. I'm an old friend of your mom."

Lucas slid down a couple of steps on his bottom, and snuggled his head into Desmond's armpit.

Fournier said, "I heard you saw a duck at the playground yesterday."

Lucas didn't acknowledge the comment, kept his face pressed against his father's t-shirt.

"Is that right, Lucas? You saw a duck?"

At the pizza place Desmond had already quizzed Lucas about everything the man had said, as well as his hair and eye colors, which Lucas had said were, "all brownish, I think." Lucas had said that he'd gone to collect acorns under the trees and found the man lurking there, with his back turned to the trail. As Lucas approached, the man had asked if he wanted to see a duck, had jogged down the trail, pointed at the puddle, and said that it was a Daddy duck, you could tell because of the green head. Lucas had asked, "Where's the Mama duck?" And the man had replied that she was gone. Then he had turned to look at Lucas, and that was when Lucas saw that he had "a mad face," and it scared him. That was when Desmond had arrived, and the man had run away.

Fournier said, "Lucas, if I came to visit you again, with a man who draws pictures, do you think you could tell him how to draw a picture of the man who showed you the duck?"

Lucas nestled his head deeper into Desmond's breast and gave a negative shake. Then he pulled his chin back and said, "Daddy?"

"Yes, buddy?"

"It broke."

"What broke?"

Lucas lifted his toy up to his father's face and said, "Rocket Boy Bob broke."

The figure's head was gone, snapped clean off. Lucas started to cry.

* * *

At the police station Desmond waited with stale coffee and a stack of even staler magazines. The coffee was his third cup of the day and he was drinking it mostly just to keep himself occupied, even though he knew it would only make him jittery and probably more paranoid than he already was. If that was possible. Fournier had suggested that Lucas might give a more accurate description if his father wasn't watching him. "Kids try to say what they think their parents want to hear. Don't worry; this guy is good with kids. He won't scare him; he'll make it like a game."

Desmond didn't know if that was the real reason they were interviewing Lucas alone. Probably only part of it. He had regretted consenting as soon as Fournier disappeared behind a frosted glass door with his hand on Lucas's shoulder, and now he waited with his leather laptop bag resting between his feet like a napping dog.

When the door opened again and Fournier waved him in, he found the room empty except for a table with a manila folder on it. No artist, no pencils, no Lucas.

"Where's Lucas?" Desmond asked, stepping around the table toward the only other door.

Fournier raised a placating hand. "He's fine. I just want to talk to you about the sketch."

Desmond pointed at the folder. "Is that it?"

"Yeah." Fournier pulled a chair out for Desmond to sit in, but Desmond ignored it. He'd been sitting for over an hour and he didn't feel like settling now. He just wanted to satisfy his curiosity and then see Lucas as soon as possible. He felt Fournier's eyes on him as he opened the cover of the folder. He was thinking that the whole presentation was typical police theater, that the only reason to have the sketch in a folder was to frame his reaction to it when he flipped it open, but he'd no sooner formed the thought than he saw the page inside and recoiled in shock.

There was nothing ordinary about this face.

He had a mad face.

Desmond had chalked up the description to a four-year-old's limited vocabulary, but now he saw that it was spot on. The face was mad, all right. Mad in every sense.

"Have you ever seen this before?" Fournier asked.

"No. I don't think so."

"What does that mean?"

"I mean not this one in particular, but I'm sure I've seen something like it."

"Where?"

"Same as you… movies, art, I don't know, maybe a museum."

"And what would you say it is?"

"It's a samurai battle mask. The guy in the hoodie was wearing a samurai mask?"

"That's what Lucas saw."

"And the dolls. The decapitated dolls, and the haiku. Chuck… it has to be the guy. It has to be Sandy's killer."

"Whoa." Fournier rested his knuckles on the table and leaned in. "Even *if* I was willing to consider that we put away the wrong guy—"

"What other possibility is there?"

"Could be that some sicko who followed it in the news is playing a cruel trick on you…. Or it could be more complicated."

Desmond tore his gaze away from the drawing and squinted at Fournier. "You mean like me planting the haiku and headless toys and working with an accomplice in a mask to manufacture a suspect?"

"You came up with that scenario pretty fast. Anything to it?"

"I have a wild imagination, but yours is…. I want to see my son. Now."

"I'm afraid that's not possible."

Chapter 3

Shaun Bell climbed the basement stairs. His steps slowed as he reached the top, his calves heavy, his muscles sore from training and lifting. He thought about how the high ceiling of the basement meant that there were more steps to climb. It wasn't easy finding a house with a high-ceilinged basement, but they had done it twice now, once on each coast. It made for some inventive conversations with realtors. Of course, a deep basement wasn't the only important criteria; there were also privacy concerns.

Sensei had handled the realtors, but Shaun had listened attentively. There was purpose in everything Sensei did and said. Nothing lazy, no words wasted. Even what seemed like idle chit-chat served a purpose. So Shaun Bell had learned the art of negotiation just as he had learned the art of tea and the art of harmonizing body, mind, and blade. In all of these, the *kihon*, the fundamentals, were the same: composure, intent, gauging proximity, and acting mindfully.

But lately, hesitation had crept into his heart like a black-clad intruder. Some of his actions these past few days had been spontaneous in the wrong way, arising from impulses that were at odds with his sworn purpose. He reached the landing, took a rag from his back pocket, and wrapped it around the doorknob. He drew a long cleansing breath before opening the door and banishing the betrayals from his mind on the exhalation.

In the kitchen he washed the blood from his hands. From the sink he glimpsed Sensei, seated in the kneeling position on the *tatami* mat in the empty den. Sensei had already changed into his black *gi* and *hakama*—the elbow-length sleeves and pleated skirt-pants of a warrior. His eyes were closed in meditation, and his short sword lay beside his knees on the mat. A dissonant tingle ran down Shaun's spine at the sight of it.

Shaun prepared the white tea in the ceramic kettle. There was a coffee maker on the counter as well, but they never used it. Shaun supposed they kept it as a prop, like the television and so many other things Sensei had acquired to dress the house in the trappings of an ordinary western life: photos of grandchildren who did not exist, gadgets, magazines, and DVDs. All purchased for the same reason as blue jeans and sneakers—to complete a disguise. Just as one couldn't walk the streets in a *hakama* without attracting unwanted attention, neither could one keep a house adorned with nothing but calligraphy, an incense burner, and an antique tea set. If the police should come calling on people of Japanese ancestry, it was best to be able to offer them a cup of coffee.

Shaun had been nine years old when 9/11 happened. By the time he got to high school there were already paragraphs in history books about racial profiling. He knew the issue was sensitive, but he wasn't naïve. When a killer telegraphed an obsession with the symbols and weapons of a particular race, the FBI would have no compunction about interviewing local people who belonged to that race. They would come knocking; it was only a question of when. When they did pay a visit to the old Japanese man and his young Caucasian tenant, a house devoid of all Japanese culture might be just as suspicious as one with no American junk. So the grass *tatami* mats shared the den with a throw rug, the rock garden coexisted with the statue of St. Francis the previous owner had left beside the doorstep, and the painting of the bodhisattva Fudo Myoto with his chain and flaming sword added color to the hallway among the fake family photos. Shaun walked past these now on the way to his bedroom where his own *gi* and *hakama* hung in the closet.

There was just enough time to dress before the tea was ready. Shaun didn't wear a watch, but he had an innate sense of how long the leaves needed to steep in the same way that a man who wakes to an alarm every morning will eventually find his eyes opening at the same time even when the clock is removed. There had been a time, long ago, when he'd used a thermometer to make the tea. That was back in California. *When I was an American*, he thought, and caught himself. Of course, he was still an American by law—an American who could tell when the tea was ready by its color and aroma and, if he was out of the room, by the clock in his gut.

He slipped into the kimono and tied the elaborate straps of the *obi* sash and *hakama* pants with quick, nimble fingers. He straightened the pleats, swatted lint from the black silk, and appraised himself in the mirror. His dirty-blonde hair was getting long. He would have to cut it soon. Or maybe let it grow out so he could put it in a topknot. Never in public, of course. His stomach fluttered. Time to bring the tea.

In the den he placed the tray on the floor between the two mats. He had bowed in the archway upon entering, even though Sensei couldn't see the gesture with his eyes closed. Now Sensei opened them, and Shaun executed the formal kneeling bow: left hand touching the floor first, then right, eyes level, but head low. He poured Sensei's tea into a cup the color of lapis lazuli and placed it into the master's hands. Sensei's impassive face moved ever so slightly with the ripple of an almost invisible smile. It was a strange smile, like a mirage in the steam wafting up from the cup. Every time Shaun saw it, he wondered if it had really been there.

Sensei waited for his acolyte to pour his own cup. Then, in synchrony, they tasted the tea in silence.

Sensei said, "You obtained the target I requested?"

"Hai, Sensei. It is prepared as you wished."

Sensei's *wakizashi* rested in its sheath on the floor between them, and Bell noticed that, for the first time in their long friendship, it was oriented with the blade edge facing away from Sensei's own body, the handle near his right hand. So *that* was what had felt so discordant. From their very first day of training, Sensei had arranged his sword on the mat according to the traditional etiquette: the mirror opposite of this, with the blade transmitting peaceful intentions, as it would be difficult to draw it quickly on the person seated opposite. Difficult, but not impossible for Sensei, and now—placed in this more threatening orientation—very easy indeed.

"Tell me again why you did not kill the boy in the woods."

"There wasn't enough time. His father found us."

"Not enough time." Sensei let the statement hang in the air. Dust motes floated in the slanting late afternoon sunlight. The notion that time was a factor for someone with Shaun Bell's training was dubious, perhaps even laughable. But Sensei was not laughing.

"There was a headless doll in the sandbox. Did you see it?" Sensei asked.

"No, Sensei. An auspicious omen, perhaps."

"And yet, it was not an auspicious day."

Shaun focused on his breathing, keeping it steady, keeping his rate of respiration down so that his heartbeat wouldn't quicken. He hoped Sensei couldn't hear the adjustment of his breath in the silent room. The doll was a peculiar coincidence. He hadn't put it there; it had just been at the scene, unearthed by chance. But it *had* given him the idea to repeat the motif with one of the boy's own toys. Of course, for the warrior, there was no such thing as chance. Did the appearance of the doll indicate that his course was aligned with heaven? But which course? He was at a fork in the path. How many of the tentative steps he had taken down the divergent way to see if his feet felt right on it had Sensei witnessed?

It didn't matter now. As always, the master was correcting his trajectory. But if Sensei knew with certainty of a betrayal, then Shaun would not be looking at the sword on the mat right now, divining its meaning and waiting for it to be drawn on him. He would already be dead. There was still doubt in the master's mind, and Shaun needed to advance into that space swiftly and decisively.

"I hesitated, Sensei. I'm sorry. My skill with the short blade is less certain. If I'd had my *katana* I would have acted, but the need for a concealed blade, a shorter blade…. I doubted my reach, and when the moment arrived and the man had found us, I decided that no cut was better than a poor cut."

The master's face was like stone as he listened to the excuse. Then he said, "You doubted the method. Did you not also doubt the righteousness of the kill?"

Shaun was silent. The accusation was plain. To try to deflect it with a lie now would be disgraceful and transparent. He might as well offer his neck and ask for a dagger. Sensei had always been able to read him like a book.

When Shaun was a boy, there had been a period after his parents' divorce when he became mute, unable to talk to his classmates, his parents, anyone. During those months, he had retained only his ability to speak to animals. His parents never knew that he talked to the dog in the privacy of his room. They didn't listen at the door, and they spent more time on the phone with the shrink discussing pills for him than they spent with him. Nor did they ever know that when the kindly old Japanese man moved into the downstairs rental, he was the person Shaun found his voice with again. In retrospect, it made sense. Sensei was in a different class of human, much more aligned with the animal kingdom; he was a pure predator.

"Remember," Sensei said, "that your actions transcend you. You are an instrument in a greater hand. You are a razor shard blown on the wind of karma. When we met, you stepped into the path of that wind, but you are not the one who stirred it, nor can you set its course."

"Hai, Sensei."

Sensei raised his right hand from his lap. Slowly and deliberately, he picked his sword up from the mat and set it down again in front of his student, orienting the blade in the proper position this time. "Do the honors," he said.

Shaun bowed deeply to the sword and exhaled. He picked the weapon up and inserted the scabbard through the straps at his waist.

"Rise," Sensei commanded him.

Shaun Bell walked to the basement door with his master one step behind him. He still half expected to hear the *tachikaze*, the wind sound, of a sword behind him as he descended the stairs.

He drew a deep cleansing breath as he set foot on the concrete floor at the bottom. His left hand was curled around the mouth of the scabbard, his right resting at his side. Striding silently across the room, he moved his left thumb to the drawing position and used it to push the handguard, loosening the blade from its snug fit in the *saya*, freeing it up for a fluid drawing cut. Once the body was in motion, there might be pauses in the lethal dance, just as there were silent beats in the rhythm of music, but there were no stops and no discrete movements—everything flowed into everything else. The stride, the draw, the cut, the *chiburi* in which blood and tissue were jettisoned from the blade in a sweeping arc, all of it was one dance.

The black folds of the *hakama* swirled around his feet as he quickened his step, giving the feeling that he was not walking but gliding across the empty floor of the training room.

Mindful of every nuance of posture and grip, alignment and bearing, he drew the blade in a fluid, accelerating flash, rolling the scabbard with his left hand just before the steel cleared the oiled wood, allowing the curved blade to travel upward from his waist to his shoulder, slicing clean through the flesh of the pig carcass mounted on the wooden stand in the center of the room.

The top half of the animal slid toward the floor with a sucking sound, but before it hit the concrete, the blade had already come down again, retracing its path from ceiling to floor, and severing the pig's head clean off at the neck.

Bell took a step backward into a long stance, and completed the form with the wet umbrella *chiburi*, sending a rain of thickening blood to splatter against the concrete wall.

He re-sheathed the blade with a graceful gliding maneuver, drawing the flat edge across the crook of his left arm and over the webbing between his left thumb and forefinger where he gripped the mouth of the scabbard, a long exhalation of breath synchronized with the sliding of steel into wood.

Sensei paced around the pedestal, examining the remaining section of carcass still fastened to it and the two pieces that now lay on the floor.

"It was the same height as the child?"

"Hai, Sensei."

The master nodded, appraising the clean angles. "You will not fail again."

Chapter 4

"What do you mean it's not that simple, Chuck? I came here of my own volition. Now bring me my son. We're leaving."

"There's some doubt about your fitness to take care of him."

"*What?*"

"I called your father-in-law. He's on his way with a lawyer. You should call yours too before we all sit down and discuss what's best for Lucas in light of recent events."

Desmond felt his face flushing hot with anger as his mind reeled. The entertainment lawyer he'd used a few times to look over contracts was unqualified for the job. And what *was* the job, exactly; a custody battle with the Parsons? His hands clenched, and he realized that in a situation like this, a man could lose control very quickly. He knew he had every right to be angry. It was normal to be angry, accused of unfitness when there was a real threat out there. But if he showed his rage, he would only look more suspect, more like a man capable of violence.

"Where's Lucas?" he said, struggling to keep his voice steady.

"He's with an officer, playing with puzzles. He's fine. I gave him juice and a snack from the vending machine."

"What kind of snack?" Now this fucking guy was feeding his kid? He didn't know the first thing about Lucas. What if he had a peanut allergy?

"A bag of Cheez-its. That okay, Pop?"

"What did you tell him?"

"I told him I wanted to talk to you alone about the drawing, and that his grandparents are coming to see him too."

Desmond closed the space between them and reminded Fournier that, although he didn't have the same weight to throw around, he was taller. "What game are you playing, Chuck?"

Fournier angled his eyes up and locked them on Desmond's. "You've been under a lot of pressure as a single parent."

"What's that supposed to mean?"

"Just what I said."

Desmond took a step back. "You think I did it."

"Do you still have that sword hanging on the wall of your writing room?"

"You saw my writing room. It's my den. And I don't keep weapons around in a two-bedroom apartment with a toddler."

"Where do you keep 'em?"

"If I can't see Lucas, this conversation is over."

Desmond sat down at the table, folded his arms and stared at the sketch of the samurai mask until he heard Fournier leave the room. He tried to remember everything he'd seen on TV about interrogations and police procedure. He didn't write crime fiction, so he hadn't done the research, but he knew they couldn't hold you if they weren't bringing charges against you. He could get up and leave. But he wasn't going anywhere without Lucas, and Fournier knew it.

A paper cup of water from the cooler sat on the table between Desmond's laptop and the Xerox copy of the sketch. Desmond figured Fournier and his partner were probably sitting on the other side of the mirrored glass watching him. He opened the laptop and read the haiku again. It reminded him of that old saying about the early bird getting the worm. Was it supposed to evoke that? He often found that phrase kicking around the back of his head in the morning when he was dragging his ass around the apartment, making coffee, and trying to retrieve some scrap of story from the receding tide of REM sleep. And the message had been put on his manuscript, right where he would see it first thing in the morning while trying to get the worm *du jour*. So what did that mean?

Solitary. The solitary drake, the solitary dragon…dives. An animal with no mate, that part was obvious, but no duckling either. Was that a threat? He looked again at the pencil sketch. It really was the epitome of an angry face, a *demonic* face, with steeply arched eyebrows that morphed into fiery clouds above round eyes glaring over high cheek bones pushed higher by a wide-open mouth, downturned at the corners in a grimace that seemed to scream for vengeance.

He didn't know what words Lucas would have used to articulate these details or how he might have helped the artist revise what would have at first been a rendering of a human face, but however they had arrived at it...this was a picture of a mask. No man could sustain an expression as extreme as the one on the page. And he knew he had seen its like before—it was a classic samurai battle mask.

The door clicked open and Fournier came in, followed by Phil and Karen Parsons and a tall lanky guy who resembled an undertaker in a suit that looked expensive but too short for his frame, as if he had outgrown it.

"Hello, Desmond," Phil said, looking down at him, eyes lingering on the sketch. Karen wore a tight smile that clashed with her beauty like a tacky plastic watch worn with an evening gown. Desmond had always liked her, and he still thought she was too smart for this shit, but Phil had probably cozened her into it. Then again, maybe not. She had changed since Sandy's death, in some ways that were obvious (like her true age catching up with her face all at once) and in others that Desmond could only speculate about. All he knew for sure was that his easy rapport with her had been winnowed away with her daughter's ashes.

No one introduced the thin man, but Fournier did ask Desmond, "Did you lawyer up?" It came out in a jovial tone, as if the detective were asking a houseguest if he needed a beer.

"If you're not charging me with something, I don't believe I need one."

Fournier opened the door on the far side of the room and ushered them across the hall into a larger room with a long conference table. There was no mirrored glass in this room, just a window that looked out onto downtown Port Mavis. The city was waking up now, cars idling in illegal parking spots right across the street from the police station, while commuters clamored to grab a newspaper, a pastry and a cup of coffee at Tradewinds—the newsstand and café that had been called a "soda fountain" back when Phil and Karen were dating and Sandy existed in some quantum state, a mere potential, waiting for a spinning vector to collapse, like a coin revolving on a countertop.

When they had taken their seats and turned their attention to Fournier, the detective tipped his hands in the general direction of Phil Parsons. Desmond's father-in-law was no stranger to the station; he was an ex-cop who had retired early when a chunk of flying rubble jettisoned by a jackhammer had taken out his left knee at a night construction site. Fifteen years later, now past his normal retirement age, he still walked with a limp. He was balding, in a handsome way, probably because his square jaw and bright eyes were accentuated by the absence of hair. Phil was the type of man who would always show the remnants of the physique he had built in his youth, even as the skin overlaying that frame wrinkled, the sinews sagged, and the inevitable paunch expanded. But his personality was leaner than his body. If Phil Parsons were a canned food, his label would have listed bullshit in the less than 2% category.

"Desmond, just to be clear, I don't think you killed my daughter," he said with no change in posture. "That piece of trash is doing life, and there isn't a day that goes by I don't wish we lived in a state with the needle. But it does sound to me like you're losing your marbles. Typing spooky poems to yourself and trying to convince people that you and Lucas are being stalked…that what I'm hearing?"

"Yesterday I found Lucas with a stranger at the edge of the playground. The man had his back turned to me, but it seems he was wearing a mask. You were a cop, Phil. Does this…I don't know, raise your hairs at all?" Desmond shot a quick look at Karen, then added, "There were also decapitated toys, at the playground and the apartment. Did Chuck tell you that?"

Phil nodded. There was a brief silence. Karen folded her hands on the table and leaned in, but she gazed at a blank space on the Formica as she spoke. "Desmond, please understand that we are only here out of concern for Lucas. This may not be easy for you to hear, but…you're a creative type of person, that's just who you are, and…." She met his eyes now. "You must understand that in getting to know you, I've seen you at times when you just seem to be elsewhere."

Desmond drew a deep breath to make up for how shallow his intake had become while listening to this setup. He knew where this was going.

She raised a hand slightly to keep him from launching in, and continued. "I've heard you say in interviews that you listen to your characters like voices in your head. You make them sound like they have a...I don't know, a *will* of their own, or an agenda that isn't necessarily yours."

"Karen that's different. Don't use my work against me."

"You have a vivid imagination."

Desmond scoffed at the idea with a short laugh. "That's like saying that cops are paranoid all the time, even when they're off duty. And ironically, you guys aren't paranoid enough right now."

Phil said, "You've been coming unraveled since we lost her, Des. You were barely there before, and now your daydreams are taking over."

"So what exactly do you think? You think I wrote myself a cryptic message, pulled the head off of Lucas's toy, and had my computer dusted for prints...why? Why would I do those things?"

"You feel guilty," Phil said, like he was pointing out to Desmond that he had some mustard on his shirt.

"But you don't think I *am* guilty."

No."

"Well, *he* does." Desmond nodded at Fournier. "Right, Chuck? Deep down, you still think I killed her?"

"Doesn't matter what I think."

Karen looked at Chuck Fournier with something new in her eyes.

Phil said, "It's not uncommon. It's a form of survivor guilt. You think you should have been able to save her, so you convince yourself the killer is still out there. This time he's threatening Lucas, and you get a second chance to be a hero."

"You're a shrink now, Phil?"

"No, but I can refer you to one."

"Desmond looked at Karen. "Is that what *you* think? I'm so delusional I'm mistaking my own shadow for a monster?"

She returned his gaze but said nothing.

"What about this drawing?" Desmond said. "Why would some innocent stranger be wearing a mask at a playground, and why did he run when I found him with my kid? How does *that* fit into your theory that I'm delusional?"

There was another moment of silence and when no one else spoke up to fill it, the lawyer shot a glance at Phil for permission, then cleared his throat and said, "One reason why a man might wear a mask would be so that his own son doesn't recognize him."

Desmond didn't even know how to begin responding to the accusation. They had made up their minds about him and anything he said now would only dig him in deeper. He wondered if the microphones in the room were on, if the conversation was being recorded. But aside from the break-in at his apartment—which no one took seriously anyway—there had been no crime committed. He had started the whole chain of events himself by calling Chuck Fournier. And he could end it right now by walking out. He stood up. "Bring me Lucas," he said to Fournier, "We're leaving."

The lawyer looked alarmed. "Mr. and Mrs. Parsons are initiating a guardianship case against you on the grounds of instability and unfitness. You could spare your son a great deal of discomfort and stress by reaching an agreement outside of a courthouse."

Desmond waved his finger. "I'm not having any such discussion. You have *no* authority. None of you do."

The lawyer continued, "If you call on counsel, we can hammer out a temporary solution whereby you would retain visitation rights contingent on submitting to a psych evaluation—"

"Fuck you, Lurch." Then turning to Fournier, "*Where is my son?*"

"Desmond, if you leave this meeting…," Fournier said with no sign of rising from his chair, "You're gonna have to start asking yourself things like are there any retail records for the purchase of a hoodie sweatshirt that Lucas wouldn't recognize? Is there a web search history for samurai masks from your IP address? Think about it, Desmond. A warrant wouldn't be hard to get."

"Really? Somehow I doubt that. You don't even have enough for protective custody. If you did, you'd be telling, not asking. Get Lucas. *Now.*"

Fournier grudgingly hauled his bulk out of the chair. In the doorway, Desmond turned to face Phil and Karen. "You'd better think hard about what you're doing to your grandson. He's been through enough already."

Desmond followed Fournier down the hall. They rounded a corner and Lucas came into view, sitting on a chair, swinging his feet back and forth. At the sight of his father, the boy did the same thing as always when they'd been apart for a while—he shouted, "*Daddy!*" and came running, collided with Desmond's thigh, and wrapped his small arms around it.

Same as always, only this time it felt different.

Chapter 5

Desmond drove. He didn't have a destination in mind, but neither was he ready to head home just yet. All he knew was that he wanted to get Lucas away from the police station parking lot before Phil, Karen, and their lawyer left the building. From the backseat, Lucas was chattering about all manner of trivia, with a few relevant questions mixed in, questions that Desmond also wanted answers to. It was always harder to think clearly with a toddler volleying repetitive queries from the back seat, so after answering a few, Desmond reached for the CD wallet in the glove box. "Lucas, you want to listen to your favorite songs?"

"Yeah. 'Let It Be,' Daddy. Play 'Let It Be.'"

Desmond jabbed the power button on the radio. It came on midway through one of those acoustic songs by Billy Moon that somehow sounded even more haunted than it would have if the singer hadn't jumped from the Golden Gate Bridge shortly after recording it. Desmond cut it off by feeding the Beatles disc into the slot.

"Twelve, Daddy. Track twelve."

"I know, buddy, I know." It was a *Best Of* collection, and Lucas had memorized all of the track numbers. 'Let It Be' was a favorite; Lucas even tried to sing along to it. Desmond knew that the main reason the boy had latched onto that particular song was because he loved to watch the track numbers come up on the display and had become fascinated with the number twelve ever since Desmond had pointed out its prevalence: on clocks and calendars, in boxes of donuts and cartons of eggs. Lucas wasn't in school yet, but he had a big appetite for information. Sometimes Desmond worried that by the time the kid got to kindergarten, he would already be pegged as a geek, chattering about twelve-based systems having their origin in the

Babylonian zodiac. It was probably an unfortunate side effect of having a writer for a single parent.

In time, Desmond became aware that he was driving out toward the southeastern edge of town. If he didn't change course the road would lead him to the strip mall, beyond which a wooded hill sloped down to a derelict railroad track and the riverbank where the town's homeless had encamped before the police discovered Sandy's murder weapon in the tent of a deranged vagabond.

Maybe he should have thought things through before coming out here. He couldn't just go poking around on the trail in search of stragglers with Lucas in tow. According to the local paper, the camp had been cleared out by the police after the murder. A few small articles profiling the tribe of destitute wayfarers had seen print around the time of Harwood's arrest, and again during his trial—the sort of press that causes a stir around a threat already gone. The chances of the same camp producing another psycho were slim, but the surrounding community had wanted them out. So the cops had trucked all of the weather-stained furniture to the town dump and set about patrolling the river bank periodically for a while, shooing away or arresting any squatters they found until they could say with some confidence that the untouchables had been vanquished. To where, who knew? Maybe some were now spending their nights in barns and sheds in the backyards of the same people who had wanted them flushed down the social drain in the first place, like a piss stain hosed off a concrete wall.

Desmond figured most of them would have reconvened on the old turf sooner or later, after public attention had shifted elsewhere. People, even those without jobs or homes, were creatures of habit.

There was plenty of parking available in the shopping center when Desmond pulled the car in. The Aikido studio at the end of the strip wouldn't get busy until school let out. Apparently a recent spate of school bullying cases had resulted in a rise in enrollment. Desmond had read about it in *The Tribune* and was reminded of the last time he'd seen Sensei Salerno in the news, during the blur of pain and confusion and autumn rain that had surrounded Sandy's death.

Salerno had been one of the only people who knew the suspect's name. He came forward early in the investigation, admitting that he sometimes spoke with Greg Harwood during walks he took in the woods between classes, along the old rail trail. If Desmond remembered correctly, the paper had quoted the Aikido instructor as being "shocked" by the allegations brought against the man, whom he had perceived as a "gentle, if troubled soul." The reporters had made much of the fact that only the proprietor of a self-defense studio had any business wandering alone in those woods and then moved on to other locals who claimed to have seen Greg Harwood dumpster-diving and staring lewdly at women around the parking lot.

Desmond chose a space close to the dojo, in the shade of a tree. He would be able to see the car from the entrance, but he didn't want to unbuckle Lucas from his seat until he knew the place was open. Ushering the boy across the lot and back just to rebuckle him while he fussed would hardly be worth it if he found the front door of the dojo locked, the place closed.

"Listen, Lucas, you see that door right there with the white letters on it? I have to run over there and see if it's open. Can you wait for me? I'll be right back."

"I want come."

"You can watch me the whole time, okay? If it's open, you can come in with me."

Lucas gave him a skeptical look that reminded Desmond far too much of Sandy. He had her deep brown eyes.

"Tell you what. If you say the alphabet slowly, I'll be back before you get to Z, okay?"

Lucas shook his head.

"I'll be right over there."

"Daddy?"

"Yes, buddy?"

"What if the man with the mad face comes?"

Desmond felt a chill ripple over his skin like a low-grade electrical charge. "Okay, buddy...we'll go together."

When they reached the door, Desmond pulled on the handle and was surprised to feel no resistance; it swung open on an unlit, vacant room. Ambient sunlight from the storefront windows scattered across blue mats that covered most of the floor. The only decorative items were a framed photo of an old man with a wispy white beard, and a calligraphy scroll hanging at the front of the room above a low shelf upon which a bowl of fine white powder—possibly sand—and a few smooth river rocks rested beside a wooden sword. On the far side of the room were a pair of locker room doors (his and hers) and a dark blue curtain, drawn aside, allowing light to spill out of the room beyond it.

Opening the front door had caused a string of chimes to sound, and as their bright reflections rolled across the empty room like a bag of spilled marbles, Lucas let go of Desmond's hand and, seeing the expanse of blue-padded floor, took off at a run just for the sheer joy of racing through an obstacle-free zone. *"Lucas! Wait!"* Desmond commanded in his fiercest whisper-yell. Lucas looked back, and Desmond pointed at a pair of shoes on a carpet runner by the door. He reeled his son back in with two wagging fingers. "Take your sneakers off," he said as he pinched the heel of his own left sneaker with the toe of his right and stepped out of it.

A figure appeared in the doorway of the curtained-off room, a large man with a goatee, dressed in sweatpants and a t-shirt with writing too faded to read. Sensei Salerno. Desmond recognized him from the news, and—judging by the way the man's face changed in an instant—it was mutual. Whenever strangers recognized Desmond, he always hoped it was because of his books, but this close to home it was almost always because of Sandy's murder.

"Hello there, friend." Salerno said. "How may I help you?"

"My name is Desmond Carmichael, and this is my son, Lucas."

"Hello, Lucas, I'm Peter. But if you're here to sign up for the kids' Aikido class, you'll call me Sensei. Did you want some information about the classes?"

"Actually, no...I was hoping I might ask you a few questions, if you have a minute, about Greg Harwood."

Salerno sighed. "I thought that might be what brought you here. I knew your name before you told me."

"And you knew Harwood?"

Salerno looked down at Lucas and nodded. "There's not much to tell. I didn't know him that well."

"You knew him well enough to think he wasn't guilty."

"Sir, I'm not sure we should be having this kind of adult conversation...."

"I'm pretty good at leaving certain words out."

Salerno walked to the front door and turned the lock. He raised his index finger as he crossed the room: *just a minute.* He ducked behind one of the curtains and reappeared with a giant green fitness ball. Desmond felt the bottom of his stomach drop out. The sight of the ball hit him as hard as if Salerno had emerged from behind the curtain holding a sword. It was always the little things that still messed him up in a heartbeat, ordinary things. He knew people used the balls for yoga and the like, but they would only ever remind him of the hours Sandy had spent bouncing on one both before and after Lucas was born. He thought of it as a kind of pregnant lady's throne that provided relief while carrying a child and then helped to lull the same child to sleep after birth. Desmond had himself logged his share of late night hours on the ball, praying that he wouldn't fall asleep before Lucas did and roll off the damned thing, dropping his newborn son to the floor.

Salerno bounced the enormous green orb against the floor like a giant basketball. The sound reverberated with a metallic ring. "Lucas, how would you like to roll this ball around the room while I talk to your father in my office?"

Lucas smiled and looked at Desmond.

"Go ahead, kiddo. Have fun. Just stay on the blue mats."

Lucas ran to the ball, collided with it, and laughed. He could barely get enough of his arms around it to lift it, and when he did, he disappeared behind it. Desmond felt his grief breaking under the comical sight of the giant ball running across the room on stubby legs and stocking feet. Salerno was smiling too, as he held the curtain aside for Desmond.

Inside the office a wide, paper-cluttered desk with an outdated PC occupied one wall. Black-and-white photos and tournament posters hung above it. Another wall held racks of wooden swords and staves of various sizes and hues. Padded gloves and scuffed up pieces of body armor spilled over the edges of a crate in the corner. Salerno settled into his office chair beside the desk and gestured for Desmond to choose one of the folding chairs across from his.

"Why are you here, Mr. Carmichael? What do you hope to accomplish?"

"Call me Desmond, please. I haven't been Mr. Carmichael since I lost my teaching job."

Salerno allowed the silence to spread, placing the burden of conversation on his visitor. At last, Desmond said, "Between you and me, I'm beginning to think the police may have pinned my wife's murder on the wrong man. Since you knew him, I'd like to know why you thought he was innocent."

"I don't know if he's innocent or guilty. I've never said one way or the other."

"I saw you on TV after they arrested him. You looked incredulous, to say the least."

"The news took me by surprise, sure. But we don't always know what people are capable of, do we? That's a fact that has probably kept me in business."

"So Harwood didn't strike you as the violent type? The prosecution had a lot to say about a history of mental instability."

"He had problems, yes. Most homeless people have serious problems. If it isn't substance abuse or PTSD, it's usually something like schizophrenia."

"Which was it for him?"

"I don't know his history, maybe a combination. If you attended the trial, you probably know a lot more than I do."

"But you interacted with him…how often?"

"I'd see him hanging around behind the building sometimes, rooting through the dumpster. I never actually spoke to him until one day when he filched a bo staff from the dojo while the students were in the changing room."

"What's a bo staff?"

"One of these." Salerno waved at the wall of wooden rods. Some were adorned with dragon graphics, but most looked like simple oak or mahogany dowels. "We use them as training weapons. The staff Harwood stole belonged to a young student who didn't have much money to replace it. I felt responsible. I could have given the kid one of my own staves, but the theft became sort of a watershed moment for the class. If someone could just wander in and violate our safe place, the place where we were learning how to deal with conflict in a direct and upright way…well, I said I would get it back, so I went to the camp and asked for it."

"And Harwood admitted taking it?"

"I knew they were desperate people, and I wanted to resolve things peacefully, so I offered a twenty dollar reward for the staff. It probably retailed for thirty."

"And?" Desmond could hear Lucas laughing and slapping against the mat, probably rolling off the ball. He couldn't remember the last time *he* had laughed, but it was good to know that his son still could.

"He fetched the staff from his tent and traded it for the bill. Said he only took it because he needed a walking stick more than some rich kid needed to learn how to clock somebody with it."

"What was your impression of his personality?"

"He did seem…agitated, a bit twitchy. That must have been evident at the trial."

"Honestly, I couldn't bear to watch much of it. But I know he wasn't allowed an insanity plea."

Salerno cleared his throat. "The DA wanted him in that sweet spot: crazy enough to kill but not too crazy to pay for it. Deemed fit to stand."

"Disturbed man plus possession of the murder weapon equals guilty."

"They wanted me to testify that he had stolen a martial arts weapon. It was true, so I signed a statement, but I was relieved when they didn't subpoena me."

"Just a walking stick to Harwood?"

"Maybe."

"You're holding something back," Desmond said. "What is it?"

"I started going down to the river now and then to leave food for them. Bread, stew, ramen noodles. Most times they hid from me, but I did have one more run in with Harwood at the dojo. He was hanging around in the open doorway on a summer night, watching the Iaido class." Salerno didn't look away from Desmond, but he seemed to be listening for the sound of Lucas, maybe wishing the boy would interrupt so he wouldn't have to tell this part.

"What's Iaido?"

"Japanese sword art. We used to have a visiting instructor come in to teach it one night a week. Kendo too, that's the fencing version with armor and bamboo swords."

"And this…Iaido is done with wooden swords too?"

"No. They're usually aluminum or unsharpened steel."

"So you actually taught a samurai-sword class here?"

"*I* didn't, Sensei Masahiro used to, but it was a long drive for him. When we didn't have enough students enrolled in the class we dropped it."

Desmond stood up and sat down again. He cupped his hand over his mouth and slid it down his chin, looking at the ceiling. How had he ever doubted Harwood's guilt? But the homeless man had a home now—Walpole State Penitentiary. Crazy or not, fascinated with swords or not, he sure wasn't cavorting around playgrounds in a samurai mask. "Did the police know you hosted a sword class that Harwood used to watch?"

"We had already dropped it by then, but they took a list of all the students who had attended and interviewed them. I didn't volunteer the information that Harwood had observed a class. It was only the one time, and he was never in the building. I'd sent him away, told him that me bringing meals to the camp didn't mean he was absolved for stealing the staff."

"You *do* think he's innocent."

"I don't know, Desmond. When he asked me about the sword class he seemed indignant about the whole idea of martial arts; why people would want to learn how to hurt each other. I tried to explain, as I often do with parents, that in addition to the self-defense techniques we teach in Aikido, the weapons lessons have more to do with harmonizing body and mind. The opponent you are really trying to defeat is yourself, your own clumsy, unconscious tendencies. The martial arts are about mastery of the self and meditation on your own mortality."

Desmond thought that sounded like a nice New Age sales pitch to gloss over a tradition of macho posturing, but he had to admit that he liked Salerno. The man had a gentle and intelligent presence. Not what he had expected when he ventured in here. "So Harwood was offended by the school, by the idea of teaching violence."

Salerno nodded. "And I didn't want the police to be able to suggest that he was fascinated by it, nor did I want to argue for his innocence. For all I know, he did kill your wife, and I wanted to keep my hand off the tiller."

Desmond sat back in the folding chair. It creaked under his weight. He listened for Lucas and didn't hear the bouncing ball. "What are the chances of the sword that killed my wife being found within a mile of a martial arts school with a sword class?"

"The police asked that very question. I think they knew that none of our students would have risked ditching the weapon so close to a place where it could be connected to them. But, correct me if I'm wrong.... Didn't the sword that killed your wife belong to you?"

"Yes. Sandy's grandfather brought it back from World War II as a souvenir. When he died, her father gave it to me. He figured since I write fantasy stories, I'd like a sword. I hung it over my desk, out of Lucas's reach, and pretty much forgot about it."

"I heard the killer broke into your house, saw the sword on the wall, and then decided to use it when your wife encountered him."

"Yeah. They called it a 'weapon of opportunity.'"

"What was she doing in the backyard in the middle of the night?"

"Our dog always whined to be let out around four in the morning, and she'd gotten up to let him out. Usually she'd wait by the sliding glass door to let him back in when he was done before he could bark. When he didn't return that night, she must have stepped outside and gone looking for him...the dog was killed first."

"And nothing was stolen?"

"Nothing. Just the sword, later found in Harwood's tent with her blood on it."

"It sounds like maybe someone disposed of it in the perfect place for a variety of suspects: some of them martial artists, some of them vagabonds."

"That's what I'm beginning to think."

"Why now? What brought you here after all this time?"

Lucas pushed through the curtain and crashed into Desmond's lap. "Daddy, I'm hungry."

"Okay, buddy. We'll go soon." Desmond tousled Lucas's hair. It was stiff. The kid was overdue for a bath. "Would you please go get Peter's ball and bring it back to him?"

"I can do it!" Lucas ran out of the room, and Desmond almost wished he could afford to enroll him in classes. The change of scenery seemed to have done him some good.

"He's a good boy," Salerno said.

"Yeah." Desmond flashed a rueful smile. "Looks like time is short, but if I could squeeze in one more question: you mentioned fencing armor? Do you guys ever use samurai face masks?"

Salerno looked confused. "Not sure what you mean. The Kendo helmets have a wire grille."

"So nothing like a wrathful face plate?"

"No. I think I've seen what you're talking about in books, but no, we don't have anything like that, why?"

"I get the feeling you and I will talk again."

"My door is always open to you."

"To be continued? Gotta feed the boy."

"To be continued."

At the front door, as Desmond and Lucas stepped out into sunlight, Salerno handed Desmond a business card. "Call me anytime. And, you know, Sensei Masahiro might be able to tell you more about those masks. He *is* Japanese. His number's on the back. Super nice guy. Very approachable."

Chapter 6

The wooden guard tower was the only landmark on the road to indicate that the site had once been an internment camp. Agent Drelick pointed through the dusty windshield. "That's it," she said, "pull over."

Pasco eased up on the gas and pulled the government-issued Crown Vic to the side of the road where it churned up a cloud of yellow dust that was immediately shredded by the wind. The tower was separated from the highway by a four-strand barbed-wire fence running along galvanized T-bars. The fence was mostly for show, the wires spaced far enough apart that the agents could have climbed through if they didn't mind tearing a few holes in their clothes. Someone *had* climbed through last night.

Pasco parked behind a police cruiser that had been posted to keep the traffic moving. The local law hadn't shut down U.S. 395, but Drelick thought they probably should have. She shielded her eyes and looked up, saw a young man moving around on top of the tower. There was an aluminum ladder inside the x-braced frame of the structure, propped up against a wooden ladder built into the tower but that didn't extend low enough for anyone to reach from the ground. The top of the tower was a simple cube: a guardhouse made mostly of windows, the roof constituting a platform surrounded by a 2 x 4 railing. The figure she'd spotted moving around up there was the forensics photographer, now leaning back against the railing to get a wide shot of the area where the bloodstains must have been.

A young officer with a pockmarked face climbed out of the cruiser and came to stand beside Drelick as she stared up at the tower. Pasco stayed in the car with the engine idling.

"Are you with the FBI, ma'am?" the officer asked, appraising her black trench coat and polished shoes, and thinking, no doubt, of some X-Files episodes he'd seen on Netflix. She knew her haircut didn't help, but fuck it; she wasn't going to change what looked good on her just because of some actress who wasn't even on the air anymore.

She nodded, flashed her ID, and read it to him, "Special Agent Erin Drelick." She tilted her chin toward the tower. "Was that ladder here before today?"

"No, ma'am. When they reconstructed the guard tower they only went halfway to the ground with the built-in ladder. Didn't want to encourage the local kids, you know? Stunts, graffiti, etc. We brought the other ladder in this morning."

"'We? Were you personally here when the ladder was brought in?"

"Yes, ma'am."

"Did you check the ground under the tower for impressions from another ladder used by the perp?"

"There weren't any."

"How about shoe prints?"

"Negative again."

"Anybody take a picture of the ground before stomping around on it and erecting a ladder?"

The officer pulled his hat down to shield his eyes and looked up. "We went up before the CSI got here. There was nothing on the ground to take a picture of, Agent."

"And what did you find up top?"

"Just blood. Mostly soaked into the wood and not much of it considering what we found in the park."

"Do you think whoever went up there last night climbed the bracing to reach the half-ladder?"

"Must have. Probably had the head in a backpack or something so he could use both hands for climbing."

"Where's the head now?"

"On the ground over there in Block 20 where the birds dropped it." He pointed beyond the barbed wire at a spot in the patchy sagebrush where two figures stood over a white canvas sheet held down with stones. One of the figures was driving a pole into the ground with a hammer, but the wind was pulling the clanging in some other direction so it sounded out of sync with the blows, a dislocated sound, like the tolling of a phantom bell. "If it wasn't for the crows fighting with him, that turkey vulture pro'ly woulda got away with it. Then all we'd have would be a little blood up there that wouldn't be found until God knows when."

Drelick nodded. "Thank you, Sergeant...."

"Wilkes, ma'am. Sherriff Knowles is waiting for you at the main entrance."

She climbed back into the car, and Pasco crawled up the gravel shoulder. They passed a wooden sign suspended from a pair of posts by rusty chains at the four corners: MANZANAR WAR RELOCATION CENTER. She recalled seeing a heated debate in the *Los Angeles Times* a few years back about the use of the phrase "concentration camp" at the site. Apparently, the more conservative party had prevailed. The park featured an auto tour but not today; another police cruiser blocked the entrance. Pasco flashed his ID, and they drove between a pair of stone huts to where the sheriff's car was parked. Knowles started his engine at their approach, pulled out in front of them, and gave a curt "follow me" wave out the window.

Drelick had looked at the web site, so she knew that the white building going by on the left had once been the school auditorium and was the only building that remained from the original camp. With a modern facelift, it now served as the Information Center housing artifacts, photographs (including the famous Ansel Adams set), and little theaters that screened short documentary films for visitors. All that remained of the rest of the village amounted to a few stone foundations, piles of rocks amid the sand-blasted scrub, and signs indicating the places where numbered barracks blocks had once stood. They cruised past a replica of a tarpapered plywood barracks near Block 20 and parked in the scant shelter it provided from the dusty wind, behind the sheriff's car.

Sheriff Knowles shook their hands while shouting over the howling wind, "Welcome to Manzanar. What have you been told about this crime scene and your role here?" As a national monument, Manzanar fell into a weird jurisdiction where the Department of the Interior, the California State Police, and the FBI all played in the same sandbox.

"We were told you have partial remains," Drelick said. "Remains of a victim we may have the rest of. We're here to make an ID."

Knowles nodded. "If it's a positive, he's yours. If not, he goes to the morgue in town. I sure as hell hope he's yours because I'll be damned if I know where to start looking for the rest of him."

"Let's have a look," Pasco said.

Following the sheriff to the spot she had glimpsed from the road, Drelick felt like she was fording a river against a strong current. A ribbon of yellow police tape broke free of the barricade stakes that cordoned off the area, flashing past Drelick's wind-lashed hair and snagging in a tree where it trilled with a staccato flapping sound. Dust as fine as flour filled her nostrils, and she wished for a bandana to tie over her face like a bandit in a spaghetti Western.

Knowles gave a nod, and an officer rolled one of the boulders aside with his boot. The canvas flew up on the wind, releasing a cloud of black flies and wrapped tight around the torso of a park ranger who was caught off guard—holding his hat down on the crown of his head while batting at the canvas with his free hand. For a fleeting second he looked like a man fighting a ghost while he wrestled the fabric into a bundle.

A severed human head stared up at Erin Drelick from the dusty ground, its skin painted in the purple-gray palette of death. The eyes and nasal cavity had been picked over by carrion birds, leaving ragged white necrotic tissue where the eyelids and nostrils should have been. The red cut along the neckline, however, was laser straight.

"You have that photo?" she asked Pasco.

He took a 2 x 3 from his pocket, a headshot of Geoffrey Lamprey, age 37. Pasco's thumbnail blanched white as he squeezed it to keep the wind from stealing it. Drelick nodded and said, "It's Lamprey. Confirm?"

"Confirmed," Pasco said.

"Thank you, Sheriff. That's our head. Have your men bag it. There's a cooler full of ice in our trunk."

Sheriff Knowles worked his jaw through a couple of rotations like he was chewing on something. "A cooler of ice? You're just gonna put it in the trunk of your car?"

"You think we should FedEx it to L.A.?" Pasco said. "Taxpayers already put the gas in our car to come up here."

"Alrighty then. Officer Cook, you heard the lady; evidence bag."

Drelick turned to the park ranger in the straw hat and insulated vest. "Are you the one who saw it drop?"

He nodded, still holding the bundled canvas to his chest.

"Give us the play-by-play," Pasco said.

"I saw the birds from the road before I got to work this morning. They were fighting over something up on top of the tower, but I couldn't see what. I drove right over there as soon as I was inside the park. Maybe seeing me coming made the vulture decide to take off with the head. He flew right over me, and a couple of the crows tried to dive-bomb him. That's when he dropped it right here."

To the Sheriff, Drelick said, "Did you find anything on the tower?"

"Just a little blood on the top platform where the head must have been left. Nothing in the guard booth. No prints, no fabric on the barbed wire. You can go up and have a look if you'd like. But tell me, Agent: what makes this a federal case if the rest of the victim was also found in sunny California? Believe me, I'm glad it is, but I'm also curious."

Drelick stepped closer to him and, speaking under the roaring wind so that only he could hear her, said, "There's a resemblance to a case in Arizona."

"Huh."

"You have any leads on witnesses who may have seen a car parked near the tower last night?" Pasco asked.

"Not yet, but I'm sure you noticed we are in the middle of bumfuck nowhere. We'll see if anyone comes forward when it hits the news. So far no reporters have noticed we've closed the park, and I'm in no hurry to bring it to their attention."

"Good," Drelick said, "Hold off until we're gone."

The ranger shifted on his feet, suddenly looking uneasy. "Who did you call?" Pasco asked him.

"Just my wife."

"She a gossiper?"

The ranger shook his head. Drelick read his brass nametag. "Mr. Abath, my partner and I are going to need a tour of the grounds. Will you ride with us?"

"Of course."

"Sheriff, did your men check the barracks replica for evidence?"

"Clean as a whistle. The beheading wasn't done here. And if the head belongs to your victim, then my understanding is there aren't any other missing parts…are there?"

"No," Drelick said, "but whoever put the head on the tower wanted to frame it for presentation, to send a message or make a symbol out of it. And unless you've combed this entire square mile, there may be more to the message that we've yet to find."

"I'll get a team together with some dogs," the sheriff said.

"Mr. Abath, have you or your fellow rangers found any foreign items in the park this morning?"

"Beg pardon? *Foreign?*"

Pasco said, "A machete would be good, but she means *anything*. A hankie, a food wrapper…litter."

"No sir, but people do leave offerings at the graveyard all the time. We don't keep track of what's left there from one day to the next."

"Take us there first," Drelick said.

The cemetery was at the southwestern edge of the site, beyond the gardens and the signs marking where the hospital and children's village had once stood. It was stark, little more than a barren lot corralled by a fence of bark-stripped tree limbs in an X pattern. A few small circles of stones were the only indicators that six bodies were buried there. The desolate, snow-dusted Sierras dominated the horizon like a decaying animal jawbone under the cobalt sky. In the foreground, flanked on three sides by squat, rope-threaded posts, a three-tiered white marble base culminated in an obelisk with black-painted *kanji* characters carved into its face. Clusters of origami cranes hung from strings and huddled in the shelter of the monument, their bright colors incongruous with the somber desolation.

"What does it say?" Drelick asked, pointing at the *kanji* characters.

"*To Console the Spirits,*" Abath replied. Gesturing at the cranes, he said, "These are the offerings. People leave the origami birds, coins, rocks...all sorts of little trinkets. Hmm.... Haven't seen *that* before." He bent down to pick up a pair of wire-rimmed spectacles from the marble base, but Drelick seized his arm.

"Could have fingerprints," she said. She snapped a couple of photos with her phone while Pasco produced a latex glove and a Ziploc bag from his coat pocket. Drelick scanned the horizon and said, "The glasses were facing east, toward the watchtower."

"What do you think that means?" asked Pasco, zipping the bag shut.

"Maybe nothing. But Lamprey's driver's license says he wore glasses. We should find out if they're his." She circled the obelisk, and when she came around the south side, her jaw went slack. "Ranger Abath, do you speak Japanese?"

"That's why I got the job."

"Can you read it, too, or do you just have that inscription memorized?"

"Both. I mean, yeah; I can read kanji," he said, following her around the side of the stone slab and seeing the scarlet brushstrokes there. "Holy shit, is that blood?"

"What does it say?"

His Adam's apple bobbed as he swallowed. "*Shikata ga nai.*"

"And that means?"

"It's kind of a famous saying around here. It means, *it cannot be helped.*"

"What can't be helped?"

"Anything. Everything. The internees used to say it to express their resignation. A more literal translation might be, 'It must be done.'"

Chapter 7

Desmond put on the Beatles CD as soon as they got in the car so he wouldn't have to spend the entire drive answering questions about where they were going and what it would be like. He usually flipped the rearview mirror down so he could glance up and see if Lucas was getting into the music or nodding off to sleep, but today the mirror stayed up and he found himself looking more at the road behind than at the road ahead.

Lucas soon tired of the music and started complaining that he wanted to skip ahead to the next track or to a favorite number. Just a few weeks ago, Desmond had thought it was cute that Lucas already had favorite songs and clever that he had memorized the track numbers. Now he regretted letting the kid boss him around like a personal DJ. He had his attention on the stereo controls more than the road, and when he had to slam on the brakes to avoid hitting a pickup truck that had pulled out of a donut shop, he jabbed the power button and announced that they were done with music. He tried to remember if the dark red metallic sedan two cars behind them had been there on Ocean Road, but he didn't know. What he did know was that even grocery shopping with a four-year-old was nearly impossible for him, so why should avoiding a tail be any easier?

Before long they were cruising through tree-lined suburban streets like the one they used to live on. Lucas craned his head around to look for kids, and covered his ears when they passed a loud lawnmower. When the sound faded behind them, he asked, "Is this where Carl lives?"

"Yes, in one of these houses. I just have to figure out which one." He looked at the Post-it note on the steering wheel. He had worked with Laurie Fisher at the school for three years and considered her a friend but had never visited her home. He was just grateful that she'd made him feel welcome, even when the first call he made to her since losing his job six months ago was to ask her for a favor.

"Does Carl have trains?" Lucas asked.

"I don't know, buddy. We'll see."

"*Why* we'll see?"

"I don't know if he has trains. He might. Carl is a little older than you. He might have other cool toys. He might have trains...I think this is the place, buddy."

Laurie invited Desmond in for a cup of coffee and a look around. "I trust you completely," he said, trying to brush it off and get back in the car. It was obvious that the house was well kept. It sure was nicer than their apartment. The manicured lawn, polished floors, and antique furnishings reminded him of their old neighborhood and awakened an unexpected dissonance in him that made him anxious.

"*You* do," she said, "but Lucas has never been here before. He doesn't know me. Just come in for a few minutes while he gets comfortable."

Desmond settled on the couch and waited as she got the coffee. Lucas scanned the room with wide eyes but stayed close to his father's knee. Laurie called up the stairs for Carl, who came down with a gadget in his hand. In a whisper, Lucas asked Desmond what it was. "I don't know. Go ask *him*."

And that was all it took to break the ice. Carl started asking Lucas what characters he liked and then pulled them up on his handheld video screen. Lucas followed Carl upstairs without so much as a backward glance. Laurie handed Desmond a mug and sat down beside him. "Well, that was easy," she said. "Carl likes younger kids."

"Yeah. It's nice to see Lucas with another boy. Thanks again for watching him."

"Happy to. And don't worry; I'll get them out in the yard too. It's too nice of a day to stay in and watch videos."

"You aren't planning on taking them anywhere…out and about, right?"

"No. Why?"

"Desmond sighed. "I've just become a little overprotective around playgrounds, that's all."

"That's understandable."

He realized that she would think it was because of what had happened to Sandy, and in a way it was, but she had no idea.

Laurie took a sip, set her mug down on a coaster, and said, "So…read any good books lately? Write any?"

Desmond smiled and felt gossamer webs that had been constricting his breathing let go and float away. She wasn't going to ask him about the hard stuff. She knew better, and he felt a disproportionate gratitude welling up in response to this small kindness, this omission that he knew had nothing to do with her own level of comfort or skill when it came to heavier conversation. "Well, I'm always reading, it's a great escape. And we should definitely talk books sometime, but speaking of escape, I should really get going while he's distracted. I don't know exactly how long this errand will take."

"No worries, take your time. He can stay for dinner. In fact, why don't we plan it? Does Lucas like macaroni and cheese?"

"Loves it."

* * *

Desmond switched the car radio to a news station just because he could. When there was no weather report, he poked around and settled on a hard-rock station. He drove north toward the box stores by the highway. Bob, his landlord, had agreed to let him replace the locks, but Desmond had to do the installation himself and pay for the hardware if he wanted the expensive stuff. Desmond had protested that the place wasn't safe; there had been a break-in. But when pressed about what was stolen he had backed down, admitting that nothing was missing. He didn't want to tell Bob about the haiku.

"So nothing was stolen, but you reported a break-in to the police? I'm gonna see my address in the police log of *The Tribune?*"

"No. But the door was open, Bob, and I know it wasn't me or Lucas who left it that way."

"You've been through a lot. I'll pay for the upgrade, okay? But you're still doing the installation. Are you handy?"

Desmond lied: "You bet."

There was a hardware store not too far from his first stop.

The Blue Fort was a complex of windowless buildings with powder-blue roll-down garage doors and heavy-duty locks, surrounded by a tall chainlink fence, with no barbed wire but plenty of video cameras. Sheds could only be accessed during business hours, and a small office guarded the entrance. Desmond had moved most of the family's possessions into one of the sheds after Sandy's death when he sold the house. He knew he should have had a yard sale before packing everything up and putting it in storage, but he just didn't have the emotional grit to sift through all of Sandy's things and everything they'd acquired as a couple and then leave half of it out on the street for strangers to pick over. Even if he'd been able, he sure as hell couldn't put Lucas through that. And what if the wrong kind of people were interested? Was there a market for a murder victim's personal effects on the net? The thought had chilled him.

He liked the anonymity of the Blue Fort. Whenever he drove past it, he couldn't help glancing at the rows of sheds and thinking that one of those plain utilitarian garages was the most haunted place in town. It helped that he could never pick out exactly which unit was his; that made it easier to drive by. Lately, however, he'd been thinking about an object that was tucked away in there with all of the furniture, photos, and bric-a-brac. One item that, as Lucas's workbooks would say, was not like the others. Over the past twenty-four hours Desmond had been ruminating on how terribly easy it would be for a determined person, a person with some skill, a person who wasn't just taking a chance on robbing any old storage shed, but who knew what he was looking for with bolt cutters and a flashlight…how easy it would be for someone like that to break into his shed and leave no trace but some damaged video cameras. After all, he was paying a fair rate for storage space but not for maximum security.

Desmond pulled up to the office, thumbed the driver's side window button, and presented his card. An employee scanned it, handed it back, and opened the gate for him to drive through. "Remind me where this one is?" Desmond asked. "It's been a while."

"They're numbered," the guy in the powder-blue polo shirt said, like he was talking to an imbecile. When Desmond didn't take his foot off the brake, he said, "Third row back."

With his SUV parked in front of the unit to provide some small measure of privacy, Desmond opened the padlock and rolled up the blue door. Sunlight flooded the contents of the shed like a time-lapse film of dawn breaking on a landscape. Couches, chairs, and stacks of boxes and bins were all covered with bed sheets, adding to the brief illusion of a snowy mountain range. Desmond had told Lucas that the sheets were for keeping dust off of everything, but they were really a precaution for this day—the day when he would have a reason to come back.

He stood frozen in the doorframe, surveying the threatening shapes and shadows. He needed to remember to tread carefully. There were a few bins here that would mess him up good if he chanced upon them. Sandy's clothes would be the worst; those should have gone to Goodwill. What was he ever going to do with them but torture himself? Then there was her camera equipment: a digital SLR, some lenses and tripods, bags and filters. She had been in love with the hobby and scarcely ever went anywhere without a bag stuffed full of gear. In retrospect this provided the small mercy and sad omission that there weren't many photos with her in them left behind. Desmond hated himself for not stepping up and making an effort to take pictures of her while she was alive. He could have asked her for a lesson, could have at least tried to get a decent shot occasionally, a shot with her and Lucas. But he had always figured that was *her* thing. He didn't need to document their life because he knew that she always would. And now, with her gone, the document she had left behind was one that she was mostly absent from.

So there were few images of Sandy in this room amid the shells of their former life, but oh so many framed images of that life as seen through her eyes. In some ways it would hurt more to see what she'd seen than to see her. Desmond would need to be careful.

He walked through the minefield of sheet-draped boxes, between the couches and chairs to the corner where a folded stepladder rested against the armoire they had kept the TV in. Perched atop the armoire was a black footlocker with chrome corners and latches and another padlock. It had been hard to get it up there and it would be hard to get it down. Desmond looked back at the square of bright sunlight behind him framing his car. The motor aisle beyond was empty, just a row of blue garage doors, all of them shut tight.

He climbed the ladder, took the chest by the wide leather straps on the sides, and tried to lift it, but at this height, where he couldn't get any leverage, it was too heavy. He stepped onto the precarious top step and dialed the combination on the padlock: his wedding anniversary. The latch popped. He put the lock in his back pocket and raised the lid.

Inside, a World War II Japanese infantry sword lay atop several stacks of hardcover first-edition books, a few shoeboxes of manuscript pages, and a portable hard drive. Things he'd wanted to keep above the damp concrete floor. Things he wanted to keep under a second lock and key.

Desmond took his wife's murder weapon out of the chest, holding it hilt-up to ensure that it didn't slide out of the metal scabbard. He stepped carefully to the floor and set the sword on the sheet-draped couch. Then he climbed back up the stepladder, took one wistful look at the treasure trove of novels past, closed the lid, and replaced the lock.

The sun moved across the floor while he sat on the couch with the sword in his lap. To a passerby, he could have been a statue. When he was ready, as ready as he would ever be, he pressed the wire latch that secured the handguard to the scabbard, and taking the hilt in his right hand, withdrew about six inches of steel.

The base of the blade was stamped with a number. He had done some research last year, looked at a few of these infantry swords on collectors' web sites, and learned that if the number on the blade matched the number on the scabbard, it increased the value of the sword. In this case, they did match. He'd learned a few other things about Japanese swords, not much, but enough to know what he had here. He could remember very little of the traditional nomenclature, but he knew that unlike more expensive handmade swords, these general infantry swords had been mass produced by the Japanese military during the war. The scabbard was made of aluminum rather than carved wood, and the handle was cast from metal made to resemble the silk-wrap pattern used on a genuine *katana*.

The blade was also machine made, a product of the industrial revolution. It lacked the flowing, wavy line left on traditional blades by the clay temper process. There were collectors who analyzed the grain of the folded steel in antique blades, the carbon content, and the various styles of those wavy ghostlike lines that danced and played across the edge of a Japanese blade like incense smoke, or ripples on the surface of a lake. He had learned that such a line was called a *hamon,* and that it indicated the dividing line between hard and soft steel, a characteristic that gave a samurai sword great strength paired with a degree of flexibility. Swords forged by the ancient methods could cost tens of thousands of dollars. This one was only worth about five hundred dollars, and most of that value came from the fact that it was a war relic. Nonetheless, it had been designed with the same geometry that made the traditional swords so effective. It had been made for the same lethal purpose; it had been forged for war.

Desmond realized that he was studying the weapon that had killed his wife with the same eye for facts and details that he brought to researching books when he was avoiding the emotional commitment of writing. A defense mechanism. This object in his lap had probably killed allied soldiers in the war. Most of the history books and documentaries tended to focus on the technological advances of the war—the fighter planes, napalm, and rockets...the hydrogen bombs. But it was a lesser-known fact that more people had been killed by swords than by bombs in World War II. The Japanese hadn't worn their swords as ceremonial uniform accessories. This was a weapon built to kill, and it had fulfilled its purpose on the body of an unarmed woman in the dewy grass of a suburban backyard in the early hours of a summer day. Desmond wondered what Arthur Parsons, Sandy's grandfather who had been shot down over Okinawa, who had brought this sword home with him, would have thought about that.

Desmond had found her body in the murky light of a foggy predawn. His mind had rebelled against making sense of the shape, but there was no escaping the sight, or what it meant...and what it would mean for Lucas. That was the first crushing weight that landed on him—the unbearable fact that Lucas would be motherless and that Desmond would be charged with having to tell him, having to somehow make this make sense to his son. The poor kid didn't even know the word *dead* yet except in relation to batteries. How could you tell a three-year-old that his mother wasn't just gone but was never coming back?

Now, staring at six inches of burnished steel, Desmond knew that he hadn't done a very good job of making sense for Lucas because it still made no sense to him. It was the definition of senseless violence. All he'd been able to do was to tell Lucas that Mama had a bad accident, that she didn't want to go away, that she loved him and was still with him, would always be with him even though he couldn't see her. But he could talk to her, he *should* talk to her when he wanted to, and she would hear him. It was the best Desmond could do. He never consulted a professional or a priest about whether these were the right things to say, and for once he didn't pick up a book to find out. He just knew that he had nothing else to offer.

"I'm trying, baby," he said to her murder weapon, "I'm trying to do the things you would do for him." A tear landed on the gray metal and ran off the edge. "I know I fuck it up sometimes, but I'm trying."

She had been lying in the red grass near the shed where he kept the lawnmower. She must have bled out instantly. The dog was beside her, like they were napping together on one of the hairy dog beds that they used to kick around the floors of the old house. Sandy used to pick those beds up and move them around all day to make sure Fenton always had a slice of sunlight to lie in, and sometimes she would lie on the floor with him to stroke his head. And there his head was a few feet away from his body and hers, attached by a thin strip of flesh.

Had she found the dog like that and bent down to make sure her eyes weren't playing tricks in the foggy darkness? Had she been standing there, head bowed, comprehending the horror and drawing breath to scream when the blade came down and severed her windpipe? Desmond almost dropped the damned thing on the floor. The killer had wrapped his hands around this very handle, but left no prints. Desmond couldn't conjure a face on the shadowy figure he saw in his mind's eye, but now he could put a mask on him. *A mad face.* A face distorted into the very caricature of wrath, with fierce flaming thunderclouds for eyebrows. Maybe it was best to think of that man as a force of nature, no different than if a tornado or tsunami had swept his wife away. Equally senseless.

But there were aspects of that night that were not meaningless, God help him. There was guilt, there was failure, and there was the small betrayal that opened the door to terrible consequence.

Desmond had heard the dog whining at the door. He had opened his eyes to read the red numbers on the bedside clock: 4:36. And now he would never again be able to see those three numbers on a digital clock without a sharp pang of guilt, because he'd pretended to be asleep when she whispered his name the last time she would ever whisper it. He hadn't wanted to get up at 4:36, not with the alarm set to wake him for work less than two hours later, because he knew he wouldn't be able to get back to sleep. But if Sandy let the dog out, she could sleep in until Lucas woke up. And so he sent the girl he'd fallen in love with in an English Lit class to her execution so he could get a little extra shuteye.

When he rolled over an hour later and found her side of the bed still empty, he was confused, even a little scared. Was she in the bathroom? He listened for a flush. He waited and listened for far too long.

She wasn't in the bathroom. His stomach sank when she wasn't in Lucas's room either. He stepped into his shoes and went onto the back deck. He walked down the steps and called her name. And then her form floated out of the murk and changed everything irrevocably.

It should have been him. He should have been the one to let the dog out. He should have been the one cut down by a psycho.

Greg Harwood.

It didn't make sense then and it didn't make sense now. Chuck Fournier must have known it too, or why would he still think Desmond had killed her? The crime seemed random. Sandy didn't have an enemy in the world, but whoever had used this sword had broken into the house to take it without arousing Fenton's attention or the barking would have woken them. The killer must have entered through the back end of the first floor where Desmond's study was and taken the sword from the wall. But he hadn't simply killed them all in their sleep. Instead he had gone back to the yard and waited for her. As if he knew their schedule, knew Fenton's bladder, and knew he could count on one of them going out there alone in the wee hours if the dog didn't come when called.

Desmond had been the prime suspect until the weapon was found in Harwood's possession. Desmond, who had looked at the sword hanging above his desk every day. But neither Desmond nor Greg Harwood was expert in the use of a samurai sword, and someone had decapitated a woman and a dog with two clean, efficient strokes. Beginner's luck? Desmond doubted it now more than ever. Someone was very handy with a blade.

He slid the exposed steel back into the scabbard with a *shuck*, then fished his cell phone out of his pocket and dialed three digits. At the prompt he told the voice recognition software what he needed: "Walpole Massachusetts. Cedar Junction Correctional."

* * *

Chuck Fournier sat across the street from the Blue Fort in the maroon Honda Civic he had signed out of the impound lot. He'd been waiting too long and was getting antsy. His coffee was cold, and he was starting to wonder if the storage facility was just a ruse Carmichael was using because he'd spotted the tail. Was he even still in there, or had he just used his card to get into a private area where he could ditch the car and continue on foot? Maybe there was another way out of the lot during business hours. If so, Carmichael could be anywhere by now, might have even called for a taxi from his cell phone. And if he was still in there, just what was he up to? Checking on some piece of evidence they'd never found? Burning some document that gave him motive for Sandy's murder? Nothing had ever turned up. But now, with the Parsons' moving to take guardianship of Lucas, Desmond might be nervous, and might be covering old tracks.

Fournier climbed out of the car and trotted over to the guard booth at the entrance to the storage lot. If his timing was bad, if Carmichael was driving back out, he'd have to take cover fast. He nodded at the guy in the booth who operated the gate, and then stepped into the little glass office cube where he found a young lady in another blue polo shirt behind a counter adorned with colorful brochures and silk flowers. She was looking at a smartphone, wearing a thin smile of mild amusement, probably killing time on Facebook or sexting her boyfriend. A little bell jingled on the door at Fournier's entrance, and she stashed the phone under the counter. Seeing that he wasn't her boss, she relaxed and put a fake smile on where the genuine one had been just a moment ago. "How may I help you?" she asked.

It was time for Chuck Fournier to make a decision. This little Saturday afternoon fishing expedition wasn't authorized, not by a long shot. He was doing his surveillance on Desmond Carmichael for love, not money, and while there was no law that said he couldn't follow an acquaintance from a distance on his own time, as soon as he flashed his badge things got a lot more complicated. Without a warrant, he couldn't ask this girl to do what he needed her to do. And if he did find something incriminating here, it wouldn't be admissible in court. But his gut had more say than his brain in situations like this, and his gut was telling him to go for it because this clerk would be too dumb and lazy to even read the name on a badge. More important: his gut told him that he needed to see what Desmond was up to in there. Knowing would give him a leg up when things *were* authorized. No one needed to know where he got his ideas; they would simply be attributed to his instincts. He loved that word. If you had a reputation for good instincts, you could cut a hell of a lot of corners without ever having to fess up to doing the homework off the clock.

He flashed his badge and, instead of introducing himself, opened with a direct question as he stepped up to the counter, getting in her face to throw her off balance: "Is there another exit from the lot that can be accessed by pedestrians besides this gate?"

The girl straightened and tucked a strand of hair behind her ear. "No," she said. "Is there a problem?" Badges, words like *pedestrian*, they tended to establish a tone of authority, especially with young people who thought everything was about them, who immediately started thinking about some bag of weed they had stashed somewhere when a cop got up in their grille. Might as well seal the deal. "Ma'am, I need you to show me the video monitors for your surveillance cameras."

"Um, okay. They're back here."

Fournier was relieved to find no other employees in the back room, just a few storage cubes for employee belongings, some posters of federal regulations, coat hooks, and a bank of black-and-white video monitors on a cheap laminate desk with wires running in and out of an array of hard drives beside a grimy keyboard. "We only record at night," the girl said.

Fournier could see Desmond's SUV blocking the open door of his unit. "That's okay, just need to confirm the whereabouts of a suspect."

"I should probably call my boss."

"That won't be necessary. I'll be finished here in just a moment." He scanned the room "Do you have a piece of paper and a pencil I can use?" It would keep her occupied for a minute, keep her from making that call to her boss.

"How about a pen?"

"Pen's fine. And was that a water cooler I saw out there?"

"Uh-huh."

"Would you mind? I'm parched."

"Sure."

He stared at the screen, waiting for some sign of motion, listening to the gurgling of water in a paper cup. The parking lights on the SUV flashed and the back hatch popped open.

The girl set the cup, pen, and sheet of paper on the desk in front of him. Fournier kept his eyes on the screen. A noisy little grayscale Desmond Carmichael stepped into blown-out sunlight, clutching a bundle under his arm—about the length of a golf club and wrapped in a bath towel. Goddamn, if it didn't look like it could be the sword. The towel was a little too small, and it slipped off as he placed it in the hatchback, revealing what looked like the hilt and handguard. Of all the things to come here for when the heat was on…. Had they missed something about it in forensics? Not likely. So why did Desmond want it now?

Could be he means to use it again. Fournier watched Desmond fix the towel and slam the hatch shut. Time to boogie. He almost knocked the clerk over in his haste.

"What about your pen and paper?" she asked, "and your water?"

Fournier looked her up and down as if deciding whether or not he could trust her. "You've been very helpful, but things are developing fast and this is a sensitive investigation. Do you think you could keep my visit to yourself, not even mention it to your boss? If the suspect were to learn that we were onto him, it would jeopardize the operation and could put people in harm's way. So could you do that for me?"

"I won't say anything." She smiled, Chuck thought, in a flirty sort of way. He could tell this was the most exciting thing that had happened to her in a while. He also knew that the chances of her keeping her gob shut were slim to none; she'd probably be tweeting—or whatever the hell it was they did—within two minutes. But if that was the only way she blabbed, it might not catch up with him.

"Good luck catching your guy," she said.

He winked at her and hoped that wasn't overdoing it. Then he was through the door, hustling back to the Civic and fishing his phone out of his pocket. Time to pass the baton to someone Carmichael wouldn't recognize. Time to call that private investigator Phil Parsons had on retainer.

* * *

At the hardware store, all of the parking spaces close to the building were taken. Now that the ground had thawed, and the last of the nor'easters had passed, it looked like every man and woman on the Seacoast had spent their morning making a list of landscaping and repair materials. Desmond hoped the heavy foot traffic would be enough to keep the car secure. At least the tinted windows in the back added another layer of concealment to the towel-wrapped sword.

The place was vast, and it took him a while to find the doorknob and deadbolt sets. When he did, there were too many to choose from, but he didn't have the luxury of indecision—not enough time in the day for that. He picked one of the more expensive ones that didn't look like the tag could be attributed to fancy looks, tossed it in the shopping cart, and then hurried to gather the items he would need to dispose of the sword.

Desmond had never been much of a handy man, and it had become something of a sore spot in his marriage that whenever something needed fixing, Sandy had been quick to call her father. Desmond always felt he at least deserved a shot at the simpler projects before she called in the cavalry, but she had seen him injured or enraged over "quick fixes" enough times to know better. In the end, he was usually grateful for Phil's help, but he sure couldn't call on Phil this time. And he had looked over the man's shoulder enough times to get the gist of what was involved.

When he loaded the shopping bags into the back of the car, he found the sword undisturbed. Pulling out of the parking lot, he searched his mirrors for the dark red car he'd spotted earlier. It wasn't there. He thought about Laurie's backyard and wondered if there were woods beyond the stockade fence that bounded the property. He didn't know and now thought that he probably should have checked. The urge to drive back there now was strong, but he waited for it to pass. He rolled down the windows and breathed in a cool breeze tinged with the taste of the ocean. It helped to clear his head. He couldn't let paranoia dictate his actions. He'd decided on a course and he was going to stick to it, and when he tucked Lucas into bed tonight, he would be able to turn out the light knowing that he had done something to take matters into his own hands.

He drove past a sign for a gun shop and eased his foot on the gas pedal. The New Hampshire border was littered with them (the State motto *was* 'Live Free or Die'), and his eyes had roamed over signs like this one countless times provoking little thought beyond an inarticulate discomfort at the idea that apparently there were a lot of firearms stashed in the homes of some of the children Lucas would soon be meeting at school. Now he wondered if he should stop and buy one. But he knew that his skill with a gun would be no better than his skill with a drill. And if he went through the legal channels, he would probably have Fournier crawling up his ass. It would only complicate things further, giving Sandy's parents more evidence that the apartment was an unsafe environment and he, a high-risk parent. He accelerated past the sign, reminding himself that today's errands were all about ensuring that the one weapon he did own couldn't be used against his family ever again.

Back at the Ocean Road apartment he parked in the driveway and scanned the cars parked on the street for a human silhouette behind a windshield. They all appeared empty, but if anyone had followed him, they might be doing a loop around the block right now. Best to act fast. The towel was too small to conceal the sword completely, and he considered getting something larger from inside the house, but twenty seconds of partial exposure while he ran the sword from the car to the door seemed acceptable.

It struck him that he might be making a terrible mistake bringing this black thing into his home. He had sequestered it in a no-man's-land at the storage facility, had banished it from their lives along with the memories, so that he and Lucas could have a new start. Now, by bringing it under the roof where they slept their restless sleep and dreamed of her, was he inviting death back in? If whoever had broken in just two days ago got in again despite the new lock, and found the thing…. But he could think of no better way to hide it.

He forced his legs into motion and bustled to the front door, holding the sword vertically in front of his body to conceal it from the street. He crossed the threshold with the wretched thing buzzing in his hands like an alarm, telling him that it had no place in the home of a child, telling him that it had been made for one purpose only and that it would one day find willing hands again, capable hands.

He shut the door with his foot and laid the bundle on the desk where he usually kept the laptop. The computer was still in the car with the supplies he'd bought—he brought it with him everywhere now, even though he hadn't written a word on it since the haiku had appeared. He hadn't erased those lines, either. One more trip to the car and he had everything. He locked the front door of the apartment, carried everything he needed upstairs, and laid it all out on the dingy hallway rug.

Scenes from every movie and TV crime drama he'd ever seen flashed through his mind like shuffled cards. Where did people hide murder weapons? In this case it wasn't a matter of hiding one from the police—they had already measured its every angle, photographed it, and swabbed samples of his wife's blood from the cutting edge. It was about making sure it couldn't be used to kill again.

The police, the press, and the community all believed that Sandy's killer was locked away where he could do no further harm. Desmond no longer believed that. And he knew that whoever killed her wouldn't have done it with one of the kitchen knives in the butcher block if the *katana* hadn't been hanging on the wall. Somehow he felt sure that the killer had come to their house *because* of the sword. The poem and the mask were pieces of a puzzle that a killer adept with a sword wanted Desmond to ponder.

He reached into one of the shopping bags and removed a roll of paper tape and a folding razor knife. He set them on the carpet. Kneeling at the end of the hall, he looked at himself in the full-length mirror beside the door to Lucas's room. He looked haggard. His blond beard was speckled with strands of gray that seemed to be growing at a faster rate than the rest of it. His hair needed a trim, too. His eyes were sunken in purple shadows, and his body looked flabby under his Red Sox jersey. Who was he kidding, thinking that he could defend his son? He knew he should keep the hero fantasies in his books, where they belonged. He should be moving Lucas out of state right now, not hiding a sword in a wall.

He had considered destroying it. What Would Frodo Do, right? There was a scrap yard for wrecked cars on Samson Street that he supposed could have cut, folded, and recycled the blade. But he hadn't liked the idea of talking to whoever worked there about why he wasn't just selling it on eBay or Craig's list. They might recognize him from the news. Nor did he like the idea of Fournier being able to dig up a record of him having it destroyed. Of course a man would want the weapon that had killed his wife destroyed, but he couldn't shake the creeping feeling that the act would somehow be used against him. He could throw it in the ocean, but who would let him take a sword on a boat? Same problem: too many questions. It wasn't like a gun that could be hidden in a bag until an opportunity arose to drop it in the drink unnoticed. And what if it washed up on a beach? The feeling that getting rid of it would haunt him, that somehow it would always find its way back, was irrational but strong. He imagined a muscular man in a bathing suit and a demon mask diving to the ocean floor to claim it.

Desmond blinked, forced himself to stop staring at the sword, and removed the other items from the bag: a small bucket of joint compound, a can of white paint, a sheet of sandpaper, and a putty knife. He rummaged through the hall closet, found a Phillips screwdriver, and used it to loosen the mounting brackets that attached the mirror to the wall. He lifted it carefully, had the vertiginous sensation of dancing with himself, and then set it down, leaning it against the wall.

He picked up his new razor knife and snapped open the blade. The thin wedge of steel looked feeble compared to the sword, but sharp nonetheless. Slowly, he pushed it into the wall, and then dragged it downward with a sawing motion. Sheetrock dust drifted out of the cut and fell, like a gentle snow flurry to the carpet. He braced his wrists in front of his chest and put his weight into the cut.

Chapter 8

Erin Drelick lifted her coffee cup, tilted it toward her eye, and examined the contents: only an inch left and it had been sitting long enough to surely be cold. She was tempted to toss it back and complete the full dosage of caffeine her body needed but thought better of it. Cold coffee tasted like shit. The lab report for Geoff Lamprey's severed head lay open on her desk, and most of the lines were never going to translate themselves from Geek into English no matter how much coffee she drank. She glanced at her watch for the third time since 8:45. It was now 9:06 AM. The geeks would be at their stations by now. They'd better be. She picked up the phone.

After two and a half rings the author of the document in her hand answered, "Waraska."

"Hey Tom, it's Erin. I have a couple of questions about the lab you just ran for me."

"Shoot."

"What are these numbers that start with the letter C?"

"Alkoids. In this case they make up light petroleum. Lamprey's neck had traces of mineral oil on it."

"Were you able to identify a brand?"

"No, it's too basic. These kinds of petroleum alkoids are found in a variety of generic mineral oils. They're just gasoline byproducts used in laxatives and lubricants. The blend we found on Lamprey is fairly heavyweight, indicating a thicker oil, probably higher quality than most, but with no fragrance component to indicate a brand."

"And if it *did* have a fragrance? What would a scented mineral oil be used for?"

"That would be baby oil. Here's the thing, though: your sample *did* have a fragrance, but it was organic and doesn't match anything used in commercial mineral oil."

"Let me guess," she said, "it's the other line I needed you to translate: *Syzygium aromaticum*. What the hell is that?"

"Clove."

"So there was clove-scented oil found in the wound?"

"Yeah, trace amounts. Pure clove oil."

"Did you guys check other parts of him for it? Face and fingers?"

"Of course. There were no other traces. It wasn't some kind of aftershave or cologne, if that's what you're thinking."

"So it was left by the murder weapon."

"Sure looks that way to me. You know, if you could have waited an hour, you'd have all of this in my summary. Not like I don't have other work to do besides giving you the same info on the phone *and* in writing."

"I'll make it up to you, Tom."

"How? You taking me out on a date?"

"I'll buy your lunch today and have it delivered. How's that? What are you eating?"

"I have a brown bag in the fridge."

"So keep it there until tomorrow. What are you having now that it's on me?"

"General Cho's chicken from Uncle Charlie's."

"You got it. Now tell me why a blade would have clove-scented mineral oil on it."

"Oils are often used to protect high carbon steel from rust. That might at least point you toward a metal type for the weapon. Rules out stainless steel, anyway. The clove part, I don't know. You should talk to an edged weapons SME."

"Got a name and number for me?"

"This chicken better not be from that dump on Lindbrook Drive."

"Uncle Charlie's. I promise."

"Gimme a minute."

Pasco was sitting with his feet up on the desk, restlessly tapping a Latin rhythm with a government-issued pen against the flat of his hand and accenting every third beat by hitting his wedding ring like a cymbal. When Drelick hung up the phone he gave her a look.

"What?"

"You're really buying that little douche lunch just to get him to do his job?"

"He's doing his job anyway, but if he feels good about doing a little extra, it could mean the difference between us catching an important detail or not."

"That kind of motivation shouldn't have to be bribed. Those guys are paid to be OCD detail freaks. And you can't afford to keep buying people lunch."

"I don't recall *you* ever turning it down." She nodded at his screen, angled discretely away from her desk. "Is that your fantasy football team you were slaving over while I was on the phone?"

"Just killing time until you were done."

"Uh-huh."

He spread his hands and raised his eyebrows. "My desk work is finished, partner."

"You find anything?"

"The BFD lists more sword crimes than you'd expect."

"BFD?"

"Big Fuckin Database. You know, whatever DHS is calling that cross-referencing interdepartmental algorithmic circle jerk that would give Stalin a stiffy *this* week. I can't keep up with the acronyms anymore, so you and me are gonna go with BFD from now on. You cool with that?"

"Sure. BFD. And?"

"After you rule out the satanic weirdo teens who maybe accidentally stabbed a friend with a replica from a Hobbit movie, and the nervous college kid with a ninja fetish who killed an intruder in self-defense, you're still left with a fair amount of actual sword murders in the past decade. In most cases the weapon just happened to be on the scene as a decorative item and somebody grabbed it when things got tense. That includes one Greg Harwood, a schizoid homeless man in Massachusetts. Harwood broke into a home where a Japanese sword could be spotted through a window, hanging on the wall. Seems he tried to steal it and then used it on the lady of the house when she caught him in the backyard while letting the dog out shortly before dawn."

"He killed her?"

"And the dog. Decapitation both, which makes it the closest match I could find to the Lamprey case. But Harwood was put away in March of last year."

"Huh. Any other decapitations?"

"A couple, and not with swords. In both cases the killer was identified right away and was incarcerated at the time of the Lamprey murder. Seems most decapitations are done by sawing the head off with a knife, like in those jihad videos. The only recent instance of a single cut by a long blade is this Sandra Carmichael—the woman killed by Greg Harwood in Massachusetts."

"Okay, we should look into that one even though they apparently got the guy."

"I also ran a list of minor offenses like carrying a sword in public. Plenty of those."

"How many in California?"

"A whopping thirteen, but we *are* the mecca of film fanatics, freaks, and actor wannabes."

"True. Still, our killer could be on that list. Maybe we should make some house calls, feel people out. If nothing else, we might learn a thing or two about the culture."

"Culture?"

"Samurai sword culture."

"What makes you so sure Lamprey was killed with a samurai sword and not some other long blade?"

"Only the fact that we found his head at Manzanar. The killer was sending a clear message, leaving it there."

"Pretend I'm stupid. Spell it out for me."

"The murder has something to do with retribution for the way Japanese Americans were treated when they were rounded up and interned in the camps. Maybe the killer's ancestors were prisoners there. They may have suffered abuses. Maybe the killer even spent his early childhood in the camp."

Pasco's fingers twitched with calculation. "Nineteen forty-two, forty-three...if he was a kid in the camp, a young kid, that still puts him in his seventies now. A little old to be jumping fences and chopping heads off."

She shrugged. "Probably. Or it could be someone younger who has some obsession with the subject. Channeling psychopathic violence through a cultural filter, a historical event, to give it meaning so he feels like he's dealing social justice instead of just getting his rocks off."

"Wow, that's deep."

"Just a guess."

"But why Lamprey? He wasn't even born when Manzanar was operational."

"Which brings us to today's tasks. I need you to research Geoff Lamprey's family history. Look beyond the locational. If you find an obvious connection to Manzanar, great, but it could be something less direct, like political support for the camps by an ancestor."

"Yay, more desk work. And what will you be doing while I'm having all this fun?"

"I'm going to visit a Subject Matter Expert and pick up Chinese food."

"What's the subject?"

"Edged weapons. Waraska gave me a number for a martial arts instructor who trains cops in knife defense."

"Great. I'm cramming Genealogy and American History while you watch dudes throw each other around a dojo? No fair. Let me come with you."

"Because the director just loves to pay two people to do the job of one. What do you want from Uncle Charlie's?"

"The usual."

"One spicy beef and broccoli, you got it. You know feeding people earns you more loyalty than paying them?"

"Is that right?"

"Taps into the tribal family part of the brain."

"Did you always know you'd end up using your psych degree mainly to get favors from lab rats?"

She grinned and nodded.

"Well, here's a psych tip for you: Want to tap into the primal brain, flash them some cleavage. You're an attractive woman. It's cheaper and just as effective." Pasco ducked before he'd finished the sentence, just in time for the flying pen to miss his face. It wasn't a government-issued Bic; Drelick favored steel-tipped rollerballs, and this one stuck in the corkboard behind him, shaking a Post-it note loose to drift like an autumn leaf to the floor.

* * *

The dojo was in a bad part of town. Agent Drelick could see right away that it wasn't thriving on after-school programs. The entrance was just a metal door in a graffiti-stricken cinderblock wall. The studio itself occupied the second floor of a warehouse. A mongrel dog and her litter of pups sniffed human-height piss stains on the concrete at the end of the alley. To reach the door, Drelick had to step around a truck tire lying on the ground beside a sledgehammer—the hammer presumably to be used for beating on the tire to build muscle. To Drelick it felt like the tire should be on fire and the cinderblocks riddled with bullet holes. That would have completed the urban blight. A plate bolted to the door read: JOHN MARSHALL'S KENPO KARATE.

Inside she climbed a staircase papered several times over with faded tournament posters and flyers for self-defense seminars. The sound of someone hitting a heavy bag punctuated the air, and as she ascended the smells of urine and garbage gradually gave way to the smell of sweat. She ruminated on the fact that the sledgehammer hadn't been stolen and decided that that was ample testament to the dojo's reputation in the hood. It was probably common knowledge that Marshall taught cops how to take down knife-wielding crack heads.

Afternoon sunlight flooded the wide-open room from a bank of opaque windows and formed wedges in the thick, dusty air. A skinny young man dressed in a sleeveless shirt and sweat pants was pounding on a heavy bag. He shot her a quick glance without losing rhythm. In the middle of the room, an older man with a receding hairline and a handlebar moustache knelt in front of a plastic bin from which he was removing pieces of a black combat suit. At Drelick's approach, he tossed an arm guard at her face; she caught it, surprising herself with her own dexterity.

"Tell me if that's too big for you," he said.

She almost turned to see if there was someone else he might be addressing, but she knew there wasn't. "Mr. Marshall? I'm Agent Drelick. I called about picking your brain on Japanese swords."

"I know. Pleased to meetcha. Will that fit?"

She glanced at the pad in her hand, slapped it idly into her left palm. "I'm not here for a lesson. Not a tactical one, anyway."

"Sure you are. Your partner Pasco's paying for it."

"Oh, no. Thanks, but…I'm not exactly dressed for training."

He looked her over, his eyes lingering on her curves, then looked at the gear in the box and picked out gloves, a vest, and a set of elbow guards. "Slacks are fine," he said. "I'll get you a t-shirt, and you can lose the shoes."

"Really, I only have an hour."

"Your partner seems genuinely concerned about you keeping your field skills sharp. We can talk in between drills and some more after. The lesson's already paid for. Don't worry, you'll get what you need in under an hour."

She hadn't put on a combat suit since the academy. Part of her wanted the workout, the exhilaration of sparing. At the risk of sounding like a wimp, she said, "It's a little cold in here, can I keep my socks on?"

"Sure," Marshall said, and tossed a t-shirt emblazoned with his logo at her. "You can keep that; it's good advertising for me. Locker room's over there."

* * *

When she returned, Marshall was already wearing a full suit. He nodded at the pads on the mat at his feet. "Those should fit you," he said. "You can ask me about swords while you suit up."

"I'm not so sure about these pants," she said. "Limited range of motion. Maybe I should come back for the session on another day."

"Right, because when a perp attacks you in the course of your duties, you're gonna be wearing some nice roomy sweatpants or a karate *gi*."

"Okay, point taken. But if they rip, I will not be happy with you."

He nodded but didn't make any promises.

Drelick remembered the basics of hand-to-hand training gear, and in a moment she was outfitted with pads and feeling like a clown. But she'd found it impossible to start interviewing Marshall while stepping into a groin protector and adjusting various lengths of Velcro strapping on her arms and legs. She rose from the crouching position in which she'd been adjusting the last shin guard and peered into the helmet, wondering how much fermented sweat glazed the interior. It was equipped with a face shield. Marshall's was in the up position.

"We'll use the face shields instead of mouth guards so we can talk," he said. "What's your first question?"

Drelick tucked the helmet under her arm and gathered her thoughts. He was driving everything, and she didn't like that. She figured he was the type who not only preferred to have authority figures approach him on his own territory but who also needed to upend the hierarchy by throwing them off balance and establishing his own top-dog status as early as possible. Of course, she did have Pasco to thank for enrolling her in the lesson, and she resolved to inflict something equally uncomfortable on him in the near future.

"Do you know much about Japanese sword culture?"

"Of course. Edged weapons are my specialty, and the *katana* is the ultimate blade."

"Do you teach it?"

He snorted. "No. I teach knife defense, but nobody uses swords in a street fight. I've consulted in a few movies where they wanted the sword fighting to look real, but in a real knife fight you're dealing with a concealed weapon and a style derived from prison shanking."

"Actually, some people do still use swords. Maybe you saw Geoff Lamprey on the news?"

"The guy they found with no head?"

"Yes. That's my case."

"What makes you think it was a *katana*? Put your helmet on, let's get started."

She put it on, adjusted the strap, and lowered the face shield. "Just a hunch, really, but maybe you can confirm it. Steel blades are oiled for preservation, right?"

"And for lubrication…quick draw. A blade that isn't worn upside down for gravity release usually needs a little grease."

"Can you tell me why a sword might have clove oil on it?"

"You could have learned that from the internet."

"I like to do things the old-fashioned way, with human experts."

Marshall lowered his face shield. It darkened his tone of voice. "And that's why they say the government is inefficient."

Drelick brought her own shield down. She wasn't even stretched. This—whatever it was—was going to suck.

"While we're talking I'm going to spontaneously attack you," Marshall said, "Like a suspect might do during an interview. I want you to just react the way you would. Defend yourself. Okay?"

"Got it."

"Japanese sword oil is called *choji*. It's just mineral oil with a few drops of clove oil added for fragrance. The samurai wanted to give his sword oil a smell that would set it apart from the cooking oil. Mineral oil is a laxative, so if his wife mixed them up and put the sword oil in the wok, the poor guy would end up with a raging case of the shits."

Drelick laughed. Marshall seized the unguarded moment to throw a few punches at her midsection. They were controlled, but still carried enough force to throw her off balance. She regained it quickly by sidestepping, but he closed the distance fast, swinging a hammer fist at her from the side and connecting with the padded collar around her throat. That hurt. She jumped backward while launching a front kick to his chest, driving him back but failing to knock him down.

Drelick caught her breath and, keeping her fists up in a guarding position, asked, "Why would a modern martial artist still use clove oil on a sword? It's not like they're living in one-room huts anymore."

Marshall grinned. She wasn't sure if he was amused by her defense reaction or her question.

"You should meet some of my students," he said. "One-room huts are now studio apartments. But you're right; no real need with labels on everything. Still, *Iaido* practitioners are fussy about details. Hung up on ceremony and tradition."

"So it's more like a ceremonial thing these days, the oil?"

"Still keeps the blade well lubricated, but the scent? Yeah, that's like incense. Reminds them of the tradition."

"Sounds ritualistic."

"Absolutely. Some of them practice in front of mirrors," he said, gesturing at a wall of mirrors opposite the pale windows, "to make sure they're radiating enough of a fierce warrior gaze. Supposedly the whole practice is a meditation on death."

Drelick looked at herself in the mirrored wall. There were white lines streaked across the black fabric covering her neck and abdomen. She turned her right arm over and examined the underside of the black forearm guard. More white lines. Chalk.

Marshall turned his palm out and revealed a silver-painted plastic training knife with a chalked edge. "Didn't even know I had it in my hand, did you?"

"How did I not see that?"

"In the real world you won't. Movies always show you the knife. Criminals don't. You'll think it's just another punch when they stab it into you. And with the adrenaline, you won't feel it right away, either."

Now he had her attention. Now she wanted the lesson.

"*I* use some oil for training, too: baby oil, but here it serves a different purpose. If someone attacks you with a knife, you will almost definitely get cut. That's just something you have to accept and work with. Any self-defense move you can't do with oiled hands and forearms isn't going to work in a real knife fight when your blood will be lubricating everything."

She still had other questions for him, academic questions, but now the most pressing was, "What's the best way to disarm an attacker with a blade?" The training she had received at Quantico suddenly felt woefully inadequate.

Chapter 9

Desmond parked on the street in front of Laurie's house. He didn't know when her husband would be getting home and didn't want to be blocking the driveway, even though he planned on picking Lucas up as quickly as he could. It was getting close to bedtime.

When he called to let her know he was running late, she sounded perfectly happy to be entertaining Lucas, but that had been two hours ago. The wall patch had needed several thin coats of spackle with sanding in between to ensure that it wouldn't be noticeable if anyone took the mirror off the wall. But he didn't bore her with the details of his day hiding a murder weapon in his apartment. He had pressed the END button on his phone with an overwhelming sense of relief that Lucas hadn't been snatched from her yard by a man in an indigo hoodie.

Before Desmond was out of the car, he could see Lucas in the front bay window, standing on a couch and staring out at him. By the time he was halfway up the brick walk, Lucas was framed in the storm door with Laurie standing behind him, smiling. She opened the door, and Lucas yelled, "Daddy! Me and Carl played space ship in the tree fort and I got bubbles, look!" Lucas held a bottle of bubble juice aloft as if it were the elixir of life.

"Space orbs," Laurie said, setting a hand on Lucas's shoulder, and for a moment, Desmond had to catch his breath against one of those emotional flash floods that sometimes washed through him without warning. The sight of Lucas all lit up with delight over a game that someone else had played with him, a gentle, generous woman…. Desmond bent down on one knee, took the blue plastic bottle and examined it closely until he was sure the moisture gathering in his eyes and sinuses wasn't going to spill over. "Wow, real space orbs, huh? That's awesome."

He stood up and tousled Lucas's hair. Laurie was still smiling. "Thanks," Desmond said. "I owe you one. Did he behave himself for you?"

"He's a perfect gentleman, just like his father."

"And he ate?"

"Some. He says he likes the mac and cheese from the box better."

"Yeah, we eat a lot of that."

Lucas's knapsack was sitting by the door. Desmond picked it up and slung it over his shoulder. "Okay, buddy, it's getting late and we need to get home for story time. Did you say goodbye to Carl?"

"Bye, Carl!" Lucas called down the hall toward the den, from which the sounds of a laser gun shoot out could be heard. "Seeya, Lucas!" echoed back.

Lucas tugged at the straps of the knapsack hanging at Desmond's hip and said, "Daddy, I want to show you something."

"How about when we get home?"

"I want to show you the paper airplane."

"I think it's a butterfly," Laurie said.

"When we get home, buddy. Let's let Carl and his Mom get some rest. C'mon, take my hand."

Laurie watched from the doorway until they were in the car. Desmond turned the key and put The Beatles on. By the time the SUV rolled into the beach apartment driveway and Desmond killed the engine and the music with it, Lucas was fast asleep in his car seat. Desmond carried him to bed without waking him, thinking as he did so that it wouldn't be long before his son was too big to be transferred like this. Carrying Lucas up the stairs and down the hall, he watched his own reflection in the full-length mirror, growing larger as he approached it with Lucas's body sagging in his arms. He thought of the sword in the wall behind the mirror, sleeping in the dark.

He laid Lucas in bed, brushed the sweaty hair from his brow, and gently kissed his forehead. A flickering motion caught his eye, and as he rose from the mattress and reached to switch off the bedside lamp, he saw the unmistakable play of blue strobes splashing across the ceiling and a high corner of the wall. Desmond felt something in him clench tight at the realization that the flashers weren't moving across the ceiling the way they would if a police cruiser were passing by. They were fixed in one spot. The police were parked outside, and apparently they weren't here to discretely stand watch for a hooded prowler in a samurai mask.

Desmond clicked off the lamp and moved to one side of the window. There was a single black-and-white cruiser parked on the street. A uniformed officer was walking up the driveway beside Desmond's SUV with the white circle of his flashlight floating ahead of him like a rising full moon, his partner climbing out of the car behind him. The wind picked up and sent a scattering of sand across the street, drawing Desmond's gaze to another figure perched at the edge of the property beside a silver Impala. He knew that car, and the lines of that silhouette—Phil Parsons.

Desmond looked at Lucas. His first thought was that they couldn't come in, it would wake him, and then it would take most of an hour to get him back to sleep. They couldn't just show up at any hour and disturb his sleeping child. They had no right. But, of course, they wouldn't be here with flashers on if they didn't have some kind of right. An animal urge to wrap Lucas in his arms and flee out the back door like a fugitive stirred from dormancy, dumping adrenaline into his system. He recognized the feeling for what it was—a primal instinct to protect his own. And what exactly did they think *they* were doing here...protecting Lucas from *him?* "I don't fucking think so," he whispered at the windowpane.

Desmond took one more look at Lucas, then vaulted down the stairs and pulled the front door open before they could knock on it. They could talk to him on his doorstep.

Phil had advanced some way up the driveway, but he was still hanging back behind the uniforms, blue light painting his face in rapid intervals between the shadows. Desmond looked past the officers to the flickering form of his antagonist. "What are you doing here, Phil?"

Phil Parsons didn't answer the question; he just shoved his hands into his pockets and looked up at Lucas's bedroom window.

The first officer to reach the steps addressed him. "Desmond Carmichael?"

"Yeah."

"We have a citation to remove your son Lucas Carmichael from the home. Mr. Parsons has been granted an emergency temporary appointment of guardianship, and he has a child safety seat in his car for the transfer."

"Show me the paper."

The cop held out an envelope. Desmond took it, removed the document, and set his eyes on it, but the adrenaline made it hard to focus.

Sua Sponte Order for Transfer of Care and Custody

After taking in the title, his head swam, and fragments of the document flashed up at him, raising his heart rate: Docket #...Lucas's name and date of birth...without proper guardianship...incapacity or unfitness of the parent or guardian...where it was determined that this child's safety and welfare required that he/she be placed in the custody of the Department of Social Services pending a further hearing.... Chapter 119, section 23C...continuation of the child in his or her home is contrary to his or her best interest...signed by a Justice of the Probate and Family Court.

"How did you do it?" Desmond asked Phil.

This time Phil looked at him but didn't reply.

"You have some old dirt on a judge? Is that how you got this? Because this is bullshit. It won't stand, and I swear to God, if you put him through this for something so thin that I can rectify it on Monday...." He shook his head, didn't even know what to threaten, and now he could feel the cops staring at him.

"You can't rectify this, Desmond," Phil said, "and you know on what grounds."

Desmond could feel the tension in his neck muscles, the grinding of his teeth. "Enlighten me," he said.

"I had a private eye take pictures of you bringing that godforsaken sword into the house. You're not fit, Desmond, not anymore. It's an unsafe environment."

Desmond finally looked at the cops. "Search the house," he said, "You won't find anything. No weapons, nothing. See for yourselves."

"Sir, we're not here on a search warrant."

"I'm inviting you in."

"We're just here to pick up your son."

Desmond was surprised by the fire those words stoked in his gut. They couldn't take Lucas. A monster had taken Sandy, and now the men who were supposed to protect people from monsters were going to take Lucas from him, too? He would have nothing left."

"Is your son in the bedroom, sir?"

"He's sleeping. Come back in the morning."

"I'm afraid we can't do that," the officer said. "Please wake him and bring him to his grandfather."

Desmond took a step forward, but the two uniforms blocked his advance. "You know I didn't kill her Phil. You do know that, don't you?"

Phil Parsons' stoic façade caved in a little, and Desmond could see a flicker of bright pain beneath the awful aging loss had inflicted upon him. "You're making it hard for me to know anything, Des."

"You can stop this before it starts," Desmond said. "He lost his mother, and now you're going to confuse him, you're going to hurt him again. Don't."

"I'm not going to lose all that's left of my daughter just because you're unstable."

"*Unstable?* Someone is stalking us! What more has to happen for you to accept that?"

"Let it go, son. Don't dig yourself deeper."

Desmond shook his head as Phil continued, "You've lost your job, you're scaring him with a mask and God only knows what kind of stories. You want to be a hero like in one of your books? Then don't go making up monsters. Don't bring the thing that killed his mother into the house like you're gonna slay a dragon with it or some crazy shit. Be a man and get him out of this dump."

"*You* gave me that fucking thing in the first place, Phil. *You* brought it into our home. You're one to talk."

The second cop, the one who hadn't spoken yet, put a hand on Desmond's shoulder and said, "You two can save all this for the court date. Right now, I need you to get your son and put him in Mr. Parsons' car, sir." The cop turned sideways and placed his body between the two men, ready to start pushing them away from each other if it came to blows.

With a quieter tone than the one he'd been using, Phil said, "He's still sleeping, Des. There are two ways this can go. Think about it."

It was true. There were only two ways for Lucas to leave the house tonight, but he *was* leaving. He was leaving because men with guns were here. Desmond took a step backward, felt his shoulders crumble inward, fumbled with the door, and opened it slowly. "Okay. I'll get him," he said.

"Don't dally, sir, or we'll have to come in."

Desmond glared at the cop, then stepped into the apartment and pushed the storm door closed until the latch clicked. He left the inner door open so they could watch him through the glass as he climbed the stairs.

Standing at Lucas's bedside, watching the dim reflection of the pulsing blue lights on his son's cheek, he felt helpless. Lucas had been asleep for less than an hour; just enough time for him to be cranky if woken. Desmond shook his shoulder and spoke his name.

Lucas wrinkled his face, swatted at the offending hand, and tried to roll back into his original position. Desmond shook him again.

"No," Lucas said.

"Hey, buddy. Time to wake up. Papa's here."

"No."

"I'm sorry, but you have to go to Nana and Papa's for a sleepover."

"No, Daddy. I don't want to."

"You can go right back to sleep when you get there, okay? Nana will make you pancakes in the morning."

Desmond lifted him and carried him down the stairs, arms locked under his bottom to form a seat. Lucas had almost fallen back asleep when Desmond set him down on the couch to gather a few essentials—toothbrush, toothpaste, vitamins, and a favorite toy—and toss them in the knapsack with the change of clothes, still sitting by the front door under the coat rack where he had dropped it when they got home from Laurie's house.

Lucas slid off of the couch onto his knees and started crying. "I don't *want* to go to Nana and Papa's house, I don't *want* to, *I don't want to go!*" It became a mantra that quickly devolved into a mess of snot-clogged howling. Desmond tried to tune it out and focus on packing. The cops beyond the glass made no secret of the fact that they were watching. "I want to stay with *you*, Daddy. Daddy, I want to stay with *you*." It was a typical tantrum for an overtired kid, but to Desmond it felt like Lucas was playing the role of the Chorus in a Greek tragedy, giving voice to his own wretched emotions. The poor kid had no reason to believe it would be for more than one night, and he was this upset. What would they tell him tomorrow night and the night after that?

Desmond could hardly think straight, was knocking things over now, rummaging through the detritus of a living room shared by a widower and a toddler, feeling ashamed of the mess. With an armload of jumbled clothing, a favorite blanket, and a brown plastic bottle of chewable vitamins spilling over his elbow, he yanked open the zipper of Lucas's knapsack with enough force to jam the teeth.

Inside, atop the folded clothes and a baggie of Goldfish crackers, was a snow-white origami butterfly. His breath caught in his chest.

He remembered Lucas pleading with him in Laurie's foyer.

I want to show you the paper airplane.

At the time, he'd figured Laurie had done some kind of craft project to keep the kids busy. Maybe she had. Dear God, he hoped she had.

Chapter 10

If only.

Shaun Bell sat in the Logan Airport Starbucks and sipped tea from a paper cup. All he could taste was the paper, and the tea was too hot. He considered dumping it out. Rather than calming his nerves, the wrongness of the drink was only increasing his agitation, but buying it had given him a place to sit while watching the arrivals. His teacher would stand out from the crowd. Sensei had at times studied the unconscious posture and gait of those around him and imitated it to blend in, but Shaun knew how hard it was for him to break the long habit of moving through the world with the grace and purpose of a heron gliding through a flock of crows.

A cocktail napkin folded in the shape of a dog sat on the table beside the tea. The paper was poor, hardly capable of holding the form at all. The head was misshapen and ugly. He idly curled his fingers around it and crumpled it into a ball.

He was aware of Sensei's suitcase on the floor beneath the table. It had preceded the man to Boston, and Shaun had claimed it from the luggage carousel. Shaun let his shoe brush against it. It was the same one Sensei had taken with him when the two of them had embarked on their journey together from California to the east coast.

There were no weapons in the bag. Sensei would have used one of the blades they had stored years ago at the underground dojo on the west coast. That concrete room had been a place of awakening for Shaun Bell. He longed for the exhilaration and clarity of those days of first steps on the path.

Shaun's gaze moved across the concourse. A man dressed in vacation clothes was standing near the restroom playing with an iPhone while his two little girls chased each other around the terminal.

Everywhere he went he saw this same phenomenon—parents unmindful of their children, their attention fixed on little glass windows in the palms of their hands, mesmerized like drug addicts, longing for some artificial connection while their own flesh and blood careened wildly through a chaotic and violent world behind their backs. The writer was even worse. He invented false worlds and peopled them with ghosts while his motherless son scanned the horizon for a human connection. It was shameful. What did a man need to lose to be shaken from his immersion in a dream? What terminal force could liberate him from the pursuit of phantoms and engage him in the living world around him?

Shaun squeezed the napkin ball in his hand. He turned his fist over and examined his fingernails. There were no traces of the ink. Would the writer even find the message? If he did, it would take him time to decipher it. This was a dangerous game. The man should have acted already. Why did he need more than one message? It was a writer's business to speak the language of symbols. And really, what interpretation was required here? The reaper was coming. What more did a man need to know? But Sensei had taught him to treat all action as art. Shaun had brushed the message to Carmichael as a *kanji* character, obeying the master's dictum even as he betrayed him. That the betrayal was diffused in poetry, calligraphy, and origami did nothing to diminish the intention. He had strayed from the path of the undivided mind.

Surely Sensei knew that his excuses for failure at the playground were weak. He lacked sufficient *yamato damashi* to slay a child. Surely Sensei knew this and would test him again soon.

He tapped his foot against the suitcase, and thought of days of long light on the porch in Huntington Beach, recalled vividly the day when he had first seen that suitcase sitting on the planks overlooking the rock garden behind the apartment Sensei had rented from their family on Hale Street. Back before he knew the old man as *Sensei*.

Shaun had wandered down the back stairs after fixing himself a sandwich and, as on most afternoons, had settled into the lawn chair beside the downstairs tenant's wooden rocker. The old man had a faraway look in his eyes, but he didn't redress his face at the sound of the creaking steps, didn't hide whatever sorrow he'd been ruminating on the way most adults did when caught. His eyes met Shaun's and kindled with the same quiet generosity as always, as his mouth melted into a faint but honest smile. Shaun's parents never smiled quite like that, like they were *really* seeing him. They rehearsed a well-worn repertoire of faces and voices for patronizing him. He didn't know if they thought of themselves as masters of feigned interest or if they believed they were really seeing and hearing him during the few hours each week when they were in his presence. It was obvious to him, even at the age of eleven, that the only genuine expression they wore was worry.

They worried about him, and he thought that was probably a sign of love, but they worried more about their jobs, their cars, their house, their gray hairs and crow's-feet. He saw them separately now, so it seemed they hadn't worried about him enough to stay together.

The old man patted the suitcase. "I am taking a trip," he said.

"Where?" Shaun asked.

"Arizona."

"Why Arizona?"

"I looked up an old acquaintance. It will be a hunting trip."

"You hunt? Like with a gun?"

The old man smiled. "I have always wanted to try hunting, but the time never seemed right for it. When you get to be my age, you realize that it is important to try new things, to do things you have always wanted to do, or you may never do them at all."

"You're not *that* old," Shaun said, placing his half-eaten peanut-butter sandwich on the wobbly little whitewashed table between them.

"Life is like a water bubble. No one knows when death will come. We must use the time we have."

"When will you be back?"

"In a few days."

"What will *I* do? After school."

"You can come down here the same as always. Make the tea. Drink the tea and practice your *bokken* forms. Just as if I were sitting in this chair. It's good for you to be outside. Don't start watching TV."

Shaun made the same face he would have if his neighbor had suggested that he might start eating worms, and together they laughed.

A moment passed in easy silence, broken by the double honk of a car horn from the street side of the house. "My taxi is here," the old man said, rising.

Shaun carried the suitcase to the car for him. It was heavy.

After the taxi disappeared under the purpling sky, Shaun went to the kitchen and made the tea. Two cups. He drank one and let the other cool on the little white table beside the rocking chair. He took up the wooden sword that the old man had carved for him with his mother's permission. She had been happy to learn that he could still spend some time swinging a piece of wood in the back yard, even after baseball hadn't worked out for him—team sports had never worked out for him, not at any of the schools they'd tried. It would still be several hours before she was home. Enough time to practice his patterns. He walked around the rock garden and stepped onto the freshly cut grass.

It was good to have something to do in the yard while the house was empty, good to have something to keep his mind off the absence of the dog. His mother had gotten rid of the dog soon after she'd gotten rid of his father. Shaun would never know for sure if she had left the gate open intentionally....

In the airport coffee shop, Shaun Bell moved the cup to the edge of the table so that he wouldn't have to endure the inferior smell of the tea. He recalled the smell of grass and honeysuckle on late summer nights in California, the sky deepening to burnished indigo while he stepped and pivoted, adjusted his stance and grip, breathed and sweated until his eyes no longer searched the fence line for slow moving headlights, his ears focused only on his exhalations and the dull roar of hard wood cleaving the still air while the first cold, distant stars came out to watch him.

He could see Sensei now, moving down the concourse, gliding between the crows.

If only.

It was a phrase that haunted his mind lately, like a mantra. *If only the old man hadn't killed a dog that night when he killed the woman.*

* * *

Desmond slept in Lucas's bed. It was too small for him, and he had to curl up in a fetal position to do it, but he was too exhausted to care. It would have been harder to fall asleep in his own bed with Sandy's ghost beside him, judging him for losing their son. In Lucas's room he was able to succumb to sleep while still taking responsibility for the failure. He knew he could do nothing to rectify the situation in the middle of the night, knew that whatever he could do in the morning would only be hindered by exhaustion, so he'd surrendered into merciful ignorance of the conditions at the stormy surface of his life the way a diver escapes the turbulence of a rough sea by descending.

Twice before sleep claimed him for the night, he startled back to wakefulness with the jolt that comes from the body reacting to the hard tug of sleep—that alarmed bracing against the sensation of falling. And each time he surfaced, clutching the Spider-Man sheets, he imagined he could hear the bloodthirsty blade whispering to him from within the wall, begging him for the freedom to do the thing it had been forged for, to bleed all of the antagonists—some in shadow, some in plain sight—who were trying to take Lucas away from him.

The morning brought rain. Out of habit he rose early, showered, made coffee, and went to his desk in the living room. He stood in front of the laptop and stared at the lid until he realized he was holding his breath. Last night had been the first night with the new locks installed, but he'd still felt compelled to check them, and now he half expected to find a new haiku on the screen.

His brain was waking up at the same time as the computer, and he felt a curdling in the pit of his stomach as he remembered something that had evaded him while showering and putting on the coffee pot. In the predawn, his first pain-radiant thoughts of the day had been a replay of the encounter with Phil—what he had said to his father-in-law and what he should have said...but he had been holding one detail of the previous night just out of view, protecting himself from the possibilities it suggested: the paper butterfly.

The computer was awake now and displayed the white Word document, the cursor blinking at the end of the lousy couple of lines he had produced at the park. He sighed and closed the lid. He got up and went to the couch where the origami insect patiently waited for him.

Desmond picked it up and turned it over in his hands. He had seen origami butterflies before, but they weren't as common as cranes, and origami animals in general weren't exactly common enough to be produced like paper airplanes by American boys hanging out in a tree house. Common enough for coincidence? He couldn't afford to believe that. And this one was flawless. He looked at the clock: 6:19. It was still too early to call Laurie. *Why? Respect for her Sunday morning sleep?* He couldn't afford to put manners ahead of Lucas's safety. He picked up the phone. At least he wouldn't wake her husband. She had said he would be away on his business trip until Monday.

She answered on the fourth ring, her voice coated with sleep. Desmond apologized but didn't ask if he'd woken her. Of course he had. "Is Lucas okay?" she asked. She knew he wouldn't be calling unless something had happened; a food allergy, or an injury she hadn't noticed. How was he supposed to frame the question? *I was just wondering if Sandy's killer might have dropped by yesterday to deliver some party favors for the boys. You didn't happen to see a guy in a Japanese demon mask haunting your yard, did you?*

"This is going to sound like it could have waited, but trust me, it's important. I found an origami butterfly in Lucas's bag. Do you know where he got it?"

"Um...." Desmond could picture her lying in bed, an arm draped over her forehead, staring up at the ceiling and forcing her brain to work. "Yeah. The boys said they found it in the tree house. I figured the girl next door might have made it when she was sitting Carl for me last week. She's pretty creative...why?"

He didn't answer. Morning light had filtered into the room through the clouds and curtains, and even in diluted gray form, it overpowered the lamplight by which he had first examined the butterfly the previous night. Now he could see dark spots on the paper, the shadows of ink within its folds. "It might be nothing," he said, not believing the words, "but it has something in common with what happened to Sandy, so I hope you'll forgive me for being freaked out." He unfolded the paper. "Could you ask the girl if she made it? Call her and call me back?"

When the paper was no longer a butterfly, but a many-creased and softly angled paper square, he let go of it and watched it drift to the surface of his desk. It sliced through the air sideways and gently came to rest on the wood laminate. A bold, fluid *kanji* pictogram blazed up at him in black ink. He wasn't hearing Laurie's answer to his question, something about when the sun was up. He snapped back when she asked him if he was okay.

"No," he said. "I don't think I am." He pressed END.

He flipped the laptop open and ran a search for "kanji butterfly." It was all he had to go on. Most of the results were for tattoo studio websites where illustrations of butterflies combined with calligraphy jumped out at him from freckled swatches of pale skin, inflamed red around the freshly inked lines. He clicked back and tried a more traditional calligraphy site where he was able to find the *kanji* character for "butterfly," but it didn't match the ink on the paper in front of him. Another site allowed you to order a custom calligraphy scroll, but you had to type in the English word or phrase that you wanted translated. Desmond needed to go the other way—from *kanji* to English. Typing in random words to find a match would take all day. He needed human help. And for that, he would have to wait. It wasn't even 7 AM.

He poured more coffee, paced the apartment, and looked at the street through the blinds. He felt helpless. Fear droned through the silent apartment, threatening to reach a panic pitch at any moment. He tried to focus. Salerno had said that the guest instructor, the sword teacher, was Japanese. Maybe a phone call to the man, followed by an email attachment, would be enough to get a translation. He smoothed out the paper square and placed it in the circle of light from the desk lamp. Then he snapped a few photos of it with his smartphone until he got one that wasn't too blurry. The phone rang in his hand and startled him while he was looking at the pictures.

It was Laurie calling him back to tell him that the girl next door didn't know anything about origami. It was exactly what he'd been expecting to hear, and yet his dread deepened at the confirmation. "Desmond, what's this all about?" she asked, with a new kind of concern in her voice. "Frankly, you're scaring me. You seem stressed and…paranoid."

"I can't talk about it yet. Not until I understand it better myself," he said.

"Is someone stalking you? Because of your books, or because of…."

What happened to Sandy.

"The police don't seem to think so," Desmond said.

"But you do."

"I can't talk about it."

Silence from her but not consent. She didn't want to let him off the hook. Not if she thought she might be able to help.

"You're a good friend, Laurie. I'll keep you in the loop."

"Let us know if you need anything. Really, anything."

"I will. I might need a character reference to keep custody of Lucas."

"What?"

"That's why I can't get into my suspicions with you. I'm trying to find my way through a maze, and if a judge or lawyer ever asked you point blank whether or not you've heard me talking about certain far-fetched ideas…it could hurt my chances of keeping him."

"What happened, Des?"

"I'll talk to you soon. I promise." He hung up.

The *kanji* character shone from the screen in his hand in high contrast black and white.

Desmond went to the coat rack by the door, took his wallet from his jacket pocket, and plucked Salerno's business card from the fold. The sword instructor's name and phone number were scrawled on the back, barely legible. He checked the time: still too early to call a stranger or a lawyer. What to do to kill time? Writing was out of the question. He wouldn't be able to focus. Looking at the laptop he doubted that he would ever be able to focus again. How could he type on those keys knowing that Sandy's killer had touched them? His space had been violated. Everything had been violated—his home, his work, his relationship with his son. But for Desmond, writing was thinking. Even when there was no escaping into fiction, there was the hope that forming questions and potential answers in writing would calm him and show him a way forward. He used to talk to Sandy to puzzle out problems, and while he wasn't going to start talking to himself, he sort of could, if he wrote. But the laptop sat on the desk in the corner looking like a bear trap.

He climbed the stairs, entered his bedroom, and opened the top drawer of his dresser. He felt around in the back of the drawer under his socks until his fingers found a polished wooden box. He withdrew it: a mahogany case with rounded corners and invisible hinges, longer than it was wide. He slid a switch on the side, and the case opened with a weird slowness that reminded him of hydraulic levers. Inside, a jet-black fountain pen with sterling silver accents was nestled tightly into a bed of silk.

Sandy had given him the pen as a gift when his first novel sold. He had signed the contract with it, and it had always been more of a symbolic item to him than an actual tool, something to display on his desk back when he had a real desk instead of a table in the corner of the apartment—a token reminder of his calling. It had also reminded him of who he was writing for: a woman who loved and understood him.

Actually writing with the thing had always seemed pretentious to him, and a little intimidating, as if every word scratched out under its sharp quill tip had to be worthy of graving in stone, every milligram of its rarefied ink weighted against the literature of the ages. And Desmond knew in his heart that he was more of an entertainer than an artist. Sure, there were timeless mythic themes in his work, and he treated those threads seriously; but he also knew that he had inherited more from Tolkien than Tolstoy. The yarn he was currently spinning even featured a knight avenging a slain queen, and you didn't have to be Freud.... Therapeutic? Yes, definitely. Maybe even cathartic, but the act of writing about heroes didn't have to be heroic. The laptop had always been fine.

He took the pen from the case and studied it, placed it between his thumb and forefinger and gave the grip a try, scribbling on air. It was comfortable. He fetched a blank legal pad from the top shelf of his closet, carried his new tools downstairs, settled at the kitchen table, and documented everything he could remember since the day at the Castle Playground. At first the sentences formed in slow, halting bursts. He drank cold coffee, kept the pen on the page, and found a rhythm. Ink flowed.

Two hours later, he tossed the pen down on the pad as if it were hot. His hand ached.

The kitchen clock told him that he had burned the inappropriate hours, so he picked up the business card and typed the number into his phone. The voice that answered sounded relaxed, but not sleepy.

"Mr. Masahiro?" Desmond asked.

"This is he."

"My name is Desmond Carmichael. Peter Salerno gave me your number. He said you might be able to answer some questions about samurai swords and Japanese culture."

"Ah, yes. Peter mentioned that you might call. My condolences for your loss, Mr. Carmichael."

"Thank you." Desmond cleared his throat.

"Perhaps we could meet in person some time to discuss your questions."

"That would be great, but as a single parent, finding time can be a little tricky. I wondered if I might ask you a few questions over the phone. Have I reached you at an okay time?"

"Now is fine."

"Okay. Um.... I actually have a kanji character that I need translated. Do you read kanji?"

"Yes."

"Could I possibly email you an image file?"

"Of course."

"Thank you. I do have another question first, if I may.... I know this is morbid, but you'll understand why I would ask.... How difficult is it to decapitate a person with a sword? Would it require much skill and strength?"

The silence on the line stretched out long enough for Desmond to wonder if the man had hung up on him, but the air sounded too alive for that. Eventually, Masahiro said, "Not much muscle strength, no. The sword does the cutting, not the swordsman. However, it does require skill for the swordsman to let the blade do its job without getting in the way."

"How do you mean?"

"I'm speaking in general about cutting. Of course I can't speak from experience about cutting people. In the dojo, we use bamboo to simulate bone, and grass mats soaked in water to emulate the density of flesh."

"I see."

"The curve of the samurai sword makes it perfect for slicing, but the angle of the blade in motion must be straight. This requires a proper grip. If the grip is too tight, too stiff, it is a hindrance. Beginners have trouble relaxing and guiding the blade along a straight path without forcing it."

"Would someone who was relaxed by alcohol have an easier time swinging the right way?"

"No, even relaxed, it would take exceptional luck for an untrained person to cut clean through a human neck."

"Why is that?"

"Are you sure you want to discuss this in such…detail, Mr. Carmichael?"

"Please. Go on."

"All right, then. It would be easier to show you these things in person, but I will try to explain. There is a section of the blade, about nine inches long, where the curvature and tensile strength are greatest. If the target is struck too close to the tip of the blade, the sword will become wedged and stuck, or the tip may shatter against the spinal vertebrae. If the target is struck too low on the blade, too close to the hilt, there will be insufficient momentum to slice through, and again, the blade may become wedged in muscle. And if the hilt is not properly aligned at the moment of impact, if it is extended beyond the center of the target, the swing will be like that of a baseball bat, overextended, no good for slicing through."

"That's a lot more complicated than I realized."

"That is why it is an art. My students spend years refining the details of their form while cutting nothing more substantial than air."

Desmond's voice had grown thin. He cleared his throat and asked, "Could an untrained, lucky person sever a neck most of the way, but fail to cut the head entirely off?" He felt bile rising in the back of his throat and perspiration beading up along his hairline.

"Such a cut would be the mark of true samurai skill."

"Why?"

"It is the traditional method of finishing someone who is performing *seppuku*. You are familiar with the ritual suicide of a samurai?"

"Yes."

"When the suicide assistant sees the practitioner tug the dagger in his gut upward toward the sternum, it signals that the act is complete, and the assistant steps forward to decapitate, but not fully. A thin strip of flesh is left to prevent the disgrace of the head bouncing on the ground or rolling away."

Desmond thought he might vomit. He pressed his knuckle to his lips and squeezed the cell phone; his breath flared through the speaker in a cloud of white noise.

"Are you okay, Desmond?"

"Yeah." The word came out faint and toneless, the husk of a word.

"I'm sorry. These details must be deeply distressing for you to contemplate. I can get carried away talking shop, forgetting that you are not a student."

Desmond sighed. "Okay...thank you. I'll send you that character?"

"Of course. Do you have a pen handy? I'll give you my email address."

Desmond picked up the fountain pen, jotted the address down. Then he pressed END, dropped the phone, ran to the bathroom, and heaved up his breakfast.

After splashing water on his face and rinsing his mouth from the tap, he returned to the kitchen and, with clumsy, trembling fingers, emailed the photo from his phone. As soon as he heard the "sent" sound, he put the phone down on the table and went out onto the front steps to breathe in the salty air. He wished like hell he hadn't quit smoking when Sandy was pregnant with Lucas, wished he still had one last stale cigarette in the apartment that he could smoke the fuck out of right now. Just one.

When he went back inside, there was a reply from Masahiro on the little phone screen. Holding his breath, he tapped it. The reply was two words long.

Translation: *Fly*

The word *fly* written inside a folded paper butterfly? What was that? A command? A warning? He knew in the bottom of his sour stomach that it was. It was a message for Lucas, a message that a four-year-old child could never decode on his own. *Fly away, little butterfly. The dragon is coming.*

Chapter 11

Phil Parsons stared at the computer monitor and watched his sleeping grandson. Lucas was tangled in the sheets, having rotated sideways in the night, like a clock hand anxious for dawn. Maybe it had been a restless sleep, but the boy looked peaceful now, and Phil wasn't looking forward to shattering that peace by waking him or telling him things he didn't want to hear.

Karen's footsteps creaked softly on the carpeted stairs. She entered the study and set a steaming cup of coffee on the desk and a gentle hand on Phil's shoulder. He touched the hand with his own and squeezed her fingers.

"You could watch him from the chair in his room, you know," Karen said.

Lucas was sleeping in Sandy's old bedroom, where they now kept a treadmill and a guitar Phil could play a few chords on. Today they would ask Lucas what he wanted the room to look like because it would be his own room for a while. Then they would make a list of things they needed for him.

"I don't want to disturb him," Phil said.

"I don't know how you get any comfort from watching that thing."

"Can't say I do."

"Isn't it a little creepy, him looking like he's on one of those tapes you used to have to watch after a robbery?"

Phil took a sip of the coffee. "It's not like that. We haven't seen him much since Sandy died. It's just good to see him at all. He's gotten so big."

"He has. But this...him being here, it isn't about seeing him more."

"I know."

Karen's hand tightened on his shoulder, and she asked a question that Phil knew she probably wouldn't have asked if they'd been looking at each other instead of at the boy on the monitor: "Do you think Desmond did it? Do you think he killed her?"

"He asked me that himself last night."

"Not in front of Lucas."

"No, of course not."

"No you don't think he did it?"

"No, he didn't ask me in front of Lucas. I don't know if he did it. I can't rule it out, but I think...no."

"But you don't think he's stable."

"Do you?"

She sighed, but didn't answer the question.

"He's been through a lot," Phil said.

"And he has a very active imagination," Karen said, "I think that's what Sandy fell in love with."

"It's getting the better of him. His judgment's no good."

"You sound like you're trying to convince yourself of that."

"No, I'm convinced. Even if Harwood is the wrong guy, which is a *really* big 'if,' but just supposing Desmond is right and the killer is still out there...then this is the safest place for Lucas, not some slum-lord special on the beach."

"I did worry about Lucas getting into the water with the riptide while his father had his nose in a book or a laptop."

"See? No matter how you look at it, he's safer here."

"But judges don't take kids away from their parents just because the house doesn't have cameras and alarms, or because it's too close to the beach, Phil."

Phil took another sip of coffee.

Karen took her hand off his shoulder.

He cocked his head in her direction, but kept his eyes on the screen.

Karen asked, "What do you think Sandy would say about what we're doing?"

"Don't forget about the sword, Karen. He got it out of storage and brought it into the house. Tell me Lucas wasn't in a dangerous environment."

"And we only know about that because of all this spying."

"Thank heaven we know."

She left the room as quietly as she had entered.

Phil opened the home security program and changed a few settings. After Sandy's death he'd dumped a lot of money into upgrades. He'd been too tired to change the settings last night after finally getting Lucas to sleep, but tonight, and every night after, he wanted the lights to come on in the master bedroom if Lucas woke up and left his room to go to the bathroom or for a drink of water. The boy was going to be feeling vulnerable, now more than ever with neither parent around to tend to his needs. Phil would rise at any hour to make sure that Lucas didn't feel alone.

The smell of breakfast drifted up from the kitchen, and Phil's stomach groaned in reply. Within a couple of seconds, Lucas also groaned—Phil could hear the sound from down the hall while he watched Lucas on the monitor: kicking, rolling onto his stomach, and then propping himself up on his elbows, blinking at the unfamiliar bedroom. Good timing. Phil closed the security program, rolled his chair away from the desk, and ambled down the hall with his coffee mug in hand. Lucas stood in the doorway of the spare bedroom, looking groggy.

"Papa," he said.

"Good morning, champ. You sleep okay?"

Lucas nodded slightly, staring at a spot on the carpet. Then he shivered and said, "I hafta pee."

"Okay, let's go to the potty. You know the way."

Toddling down the hall with his grandfather's hand on the back of his head, Lucas said, "I want Daddy."

"We'll see about that, we'll see. You like French toast and bacon? Nana made some."

* * *

They ate in silence until the doorbell chimed. Phil and Karen exchanged a look of alarm.

"Daddy!" Lucas said as he hopped down from his seat and ran to the window. Phil made it to the door almost as fast.

"It's *not* Daddy. Why isn't it Daddy, Papa?"

Phil could see Chuck Fournier's black Corvette through the leaded glass panes. He opened the door on Fournier—freshly shaven and dressed in a pistachio green short-sleeved shirt and a yellow tie. On his way to work or church, or maybe church followed by work.

"Morning, Phil. I was in the neighborhood. Heard it went down pretty easy last night, but I wanted to check in anyway. Mind if I come in?"

Phil hesitated, then opened the door wider and stepped aside. "I thought you might be him," Phil said, and tilted his head in Lucas's direction to indicate the need for cautious words. "If he does drop by, it might not go so smoothly today if he sees your car in the driveway before he even gets to the door."

"I'll only stay for a minute. Hi, Karen. Hey, Lucas! Remember me? You helped us draw a picture the other day."

Lucas stepped behind Karen's leg and grasped a few inches of her blouse. Phil was relieved the kid didn't go whole hog and revert to sucking his thumb. But that might be next if the world didn't stop shifting under his feet.

"Something smells good," Fournier said.

"Come in and have a seat, Chuck," Karen said, "I'll zap some of that French toast for you. Would you like a cup of coffee?"

"Thanks, but no. I'm trying to cut back. Already had one. But the bacon sure smells good. And do I see eggs?" He lifted the corner of a red-plaid cloth napkin and peered into a steaming bowl while Karen laid a clean plate down in front of a vacant chair and said, "Just some left over from the French toast that I scrambled up. Help yourself."

Lucas hovered by his own chair where strips of French toast were getting cold on an Elmo plate beside a glass of apple juice. He watched Fournier settle in and frowned. "Nana, can I do my puzzle in the den?"

"Three more bites of French toast and you can."

Lucas picked up a strip and made two small, quick chomps, chewed enough to make room for the third bite, then fulfilled the contract. "Make sure you chew it," Karen said as Lucas ran from the room. Karen followed.

"You might *not* see Desmond today, after all." Fournier said around a mouthful of eggs and bacon. "I just got a call from a friend at Cedar Junction. Apparently Desmond has an appointment to visit Greg Harwood today. Set it up yesterday, and he hasn't called to cancel after what happened last night. Not yet, anyway. Must be pretty important to him."

"You're shitting me."

"No, sir."

"Why would he want to do that?"

"Well…. My *first* thought is that Des wants to see if Harwood's coherent enough to contradict anything he might say about that night now that it's under the microscope again."

"Is it? Are you reopening the case?"

"No. Not unless he does something really stupid. Which he might."

Phil took the last two pieces of bacon before Fournier could. He wasn't really hungry anymore, just didn't want to watch Fournier eat them.

"Okay," Phil said, "So that's your *first* thought…. One thing I learned on the job is that first thoughts are usually wrong. Do you have a second thought?"

"You don't think he killed Sandy," Fournier said in a low monotone that still sounded too loud to Phil with Lucas in the next room. He could hear Karen and Lucas talking about the puzzle, her leaving enough space in the conversation to maybe listen in, and no TV in the background.

Phil was getting tired of the question, but he supposed it was the price of taking guardianship. "You need to understand that Karen and I aren't trying to open that wound. That is not what this is about. It's about Lucas and keeping him safe. Desmond…he's acting erratically, and I can't say why, but I had to get Lucas out of there."

They sat in silence. Karen said something about looking for a corner piece with blue on it. Phil took a bite of bacon. It tasted bitter.

"Did Desmond tell you that he also visited Salerno's karate studio?"

"Isn't that an Aikido place?"

"Same diff. Did you know?"

"No, I didn't." This was getting stranger.

"He's revisiting the case. So am I, unofficially."

"Are you ready for the avalanche of shit you're going to bring down on yourself if word gets out that a detective thinks Harwood may be innocent?"

"Nothing's getting out, Phil."

"What if he's right?"

"I don't follow."

"What if Desmond isn't losing his grip?" Phil asked, "What if someone else did kill Sandy…someone who's still out there?"

"Think about Sandy, Phil. I knew her since we were kids, and she didn't have an enemy in the world. If the crazy man we picked up with the murder weapon didn't do it, then it had to be the crazy man she was married to, who by the way already had the weapon in his possession. A third man is one too many. You know it is."

Phil nodded.

Chuck Fournier slid his chair back, stood up, and reached across the table for a handful of blueberries. He stuffed them into his mouth and brushed the water droplets off his hand with two swipes across his pants. "I'll be in touch."

Chapter 12

It rained all the way down Route 495 and showed no signs of letting up in South Walpole. Cedar Junction Correctional Facility came up on the left, looking like it had been in the rain since the day it was built. The white limestone façade and concrete steps were stained with rust trails running from every iron light fixture and handrail. A pair of flags, limp and drenched, flanked the path. Razor wire spilled over the walls like rampant vines.

Climbing the steps with his notebook in hand, Desmond peeled a sticker off the thigh of the khakis he had bought for the visit (he had learned from the website that jeans weren't allowed). Dark raindrops speckled the fabric in pinpoints, exploding outward in a way that faintly reminded him of the flashbulbs that had left purple splotches on his field of vision the last time he'd been this close to Greg Harwood, at the sentencing.

Desmond had avoided most of the trial. He'd told himself at the time that grieving or not, he had a child to support and had to go to work. But Principal Rosenbaum would have understood if he'd taken the time off to attend. Instead, he had immersed himself in work and kept the TV off during the news hour every night. As a writer, Desmond knew that conflict and confrontation were the twin engines of character building. In life, he did his damnedest to avoid both.

Now he was finally going to see the man condemned for killing his wife, and where was his righteous rage? Where was his personal breakthrough to a new stratum of courage? He wasn't here to finally face a monster. He was entering this dungeon with pen, not sword, because of his growing certainty that the monster wasn't sequestered within its walls after all, and he supposed that made him still a coward. He dropped his hand into his pocket where the fountain pen rested (tip up to avoid staining the new pants) and jabbed his thumb on its sharp point, a self-punishing jolt that snapped him into the present moment.

Inside, the prison reminded him of every public school he'd ever worked in—all cinderblock and tile, iron radiators and plenty of clocks, every surface covered with industrial gray or blue paint that was probably applied annually to cover the grime. Not a soft surface in the place or a scrap of fabric that wasn't on someone's body. All bright, echoing spaces.

Desmond hoped the guards wouldn't confiscate his pen and notebook, but it was the first thing they did before they led him to the visitors' room and left him standing beside a plastic chair in front of a window and a metal box that cradled a beige phone connected by a flexible steel cable. Desmond sat down as Harwood entered through a door beyond the glass. The prisoner kept his eyes fixed on the floor until he was settled in his seat. He shot a nervous glance at Desmond and then looked down at his hands, folded in front of him on the counter. He was dressed in an orange DOC smock that reminded Desmond of doctor's scrubs. His short gray hair, glasses, and slim frame completed the association. If life had dealt Harwood a different hand, if he hadn't fallen on hard times and hard liquor, maybe he would have ended up in a different institution, working as an orderly or a nurse, in a hospital, taking his smock off at the end of the day, and leaving echoing halls of human suffering behind. It was a habit for Desmond to free associate like this, a writer's game, placing people in imaginary scenarios inspired by details. He couldn't help it.

Harwood picked up the phone and listened, but didn't look up. Desmond thought he looked like he was bracing himself to hear whatever the husband of the victim needed to say, had resigned himself out of duty to give Desmond a target for whatever that might be, but was limiting the interaction to simply taking the blow. He didn't have to make eye contact, didn't have to speak. He just had to show up, sit down, and take it.

"Do you know who I am?" Desmond said into the phone.

"You're the husband," Harwood said without looking up.

"*Whose* husband?"

Harwood's eyelids fluttered. "You want me say I'm sorry?"

"Are you?"

"If you want."

"Don't tell me what you think I want to hear. Tell me what you remember about that night, now that you're cleaned up and you've had time to think about it."

"Don't remember much."

"Did you break into my house and then kill my wife in the backyard?"

Harwood's fingers tightened around the phone, and his eyes met Desmond's. "You tell me. You were there, you tell me. Did I do those things? Did I kill her?"

"I was sleeping."

"Maybe I was too. 'Member waking up with that sword in my hand, all sticky from blood...."

"Where were you when you woke up?"

"My camp."

"Is that all you remember?"

Harwood looked down again, a faraway look in his eyes. He scratched the chest of his orange smock.

"Did you see anyone else? Anyone who didn't live in the camp?"

"Used to see all kinds of things when I was using. Don't anymore."

"What did you see...when you woke up, what did you see?"

"I think I told the police about it back then. Don't 'member much now."

"Tell me. *Please.*"

"Mister Carmichael, if I killed your wife, I'm sorry. I don't think I woulda meant to hurt a woman like that. I musta mistaken her for somethin' else. I have a daughter, you know."

"I know. They told me she visits you."

Harwood nodded. His skin was as pale as paper, laced with a filigree of blown blood vessels like some indecipherable script, but now it flushed scarlet. He said, "Been good for me in that one way. I don't think she'd know me if I wasn't in here."

"Who did you see when you woke up holding the sword?"

"*Reapers,*" Harwood whispered fiercely.

"Reapers?"

"Death angels in black skirts, faces like…all clouds and teeth. Like what you call *wrath o' God.*"

"Angels. There was more than one?"

Harwood nodded. "Don't angels come in pairs? Other one stood back from the firelight, in the shadows."

"Did they say anything to you?"

"Said I done the deed, killed a lady. He had my Bible in his hand; only thing I kept from my mother. Angel handed it to me, told me I should repent, confess it, else they was gonna do my kin like I done that lady."

"You're sure there were two of them?" Desmond felt the fingers on the phone going cold.

Harwood's face twisted with a wry smile. "People say drunks see double…but I never did."

* * *

When Desmond got back to the car, his cell phone was vibrating in the glove box. There was a missed call and a voice message. At first he thought it might be the Parsons or their lawyer trying to establish the rules of engagement, but the number wasn't from a local area code. He played the voicemail.

"Mr. Carmichael, my name is Erin Drelick and I'm a Special Agent with the FBI. I have a question for you related to a case I'm working on. Please call me at your earliest convenience."

Desmond took the recently confiscated and returned pen from his pocket, played the message again, and jotted down the number she spoke at the end, just in case. Then he checked it against the one in the phone's memory and hit SEND. The same soft, professional voice greeted him after one ring. "Mr. Carmichael. Thanks for getting back to me so soon."

"Sure. How can I help you?"

"Ordinarily I like to have this sort of conversation in person, but I'm with the bureau in California, so you'll understand why that's not possible."

"Okay...."

"I'm working on a case that has some similarity to that of your wife. Are you familiar with the murder of a California man named Geoff Lamprey?"

"I can't say I am."

"It's been in the national news lately because of the gruesome nature of the crime. Same as your wife's.... I'm sorry."

"He was decapitated?" The word came out in a whisper. It still hurt to say it. An abominable word.

"Yes. Forgive me if this is painful for you, but your cooperation would be quite helpful with regard to a technical detail I'm pursuing. I only need a minute of your time."

"I don't understand why you're calling me instead of the detectives in Sandy's case."

"I understand you were the owner of the sword that was used for the crime, that it was a weapon of convenience, stolen from your home and used on your wife when she confronted the intruder."

"That was the verdict, yes."

"You have doubts?"

"I was asleep. The sword was found in the possession of a local homeless man. Blood, fingerprints...I'm sure you know all about it." He looked at the squat limestone building through sheets of rain and wondered what this Agent Drelick would think if she knew he was talking to her from the current residence of said psycho killer. It wouldn't be difficult for her to find out that he'd just sat down for a little chat with the man, not if she was looking into Sandy's case with the resources of the FBI at her disposal.

"Yes, I've been over the case file. There's a detail in there that matches a finding from Lamprey's autopsy—a type of sword oil. I'm trying to track down a commercial source. You should understand that you are not a suspect in the Lamprey case."

"I should hope not. I've never even heard of him."

"I'll get to the point. Before your wife was murdered, did you ever apply oil to the blade? For preservation, maintenance, that sort of thing?"

"No. I took it out of the sheath once or twice just to look at it when my father-in-law gave it to me. Then I hung it on my office wall and more or less forgot about it."

"It was a gift?"

"Sort of. It belonged to Sandy's grandfather. When he passed away, her father didn't want it, so he gave it to me."

"Do you remember if the blade was oiled when you first received it? Maybe your father-in-law had oiled it to prevent rust?"

"I don't know, you'd have to ask him. He takes good care of tools, so maybe he would know to do that."

"I'd like you to think about the first time you unsheathed the sword. Was there a scent?"

"A scent?"

"Try to remember."

Desmond closed his eyes. He was enveloped by the sound of rain on the roof and windshield. "I don't remember it smelling like anything. The oil would have a scent?"

"Common machine oil would have a smell, yes. And traditional sword oil would have a different smell."

"Like what?"

"Cloves."

A memory flared in Desmond's mind—a park bench, the day it all came back to haunt them, an old Japanese man smoking a cigarette, and the too sweet smell of clove smoke on the breeze. The rain reached a crescendo, pounding on the car and sending the crackle and hiss of static down the line.

"Mr. Carmichael? Are you still there?"

Chapter 13

Shaun Bell tilted the *katana*. The *hamon* line glowed in the diffuse morning light. Outside, the sound of rain pattering on the rocks, dripping from the leaves. He had been meditating through the morning, listening to the rhythm of the rain, the rhythm of his breath. There was rhythm in everything. A time to watch, a time to strike, a time to withdraw. A time to reap. This was a universal *dharma*, written in the bible, written in Musashi's *Book of Five Rings*. He examined the steel, watched the play of the light along the temper line like a slow-moving wave lapping at a riverbank in the moonlight, or plasma undulating in a dying neon tube.

Musashi wrote that one must have no attachment to a particular weapon or to anything in life. If a warrior's ability depended upon his preferences, he would be lost when circumstance took them away. Sensei had demonstrated this when he used the crude infantry officer's sword to kill the woman. That weapon had symbolic and circumstantial value. Today, however, Shaun would enjoy the beauty and poetry of a true *nihonto*. Despite the council of Musashi, it was well known that swords forged by master smiths possessed souls of their own, and this was such a blade, his master's blade. To untie the silk bag was to feel it awaken. To draw it from the *saya* was to hear it breathe. To watch the light run along the *hamon* was to witness sentience in steel.

The warrior had risen at dawn. He had bathed and dressed, wound the straps around his waist over and under, tied the knots, arranged the folds, felt the board pressing into the small of his back. He had reached between his knees and slapped the fabric out to the sides, had kneeled in *seiza*, set his hands in his lap, and focused his mind. His stomach growled from fasting.

Now he wiped a few drops of *choji* oil along the length of the blade with a folded square of rice paper as the last wisp of incense smoke curled in the still air. He laid the sword on the mat and pounded the blade with the powder ball, then re-sheathed it, and examined the hilt—checked the fit of the bamboo retaining pegs, the tightness of the silk wrap, the snug fit of the silver dragon ornaments in the hand grip.

He set the sword down in front of his knees in the ceremonial manner, and bowed to it, left hand touching the floor first, then right. Rhythm in everything. A time to reap.

* * *

Vance Garrett popped a piece of chalk into his mouth, folded the extra foil under his thumb, and dropped the roll of antacid wafers into the pocket of his golf shorts. He selected an iron from his bag and swung it back and forth like a pendulum, loosening up, letting the weight of the head do the work. He scanned the putting green where the caddies were congregating around the door of the pro shop. No sign of Parsons yet. He shielded his eyes with his hand and looked up at the cloud cover. It was starting to burn off. Grass was still wet, but he was better at putting on wet grass than Phil Parsons was. Maybe it wouldn't dry too fast.

His swing was fluid and easy this morning, nice and straight. He grinned and put the club back in the bag. The grin stretched into a yawn and he covered his mouth with the back of his white-gloved hand. Funny, how fatigue improved his form. He wondered if other athletes—pro baseball players for instance—played a better game when they were hung over and tired because it loosened them up. Probably not. Most games called for more cardio stamina than this one. Golf was supposed to be relaxing, but he knew that few of his peers would say it was. It brought out the competitive temperament, and even the bucolic rolling hills and glistening water couldn't pacify that. Heartburn and hangover could. He thought of those twin antagonists as occupational hazards for a judge.

This morning the hangover was from a late night of brandy and cigars with a Masonic brother who had insisted on picking his brain about zoning law loopholes, and the heartburn was from the too large brunch he'd been treated to by a town selectman's niece who wanted to know how her husband might argue for a lesser charge when his DUI court date came up.

The clubhouse door opened, and Phil Parsons strolled out. He spotted Garrett right away and touched the brim of his tweed derby hat in salute. Garrett raised his hand—not quite a wave—then fished his cell phone out of his pocket and shut it off so no one else could pester him for advice and favors while he tried to sink nine holes to a soundtrack of carefully worded custody questions.

* * *

Lucas liked his new sneakers. They had Iron Man on them, and they lit up red and blue when he stomped his feet. Nana liked how he liked them, but she didn't like how he kept running ahead of her in them. Lucas thought that was funny. Too bad there were no puddles in the mall to splash in with the new sneakers. Maybe in the parking lot there would be some from the rain. Or the playground! Nana said they would go if he was good, and he *was* good. "I was good, right Nana?"

"Hmm?"

"I was good in the store so we can go to the Castle Playground and eat ice cream, right?"

"We'll see. And not if you keep running ahead."

"But I'm Iron Man!"

"Help an old lady out, Iron Man. Walk beside me."

"You're not an old lady, Nana."

"Already figured out how to play the ladies to get what you want, huh?"

Lucas did the thing with his eyebrows, the serious face, the Daddy face that he made when he didn't like or understand something. Nana brushed her fingers through his hair while they walked. Everyone was always touching his hair. He couldn't wait until he was tall so he could do it to them and see how they liked it. "We need to get this trimmed," Nana said.

"I don't want to."

"It's getting hot, Lucas. Don't you want short hair for summer, so you can keep cool?"

"No."

"But you look so handsome with short hair."

"Like Daddy?"

"Yes."

"When will I see him?"

"Sometime soon. We'll see."

"*When?*"

"I don't know, honey. Just sometime soon."

"If I get a haircut will I see Mommy soon, too?"

"Oh, baby...." Nana stopped walking, knelt down, and put her hands on his cheeks. "My boy. If your mother could come back she would."

"Why doesn't she?"

"She's in heaven now. But she's watching you, dear. And she still loves you so very much."

That was what they always said. Lucas broke away and ran as fast as his new sneakers could carry him to the carousel in the middle of the mall. He heard Nana yelling and looked down at the flashing lights on his sneakers. He wanted to know where heaven was. When he found out, he would run there.

* * *

Garrett made a short putt and watched the ball roll up to the edge of the hole. Right up to the edge but not in. His earlier calm was gone, wrecked by the barrage of questions Parsons didn't have the courtesy to dole out at a pace that was sensitive to a man's game. He popped another tab of chalk and answered the latest query with an edge in his voice. "No, I don't think it'll hold. Not if he gets an even halfway decent lawyer. You can't show a pattern of reckless behavior."

"But he was fired for drinking."

"He's a writer, for Chrissake. They practically get paid to drink. Still gainfully employed at that?"

"Barely."

"You said he's been off the sauce for almost a year. If he was bringing whores home, you might have a leg to stand on."

"Desmond *says* he stopped drinking, but he didn't join a program. He doesn't have a sponsor who can vouch for him or a six-month medallion to show for it."

Garrett knocked the ball into the hole and marked his card. "He's the child's only living parent, Phil, and he's never raised a hand to him. That's what's going to carry the day with a judge."

"With *any* judge?"

Garrett took a long look at Phil Parsons and didn't like what he saw. He bent and plucked his ball out of the hole.

* * *

The sound of thundering *taiko* drums rolled out of the car stereo speakers, just loud enough to mask the gravel crunching under the tires. Tree branches cast shadows over the dusty dashboard as the car rolled to a stop in the tunnel of oaks. The driver climbed out and unclipped a rusty chain with a weathered, illegible steel plate sign suspended from the middle. He tossed the chain into the bushes, got back in the car, swept the hem of his *hakama* clear of the door as he pulled it shut, and then continued up the road, which was now little more than a double-rut dirt path. He parked the car deep enough into the woods that it couldn't be seen from the road, yet close enough that he could get out fast.

With the car engine and the music off, silence settled on the woods, punctuated only by the ticking of the cooling engine and the chatter of birds. The rain was burning off of the trees now, rising in little wisps of steam. The air was still. The sword slept in an aluminum gun case in the trunk, waiting to wake, and hiss, and sing a song of blood, the *tachikaze*, the sword-wind song. A song for him alone, as the blade would travel too fast for that sound to reach living ears.

* * *

Lucas walked beside Nana and let her pet the back of his head, his shaggy hair. They were looking for the shortcut to the barbershop—the gap in the fence where the litter-strewn path cut through the woods that separated the Big Mall from the Little Mall. The Little Mall didn't really seem like a mall to Lucas because the stores weren't connected inside, but Nana said she always parked there because you could always find a good spot, and Nana liked to stop in and have coffee at the barbershop where Mary worked. Mary was okay. She cut his hair before and gave him a lollipop when he was little and used to have more days with Nana like today.

Lucas was worried. He didn't know if he'd still be allowed to have ice cream later if he had a lollipop.

Once they were on the trail, in the shade of the trees, Lucas could see the lights on his sneakers better. They were away from the cars now, so he asked Nana, "Can I run in my new sneakers?"

"Okay, but not too far."

He stomped two times and watched the lights chase each other around his soles, then he tore through the tunnel of trees toward the lattice of sunlight on the brick wall of a store-back ahead, beyond the black shadows of the low hanging branches.

The air smelled smoky and sweet.

* * *

Phil Parsons tugged on his glove and said, "You know Tom Carter, right? Isn't he one of your Masonic brothers?"

"That's right."

"Do you think he'd rule in favor of caution where a young boy's welfare is at stake?"

"That's not the only measure a judge goes by in a case like this; he has to cleave to the law. What rights does the father have? Have there been transgressions of his parental role and so forth."

"But you know him. How do you think he'll go?" Phil said, placing his ball on the tee.

Garrett was pulling various irons from his bag, examining each one before dropping it back in, buying a little time, and doing his best to avoid looking at Parsons' haggard face. Parsons who had served on the force, who had lost his beautiful daughter to an act of supreme brutality. Parsons, once a fearless man, who now kept a house like a fortress and feared for his grandson's life. Garrett had tried to read one of Desmond Carmichael's novels, even though fantasy wasn't his cup of tea—he preferred thrillers. There had been swords, yes, but it was no more violent than other books he admired. Violence drove plot. Just because a book was violent didn't mean…well, he doubted that Harlan Coben or Dennis Lehane had ever killed anyone. He hadn't finished the Carmichael book because he couldn't keep track of all the weird names, but he'd read far enough to appreciate the author's sense of compassion for his characters. Even the bad ones. He supposed judges and authors needed to have that in common if they were to be any good at their jobs.

"I'll tell him you're a friend and that I'm interested in hearing how it turns out," he said. "But that's all I can do for you, Phil. I can't pull any strings. You know that."

"Thanks, Vance, I appreciate it."

Parsons tested his alignment with two practice strokes, then brought the club back and made his drive. The ball soared over the fairway far enough off center to fall prey to the crosswind that was presently scattering the cloud cover, and sliced into the scrub.

Garrett chuckled. "Want to put down a fresh one?"

"Hell no," Parsons said. "Game's still close. I can hit it out of there."

Garrett watched Parsons stroll over to the wood line, the limp from his old injury barely visible today. He considered following to give moral support and to see just how badly the ball was trapped but decided not to. Parsons might think he was watching out of distrust, and that wouldn't be true. He didn't think Phil Parsons would move an unwatched ball so much as a millimeter. Vie for leverage with a judge? Sure, but that was part of the judicial game, and Parsons was a man who stuck to the rules of whatever game he played. He'd certainly never been the kind of cop who would dream of tampering with evidence, and Garrett knew that to a cop, the location of a trapped ball fell squarely into the category of physical evidence. Too bad Parsons had never expressed an interest in becoming a Mason. He would have made a fine one.

Parsons had only just disappeared into the thicket when a shriek ripped the tranquil air like a knife through a bed sheet. Garrett's stomach dropped at the sound, sudden and visceral. He looked around for a woman; maybe someone struck by a flying club that had slipped free of a player's grip...but he saw no one. Perspiration tingled in his armpits, eliciting a burning sensation from his deodorant. He knew exactly which direction the sound had come from. The wood. A clang of metal on metal followed.

Garrett scrambled to free his phone from his pocket with fingers that suddenly felt distant from his hands. He clicked it on, hoping, praying, for signal bars. *"Phil?"* he called to the sky, taking a few tentative steps toward the wood line.

Parsons staggered backwards out of the trees, his white polo shirt emblazoned with a vivid crimson slash. He was holding his club with one hand at each end, guarding his face with it. Garrett pulled a nine iron from his own bag and hurried down the slope toward the bleeding man. *"Phil!"*

Parsons shot a quick glance in Garrett's direction, then looked back at whatever had cut him. That half second of eye contact was enough to tell Garrett that Phil Parsons was a man about to die. A man who knew it. A loop of purple intestine squirmed out of the bottom of the gash that ran from his right collarbone to his left hip. He made an awful groaning sound and dropped one hand from the club to try to push his guts back in where they belonged. It was enough to present his attacker with an opening.

Garrett couldn't take his eyes off of Parsons. He knew he should, knew he had a camera in his phone, knew he needed to identify the attacker. But that red line kept his eyes locked. What else would fall out of that horrible red line? He saw a flurry of black and a flash of silver. It was all too fast for his eyes, indistinct like a scribbled charcoal sketch. Garrett would hate himself for it later, but at the sight of that black and silver tornado flashing out and back into the trees, he stopped running and felt his club-wielding arm go limp at his side.

Phil Parsons' head tilted back at a very wrong angle, blood gushing down his slit shirt as he fell to his knees.

Garrett dropped his club and ran up the hill. Parsons was dead, but a voice was still screaming, ragged and shrill. He eventually recognized it as his own.

Chapter 14

Desmond was packing some of Lucas's clothes and toys when he was startled by a pounding fist on the front door downstairs, followed by a shout: "Police! Open up!" He felt a surge of anger flush through his body. He'd had enough of the police. Showing up in the night to take his sleeping child and now coming back to beat his door down? *What the fuck?*

He tromped down the stairs with a stuffed penguin still in his hand. The knock and shout came again. Hearing the voice at close range he was pretty sure it wasn't Fournier, but if Fournier wasn't standing on his doorstep right now, it wouldn't necessarily mean that the man wasn't behind this somehow.

"Hang on!" Desmond yelled at the door as he reached the bottom of the stairs. But it was too late. He'd come too slowly. The door flew inward with a crack and rebounded off the jackets and sweatshirts hanging from the coat rack on the adjacent wall. Two uniformed cops moved into the entryway, pointing their guns at him, barking at him like German shepherds to get down on his knees and put his hands behind his head *now, do it now.*

Desmond was stunned by the intensity of the scene. What the hell was this anyway? His anger turned tepid in the face of the over-the-top performance confronting him, and he stood dumbstruck, not moving, not obeying, just thinking that it was weird how much this looked like the scenes on TV. But those were real guns aimed at his head and chest. Looking into the black hole in the muzzle of a 9mm pointed at his face and realizing that his own death could be in there waiting for a finger twitch to shift quantum uncertainty to bloody reality, he raised his hands and bent down on one knee. He almost regretted the submissive pose when a second later Chuck Fournier stepped into the room between the two uniforms.

Fournier didn't have his weapon drawn. He stepped up to Desmond and without a word, slugged him in the solar plexus with an uppercut. Desmond felt the wind knocked out of his lungs and thought he might vomit as he collapsed on the floor. Fournier followed up with a kick to the ribs—pain seared through Desmond's midsection. One of the officers yelled at Fournier to stop. The other holstered his gun, stepped behind Desmond, and yanked his arms back until it felt like they were about to be dislocated. The officer holding him spoke from just behind his ear, "Not the face, Chuck. Don't hit him in the face."

Fournier punched him in the gut again. His vision tunneled slightly, and when it cleared Fournier was squatting in front of him holding his head up by the hair. Desmond's arms, still pinned behind him, were going numb. The other cop produced a pair of handcuffs from a belt pouch and ratcheted them open.

"Where's the sword?" Fournier said.

"What?"

"The sword you killed Phil Parsons with. Same one you killed Sandy with. Where is it?"

Desmond felt like Fournier had just dropped him down an elevator shaft, every blood vessel in his body contracting inward and downward. Phil was *dead*? Phil had Lucas.

"Where's Lucas?" He struggled for breath. "Where is he?"

"I'm asking the questions, shitbag. Where's the sword? We have a warrant, but you can save yourself the rest of a beating by just telling me."

"Listen to me...Chuck. I don't know...what's going on here. Phil is *dead*?"

"Don't fuck with me, Des. We have enough to arrest you. You had a grudge with Parsons and you own a sword. He was cut in half this morning, and you're going to tell me where that weapon is or I will beat the filthy fuck out of you. You're a cunt hair away from being a cop killer, and we will take turns on you here and at the station if you don't confess."

"No. No, no, no. Lucas...Phil had *Lucas*. What about Karen?"

"Shut up. Where's the weapon?"

"Is Lucas okay? Did he see it happen?"

Fournier slapped Desmond across the face. "Stop acting and answer my question."

Desmond tried to clear his head, tried to tune out the pain, but merely breathing was making his abdominal muscles burn. Fournier wasn't asking *him* where Lucas was, so that meant that whoever killed Phil didn't abduct Lucas or the police would be sure *he* had. The cops would already be calling Lucas's name and looking for him upstairs if he was missing. Lucas had to be alive. *Had* to be. But if they believed that the only threat to Lucas was his own father, then soon no one would be guarding him.

"When?" Desmond asked, "When was Phil killed?" He felt the cuffs tightening around his wrists. Too tight. Fournier ignored the question and told the officer who wasn't holding Desmond, "Start tearing the place apart."

"I was at Cedar Junction this morning," Desmond said. "I'm in the visitor's log. Check it."

"We will."

"What time was Phil killed? You know how long it takes to get back here from Walpole, what time?"

"Did you ditch the blade on your way back here?"

Desmond could hear the cop who had gone upstairs, his footsteps creaking through the ceiling, and the sound of a closet door sliding open on rollers.

"I know you took the sword that killed Sandy into this apartment. Why would you do that, Desmond? Huh? Why would you want that thing around your boy?"

Fournier had been watching him, spying on him. Was that with the approval of his superiors? Was there a tap on the phone line from a court order? Desmond's head was swimming. He didn't know if the surveillance would help or hurt him, and it was too hard to think it through with the shock of Phil's death and the delirium of the beating.

He felt as if the cursed *katana* were dangling from a string above his head, like the sword of Damocles. If he told them where to find it, the string would break and the fact that he had concealed it would come down on him for better or worse. Maybe the dry joint compound would be evidence that the weapon had been placed in the wall before

Phil was killed. Or maybe not. And maybe wasn't good enough. Fournier had a hard-on for convicting him, and the two uniforms were an unknown factor.

Now that Desmond was handcuffed, the cops left him kneeling on the living room carpet while they searched the apartment and bagged his laptop. Fournier brooded over him.

"You're not going to find what you're looking for," Desmond said. "You might as well take me in because I'm not talking to anyone but a lawyer. And the first thing I'll have him do is photograph the bruises, so you should quit while you're ahead."

"Is that right?" Fournier said. His face contorted with a flash of frustration, then he sucked on his teeth and hitched up his slacks while apparently contemplating the effectiveness, or at least the satisfaction, that might be afforded by further violence. Desmond couldn't help feeling a little sorry for him. Fournier had lost a mentor in Phil Parsons and a friend in Phil's daughter. They had that in common. Only, Fournier believed that he had the killer of both right here in front of him.

Desmond opened his mouth, afraid of what might come out, but before he could say anything, the other cop descended the stairs and handed Fournier a small slip of paper, a receipt. "I found it in his jeans pocket."

Fournier studied the slip, then squinted at Desmond and held it out for him to look at. Desmond felt that sinking sensation again.

"I wouldn't peg you as the home improvement type, Des. Home Depot, huh? Just yesterday, in fact. Care to tell me why a renter like you would need…spackle, drywall tape, razor knife, sandpaper, and a lock set?"

Desmond kept his mouth shut.

"Doesn't your landlord handle repairs?"

"I replaced the back door lock after the break-in."

Fournier snorted. "Break-in…right. And what does that have to do with wall repair?"

Desmond knew that any little lies he spun now would only entangle him later. Damn, it was hard to not talk when you were being prodded by cops. When they had you cornered it was too goddamn easy to forget the Miranda. Anything he said would be remembered, written down, and used against him.

"You lose your temper with your son and punch a wall, Desmond? No crime in that, but a violent man might want to hide the evidence of it."

"I don't...."

"You don't what? Punch walls? What did you do, Desmond? Huh? Don't want to talk about wall repair. Why is that? Oh, you didn't! You sly devil...you put the sword in a wall?"

Desmond tried for a poker face and saw his failure written all over Fournier's.

"He did, he put it in a wall. Holstein, check the floors and molding for dust, and start looking behind posters and shit. Check for wet paint."

"I'm on it. Bound to be a rough job if he was in a hurry and got no skills."

"That's what I'm thinking," Fournier said.

The shorter of the two officers, Holstein apparently, climbed the stairs again, and Desmond contemplated just giving it up. He didn't have long to consider the benefits of cooperation. Only about a minute had passed when he heard a whistle from upstairs, followed by, "Think I found it."

Fournier hoisted Desmond to his feet and frog-marched him up the stairs. When they reached the landing where the staircase turned, Desmond could see that the mirror had been removed from the wall. At the top of the stairs Holstein was kneeling in front of the patch, running his hand over the smoothly sanded joint compound. His fingers came away white with fine powder. "Not a bad patch," he said with teasing admiration, "but it's not painted."

Fournier squatted and ran his fingers over the wall. "Looks long enough. But maybe too smooth for fuckface here. Could be the landlord never painted it because he knew he was gonna hang the mirror there."

Holstein shook his head. "I found it from dust on the carpet. See? Looks vacuumed but he missed a spot."

Fournier turned to Desmond. "You vacuum one spot in the whole shitty apartment and it kinda stands out, Des."

"It's dry," Desmond said. "Look at how dry it is. If you think I patched it today and had time to sand it, you're crazy." He thought Fournier would look for the razor knife, or some kind of tool to cut the wall with. Instead, Fournier just raised his knee and kicked the sheetrock in, leaving a cavity of torn paper and crumbling chalk. Through the hole Desmond could see part of the scabbard. If he'd had any doubts before, he knew in that moment that Chuck Fournier was one brash son of a bitch. No concern for preserving evidence, no concern for the possibility that the sole of his shoe might be sliced open by a bare blade inside the wall.

Fournier grabbed a chunk of sheetrock and pulled on it to widen the gap, tearing away an even larger section of wall until it folded and broke off in his hand. He brushed away some dust and peered in at the sword.

"I dunno, Holstein," he said absently, "That spackle look dry to you before I kicked it? Felt a little mushy to me." Fournier took a latex glove from his back pocket, blew into it and rolled it over his meaty hand. Then he cracked more of the wall with his elbow, ripped the sheetrock away with his ungloved hand, and gingerly removed the sword with the gloved one.

The scabbard and hilt were speckled with white dust. Fournier appraised the weapon with a grimace, wrapped his gloved hand around the hilt and drew the blade from the metal sheath, turning it over in the light that spilled into the hallway from the window in Lucas's room. Desmond knew the blade was as clean as a steak knife in a drawer, and he could see the disappointment registering on Fournier's face. No blood. Fournier slid the sword back down into the scabbard. He shone a small flashlight into the hole, up and down, making sure there wasn't anything else in there—maybe a bloody rag, a pair of gloves or a mask that Desmond might have worn for the kill. Fournier's jaw had an odd set to it, like he was grinding his teeth. He wheeled around, cocked the metal barrel of the flashlight back and clipped Desmond across the temple with it.

* * *

At the station, Desmond kept his mouth shut while they booked him. It was a pretty quick process because his prints were already in the system from his wife's murder case. He was grateful for the slight reduction in the amount of time he had to spend among men who believed he had killed a veteran cop.

They left him in the cell for what felt like an hour before moving him to one of the interrogation rooms with the mirrors and microphones. There was a sheet of paper and a pen on the table. A man was waiting for him. Desmond recognized him as one of the men who had worked on Sandy's case, but he couldn't remember the name. One of the incompetents who had put away a blind drunk lunatic and let the real psychopath run amok to revisit the family with a blade, and the best they could do now was rerun the harassment they had doled out on him a year ago.

"Take a seat. I'm Detective Sanborn. You might remember me."

"I do." Desmond said. "You're one of the guys who didn't catch my wife's killer."

Sanborn put his hands on the back of the chair opposite Desmond and looked at him with tired, hooded eyes. "Lot of people think that now," he said. "Lot of guys around here feel guilty about not being able to prove it was you. Might have saved Phil's life."

Sanborn slid the chair out from under the table and sat down, folded his hands and twitched a finger at the blank paper. "Why don't you write it all down for me, Desmond. How you killed your wife and father-in-law. Proving that you did it is pretty much a done deal, but *why* is still a matter of interpretation, and I figure you had your reasons."

"Reasons?"

"Sure. There's always a reason. You felt they wronged you in some way. You can get it off your chest now, so people don't just think you're a nut job. You're an artist, right? A writer. You think in terms of…poetic justice, right? So you probably had reasons. Why don't you share them with me? Do what you're best at, Des. Can I call you Des? Write your story, or other people will write it for you."

Desmond picked up the page, but not the pen. He said, "My son found a piece of paper folded into an origami butterfly yesterday. It had a message on it in Japanese. I don't know how to fold origami or write *kanji*...but I do know that all of this Japanese culture must mean something to whoever killed Sandy and her father. So I asked a Japanese man to translate it for me, and it said *fly*. I think it's a warning, like the haiku I found typed into my laptop. I called the police about that, but no one wanted to take me seriously. If you guys had listened to me then, Phil might still be alive. You're asking me for motive because you've got nothing."

"I have nothing? I think I have a pretty simple explanation of events. You were cracking under the pressure of being a single parent, cracking under the guilt of killing your son's mother. So you start projecting your violent urges outward onto an imaginary character, a samurai. This is something you're well practiced at—inventing imaginary warriors. You inhabit the role; wear a mask to scare your kid.... You're trying to bring this character to life. But then, when everybody sees right through it and starts to question your soundness of mind, your fitness as a father, maybe even your innocence, you get angry. Phil Parsons takes Lucas from you, and you snap. You kill again and decide to hide the weapon in your wall. That's my Cliffs Notes version. You want to flesh it out for me?"

"Where's Chuck? Did the sheriff replace him with you when he saw my temple? Or are you supposed to be the good cop, and they'll send him in to rough me up some more if I don't say what you want to hear? Is he watching on the other side of the glass?"

Desmond looked at the mirror and waved. "Hi, Chuck," he said, and frowned at the sight of his swollen eyebrow where the flashlight had clipped him. He touched a finger to it and winced. Turning back to Sanborn, he said, "There's more on my torso. You understand that I will probably sue the holy hell out of this police department when all of this is over. You guys fail to catch my wife's killer, and when he starts coming for the rest of my family, you help abduct my son, harass me, beat me.... Look, I just want to know that Lucas is safe, and that the killer can't get at him. I don't care about anything else. Just promise me you won't leave him unprotected just because you have me."

"Lucas is fine. He's safe."

"Is he in the building?"

"You know I can't answer that."

"I'd feel a lot better if I knew he was in a police station. Do you really think Karen can keep him safe? Do you have officers watching the house?"

"Let's talk about you, Desmond, how you spent your morning."

"I'll talk about anything you want, but first you need to tell me where Lucas is."

"It doesn't work that way."

"No? You guys make deals all the time. I can shut up and wait for a lawyer who will advise me to *keep* my mouth shut, or we can talk. But I need to know that my son isn't sitting in an unguarded house with just his grandmother. Do *you* have kids? Because this is on you. If you're wrong about me and anything should happen to him...." Desmond could feel his voice breaking, could see the genuine desperation he radiated having an effect on Sanborn. The inspector was getting just a little bit confused. A seed of doubt had been planted.

"You visited Harwood at Cedar Junction this morning. Made the appointment yesterday. Why? What did you talk about?"

"Tell me about Lucas, dammit! Does he know about Phil? For God's sake, he lost his mother and I don't know what he's been told about being taken from me...now his grandfather is dead. Does he know?"

"He's safe, okay? I promise. There are police around him."

Desmond stared into Sanborn's pale blue eyes and for some inscrutable reason believed him.

"Now, why did you visit Harwood?"

"I wanted to look him in the eye and ask him if he killed Sandy."

Sanborn tipped his hands to indicate he needed more than that.

"I avoided the trial, it was too painful. But now the stakes are too high. Someone is after us, maybe after the whole family. I had to see Harwood, see if he seemed innocent."

"They found the weapon in his possession, Desmond. He confessed. The only thing casting doubt on his guilt now is you hiding a sword in your wall right after Phil Parsons was seen being cut down with one."

"There was a witness?"

Sanborn shot a glance at the mirror. He had fucked up.

"Who saw it? Wait, why didn't you put me in a lineup or something?" Desmond looked at the mirror again. "Is the witness in there?"

Sanborn twisted his wristwatch as if the band were too tight and said, "We may do just that."

"Did this witness see the killer's face or was there a mask over it?" Desmond asked, sitting up straight, his eyes boring into the detective's.

Sanborn hardened his face as he leaned forward in his chair. "This is an interrogation, not a conversation. I'll humor you for the moment. Your gut reaction to Harwood was what?"

"Not guilty. Confused. But not a killer."

"If you think you can muddy the waters by visiting him, you're mistaken. If you think that signing a log and having your ID checked by the infallible eyes of the criminal justice system gives you an iron clad alibi, think again. We have you checking out of Cedar Junction at eleven thirty. If you were speeding, that's enough time to get back here and kill Parsons. You have an active imagination, but you don't have an alibi. You don't have shit unless you can give me someone who can attest to being with you at twelve twenty today."

"I was driving at twelve twenty. It's an hour and fifteen minutes from Walpole doing seventy. I was barely home fifteen minutes when the cops kicked the door in."

"If you didn't kill anyone with that sword, why did you hide it in the wall?"

"I wanted to make sure that whoever is stalking my family couldn't get their hands on it."

"Seems like a lot of trouble to take just to get rid of something. Why not sell it or toss it in the river?"

"I don't know, because I'm paranoid? You sell something on the web, there's a record of it. Maybe the killer offers whoever I sell it to a crazy sum just to get his hands on it." Desmond laughed. "Maybe the killer buys it from me and I don't know it's him. And you know we'd be having the very same conversation if I tossed it into the river."

"Why would this stalker of yours be so interested in your sword?"

"He's obsessed with samurai culture. He killed with it once before. I wanted to make it impossible to find, and I knew the one place no one could spy on me while I hid it was in my apartment."

"But you were also making sure that it was close at hand."

"If I ever found a hole in the wall, I'd know it had been taken."

"But you made sure it was in the same building as your son. Isn't that asking for trouble?"

"Trouble has been following us around. Confronting it seemed better."

"Most murder weapons get ditched in a place that can't be associated with the killer. When you hide one in your home, that's because you're attached to it, can't let it go. You keep it around for the memories?"

"Fuck you, Sanborn. I think I'd rather talk to Chuck." Desmond looked at the mirror.

"Why did you kill Phil?"

"Check the joint compound. It's been dry for twenty-four hours. I patched the hole in the wall yesterday."

"What do you think this is, an episode of CSI? You think this is a big city with a bunch of materials experts waiting around to look at crumbs from your wall under a microscope?"

"Anyone who's ever patched a hole would know that I didn't do the job right before you guys showed up. Even Fournier must know that."

"You know we do have DNA analysis, Des. The blade might *look* clean, but if they find so much as one molecule of Phil Parsons on it, you're fucked."

"Phil gave me the goddamned thing in the first place."

"They're taking apart the handle and looking at places where the blood might have run down inside the hardware. You should think hard about how well you cleaned it."

"The last time anyone handled that blade out of the sheath, it was you guys and your geeks. They cleaned it up after Sandy's death, and they're not going to find anything new but sheetrock dust." As he said this, Desmond remembered the phone call in the car at Cedar Junction, the FBI agent. In the whirlwind of his arrest, he'd forgotten all about it. She'd wanted to know if he ever oiled the blade. What was that about? Sanborn didn't even seem to know about the call. Was it a coincidence that she'd contacted him on the same day? Was she even who she said she was? He felt a creeping awareness that he was standing in a minefield.

The fact of Phil's death was sinking in now, too, and Desmond was surprised to find that it hurt. Despite their differences, he had loved the guy in his own clumsy way. Staring at the tabletop between his hands and watching the faux wood grain blur and distort as water welled up in his eyes, he said, "How did Phil die, exactly?" He could hear the thickness in his voice. "Was it the same as Sandy?"

Sanborn sighed. "I'm going to give you a minute to collect your thoughts and reconsider putting them on paper, Des."

Sanborn got up and left the room. When the door had swung shut and locked behind him, Desmond took up the pen, wrote on the paper, then walked over to the mirror, and slapped the paper flat against the glass: PROTECT LUCAS.

Chapter 15

Desmond felt sand sloshing around in his sneakers as he crested the ridge of dunes. He was climbing the thin path that wound up through the beach grass behind the apartment, the beach where they had scattered Sandy's ashes. He could smell the ocean before it came into view, the crisp salt breeze pure and clean, untainted by the dead fish smell that often accompanied low tide in the coastal marshes. He heard the surf loud and close and, sure enough, when he came to the top of the dunes, he could see the waves flooding toward him, foamy breakers churning and roiling and reaching for the wire and picket barrier fence that jutted from the dunes in a wavy line down the shore. He walked across the boundary of reed fragments, hollow crab shells, and driftwood that marked the high tide line, his sand-laden sneakers stepping over a salt-encrusted condom and a headless Barbie doll wrapped in black strands of kelp.

The wind was blowing hard, sweeping up grains of sand and stinging his hands with them. The sky darkened as a wave of ravening black clouds swept inland, mimicking the tide. The beach was empty except for a solitary dark figure wading into the surf, clothed and oblivious to the waves soaking his black jeans at the knees and splashing brine onto his indigo hoodie—no, *two* figures: walking beside the man in the hoodie and holding his hand was a boy with brown hair and a green shirt. *Lucas.*

Desmond ran to the waves, his sneakers plunging into the water, the cold ocean sluicing through his jeans. But somehow, despite the height of the tide, the beach had grown longer and no matter how fast he ran, he couldn't reach them, couldn't get to the deeper water where the stranger was now up to his waist and Lucas was bobbing on a swelling wave, beyond the breaker line. Desmond shouted with all the force he could invoke, a long holler that mutated into a ragged scream as if the grainy wind had shredded his voice in the air, perforated it with mica shrapnel, "*LUCAAAAAS!*"

The boy, who must have heard his cry, didn't turn to look, and Desmond felt a cold certainty, a lung-crushing fear, that if the boy in the water did turn to look at him, something would be wrong with his face, some mutilation, some deformity that would mark him as irretrievable and yet undeniably Lucas. The man, however, did turn to look at Desmond, and the face in the hood was a battle mask, an arch-grimace of rage, a *kabuki* horror of alabaster-white, ash-black, and blood-red lines.

Desmond lunged forward into the crashing waves, dragging his hands through the glistening water, dripping silver threads of it from his fingertips with each lumbering stride and yet coming no closer to the pair. Gulls cried on the wind, wheeling overhead, and diving from the bruised underbelly of the rippling black storm front. He traced the arc of one as it plunged and skimmed the silver sea and saw it come up with something white and angular in its beak.

The surface of the water was scattered with origami birds—swans, cranes…ducks? They bobbed and glowed in the diffuse light of a hidden sun, and Lucas bobbed among them, his head dipping below the dark water.

Something bumped Desmond's hip, the flank of an animal; he felt submerged fur glide across his skin. *Fenton?* He was almost sure it was his lost dog, his dead dog, not swimming now as he had loved to do at this very beach, but floating, drifting toward Lucas, toward the rip tide, trailing a cloud of blood from his severed neck.

There was a ringing sound now, like a metal clamp clanging against the mast of a sailboat at anchor. It grew louder, and Desmond woke on the bunk in his cell, the armpits of his t-shirt soaked with sweat. An officer was rapping his wedding ring against the bars, and Desmond almost fell to the floor as he scrambled to regain reality, composure, lucidity. How had he fallen asleep, and so deep? Shame welled up with a flush of blood to his ears, and he remembered just how little sleep he'd had over the past few days. His body had finally shut down while there was nothing he could do.

"Your lawyer," the officer said. Desmond recognized him as one of the two who had accompanied Fournier on the raid of his apartment.

Desmond's court-appointed lawyer was a short, stout man with salt-and-pepper hair and a cheap suit that looked like it could use a trip to the dry cleaners. He introduced himself as Stephen Janvrin as the cop locked the cell door behind him. Janvrin sat down at the end of the wall-mounted bed with an ease and familiarity that told Desmond he was used to meeting with clients in cells. Desmond rubbed the heels of his hands across his eyes and wondered how many of those meetings had led to verdicts of innocence.

Janvrin placed his briefcase in his lap and drummed his fingers on the lid. "So," he began, "You're the only suspect for the murder of your father-in-law, and they are awaiting some forensics results—"

"Stop right there," Desmond interrupted. "Do you know where my son is?"

"Son?"

"I have a four-year-old son. His name is Lucas. I need you to find out where he is and if he's being protected."

"Okay, but I don't know if they'll tell me. It's not the kind of thing that I need to know to defend you."

"*I* need to know it to defend *him*. Whoever killed Phil Parsons is coming after our family. My son was in the care of Phil and Karen Parsons last night after they took him from me and started a custody battle."

"I'm a criminal lawyer, Mr. Carmichael. I don't do custody battles."

"I'm innocent. If the police do their job with any competence, they'll figure that out and let me go. When that happens, I need to get my son back immediately. So I need to know if they…if *Karen* has a leg to stand on with this guardianship move. It was going before a judge tomorrow, but now that Phil is dead and I'm in here, I don't know if I'm still supposed to appear in family court on Monday morning. I need you to find out where Lucas is."

"I think you're putting the cart before the horse. Our first order of business is to get you out of here. And that may be harder than you expect."

"I didn't kill Phil. They'll know that as soon as they check out the sword they found at my apartment."

"It's not that simple. They have checked it out."

"And?"

"Edged weapons can't be identified with the same precision as firearms. When a bullet exits the barrel of a gun, there are marks left on it that are unique to that weapon. Swords and knives are a different story. Unless a little piece of the blade chips off, a sword can't be identified with a particular wound. Not unless the victim's blood is left on the weapon, like in your wife's case. This is good and bad for you."

"Why?"

"Without blood they can't prove that your sword made the cut, but *we* can't prove that it didn't. No traces of Mr. Parsons' DNA have been found on the weapon as of yet, but an expert can still testify that by its shape and size, your sword *could* very well be the murder weapon. And the fact that the same weapon was used to kill your wife when it was in your possession will not help a jury to have doubts. After all, most folks don't own a samurai sword, Mr. Carmichael."

"What about the wall, the spackle? It was dry because I hid the sword in the wall yesterday."

Janvrin was shaking his head before Desmond could finish the sentence. "It won't be admissible. No one preserved a sample, and now it's too late. It's your word against that of the arresting officers."

"But Chuck Fournier's shoe would have wet spackle drying in the treads if I only just finished the patch right before he kicked the wall in."

"That may be true, but I'm afraid it doesn't help us. Evidence won't save you. You need an alibi, my friend. Do you have one?"

"Not really."

"You're in the CJ visitor log. What time did you leave and where did you go?"

"I left the prison at eleven thirty after about twenty minutes of talking to Harwood. I drove right home and started packing some of Lucas's things to drop off at Phil and Karen's house. That's when the cops showed up."

"Did you talk to either of your in-laws on the phone about dropping by?"

"No. I didn't want to take the chance that they might say no."

"Did you talk to *anyone* on the phone? Did you stop for gas or food? If you were on the phone at twelve thirty, or filling your tank on some surveillance camera, you couldn't also be killing a man at a golf course."

"It happened at a golf course?"

"Yes. Phil was golfing with a judge friend, and he sliced it into the brush. He went in to retrieve the ball and staggered back out with gashes in his chest and abdomen."

"That's horrible."

"The judge didn't see the killer, just some black clothing."

"Do you know if he saw a mask? Like a samurai war mask?"

"I don't know." Janvrin looked perplexed, but intrigued. Desmond thought maybe the lawyer had assumed he was guilty and was beginning to reappraise that suspicion.

"Wait, I did get a call...I got a call on my cell phone from an FBI agent in California while I was at the prison. I called her back from the car before I drove home."

Janvrin blinked. "Why didn't you mention that before?"

"I figured everybody knew by now. Haven't the police been through my phone records yet?"

"They're working on it. What did this agent want with you? Did you get her name?"

"She said she was working on a case with similarities to Sandy's. I forget her name. She wanted to know if I'd ever put oil on the sword because a particular kind of oil was found on it, and she found the same kind of oil in *her* sword murder case. I told her no, I never did."

"Hmmph. So she's thinking...what?"

"I don't know, ask her. She said I wasn't a suspect in her case, but I'm guessing that may have changed by now."

"Okay, I need to talk to this FBI agent. I'll see if I can get access to your cell phone."

"Don't entangle me any further, Mr. Janvrin. It's going to be much harder for me to protect my son if I have the feds looking at me as a bicoastal serial killer."

"If you're innocent, it might be better for you to have *them* on it than a pack of townies with an axe to grind."

"*If?*"

Janvrin shrugged. He took a Blackberry from his jacket pocket and said, "You don't remember the agent's name? Try for me. First name, initials, something to go on."

Desmond tried to put himself back in the car. Rain on the windows. The female voice in his message box reminding him at first of Sandy's voice as if, impossibly, she had called him from the great beyond while he was visiting the man convicted of killing her. "Relic?" It sounded something like that. "I don't know…. She told me the name of the victim in her case. *That* I do remember because I was going to look into it: Lamprey."

"That does sound familiar. Probably getting more coverage in California. I'll look into it." Janvrin typed the name into his phone. He got up off of the bunk and straightened his suit. "Do you have anyone who would post bail for you? It's unlikely that they'll set one, and if they do, it could be quite high."

Desmond shook his head.

"I'll see you again tonight if it turns out they don't have enough to hold you."

"What if they do? I'm just stuck in here?"

"If you're the prime suspect and the evidence precludes bail, they'll transfer you to a more secure facility."

The notion was jarring; Desmond felt the ground shifting under his feet. Then he remembered the only thing that really mattered before his one link to the outside world walked out. "Please find out where Lucas is. If you do nothing else for me, make sure that he and Karen are being protected."

Janvrin looked like he wanted to say something, maybe wanted to protest. But he must have read the intensity in Desmond's eyes because he only nodded, then called for the guard to let him out.

Chapter 16

Agents Drelick and Pasco flew into Boston's Logan Airport on the Monday morning red-eye. The murder of Phil Parsons had set the stage for the Lamprey case to go national. They hadn't yet been granted jurisdiction, but the fact that Parsons had been killed within an hour of Drelick's phone call to Desmond Carmichael was enough to convince the Deputy Director that Drelick's hunch about the *choji* oil merited further investigation. They were getting close now; she could feel it. She'd had a fluttering in her stomach since LAX, and her inability to sleep in flight didn't help to settle it. Neither did the miniscule bag of pretzels the flight attendant had given her.

She closed the book in her lap (an introduction to samurai culture) and removed her reading glasses. As she folded and stowed them in the seatback pocket, she was reminded of the pair they had found sitting on the monument at Manzanar. Those glasses had been gazing east, the direction she was now flying in. The blood on the obelisk had been Geoff Lamprey's.

Shikata ga nai. It must be done.

Pasco, for his part, wasn't having any trouble catching some shuteye in the seat beside hers, but then he didn't have a phone call to Desmond Carmichael on his conscience. The very real prospect that her call had spurred Carmichael to take quick action and kill Parsons before the net closed around him was one big reason for the butterflies in her stomach. Her concerns wouldn't have been lost on Pasco if she broached the subject, but he'd seemed willing enough to leave the topic alone for now, burying his nose in one of Carmichael's doorstopper paperbacks until he dozed off.

With her partner snoring on her shoulder in the darkened cabin, she turned on her tablet and made a list of questions:

1. Was Carmichael verifiably in Massachusetts at the time of Lamprey's murder?
2. Does Carmichael have a web search history that involves swords or Japanese culture preceding his wife's death?
3. Did Carmichael ever order sword oil from an internet provider?
4. Is there a Japanese American community in the Greater Boston Area with significant ties to Manzanar?
5. Did Carmichael suspect his wife of infidelity?
6. Any evidence of psychosis in Carmichael's past?

She wanted to look the man in the eye and get a sense of him, and it perturbed her that the cop she had spoken to on the phone, Sanborn, told her that Desmond Carmichael had used almost the same words to explain why he'd visited Greg Harwood in prison just an hour before his father-in-law's murder. That was another one for the list:

7. Did Harwood say something to Carmichael that set him over the edge? Did they conspire to murder Carmichael's wife? Harwood just a patsy?

None of it made sense without motive.

The only thing the murder of Phil Parsons had convinced her of was that Harwood was probably innocent. The locals would not love her for that opinion. She would need to keep it close to the vest for a while, emphasizing her interest in the possibility that Carmichael had killed Parsons. If the Port Mavis police were wrong about the first murder, it would certainly make it easier for them to admit it if they thought they had the killer in custody now. She looked again at number 4. To introduce an unknown variable, a serial killer at large, would not win her any allies at this stage of the game.

She closed the cover on the tablet and stuffed it back in the bag between her feet. She reclined the seat and closed her eyes, but sleep continued to evade her like a crafty killer.

* * *

At the car rental counter, she handed the keys to Pasco and said, "Do you mind?

"You know I never mind driving. Noticed you favoring your foot, though. You trying to avoid putting it on a pedal?"

"Sometimes you are a real Sherlock Holmes," she said with a smile that was sixty percent false mirth and forty percent genuine admiration.

"You should really see a podiatrist about that, you know."

"It was a foot doctor that messed me up in the first place, if you recall my tale of woe."

"No, you digging in your nails like some OCD archaeologist when you were a little girl what fucked you up."

She turned on her heel away from the rental counter, letting her hair swing around and veil her blushing face.

"You know I'm right."

"Can we have this conversation in the car?" she said, walking away from him and trying not to favor the foot, which made her ingrown toenail hurt even more. She didn't know if she was heading in the right direction to pick up the car, but rolling her suitcase away from Pasco was all that mattered right now, in any direction.

He strode beside her and in a quieter tone said, "I'm not just nagging you for the fun of it. You think I want you hopping down some dark alley trying to draw your sidearm if you need to save my ass from a sword-swinging ninja? I don't want you limping for anything less than being shot in the leg." He smiled, and this time she couldn't help reciprocating with a higher content of genuine humor.

"I'll have you know I was never a little girl."

"Never ever? Hey, the car's this way."

"Never ever. Tomboy to the core."

"Boys don't care if they get dirt in their toenails. Don't even notice."

"Well my mother noticed. I wasn't going to stay out of the dirt, so I began trimming them too low. That's how it starts."

"And this doctor your mom brought you to botched the job, I know. But I bet foot work has probably improved in the past twenty some odd years. At least get a consultation."

"I will think about it. Now where's our car?"

The digital thermometer on the dashboard read seventy-seven, but the humidity was stifling compared to California's. They rolled up the windows and turned on the AC just to get the wooly feeling out of their heads. There wasn't much to see from I-95, but Drelick wanted to drive through the town of Port Mavis just to get a feel for the area. Within minutes of taking their exit, the cow pastures had given way to a cosmopolitan seaside tourist town with brick-faced shops selling a mix of nautical and New Age knick-knacks, skateboard kids idling in the concrete basin of a defunct fountain, and hip looking thirty-somethings toting laptops and book bags between the Starbucks, the news stand/cigar shop, and the library—an eye-catching, newly renovated building across the street from a dilapidated Masonic hall. The police station was also downtown, but Drelick asked Pasco to swing by Carmichael's apartment before they made their entrance.

"Looks like the kinda town a writer would live in," Pasco remarked. "Kinda yuppie, snobby...."

From the passenger seat, Drelick's eyes flicked over the buildings. "There sure are a lot of churches in New England."

"Leftovers." Pasco said. "It's just because it's the oldest part of the country. Do you know if Carmichael belonged to a church? A priest or minister might have some insight into his character."

"I don't know. I'll ask the detectives. What do you make of his book so far?"

"Well, you know I'm not very highbrow, and neither is he, I guess. Lot of weird names that make it hard to follow, but he's good at monsters."

"Sword and sorcery?"

"Yeah. I don't think I'll finish it. I like Westerns. Give me guns over swords any day."

"Does he specifically mention Japanese type swords? Or anything about Asian culture, you know, calling it by imaginary names, but describing samurai type stuff?"

"Hard to say for sure, but I don't think so. It's more like *The Lord of the Rings.*"

"*You* read *The Lord of the Rings*?"

"Saw the movies. You make calls to his agent and editor yet?"

"No. I'm starting with his old boss—the high school principal—after the police." Drelick typed a search into her phone. "After we take a look at the apartment, how do you feel about sushi for lunch?"

"Yuck."

"You could probably get fried rice or something. I figure if we have to eat anyway, we could use the time to start asking sushi chefs about their customers. If there's a real Japanese serial killer living around here, or even just someone obsessed with the culture, he's likely to be into the food as well."

"So you want to dive right into the racial profiling, huh?" Pasco said with a smirk.

Heading out of town now, following the GPS in Drelick's phone to the Ocean Road apartment, they passed seedy motels with burnt-out letters in the signs, swimming pools of cracked pale blue concrete cordoned off by chainlink fences mere feet from the road, collapsing and boarded up houses deteriorating into weed-choked lots, and a well-kept trailer park struggling to hold its chin up with small lawns and PVC picket fences.

She had the feeling that the beachfront community had at one time been an attractive location for a bygone middle class but had been reduced to a summer amusement struggling to draw vacation dollars with tawdry arcades and scrubby campgrounds. Strip clubs had sprung up amid the five-and-dime souvenir shops and pizza counters. Signs advertising a summer festival with live music, fireworks, and sand sculptures shouted colorfully over the low hum of failure and vice that seemed to waft from every concrete alley and peeling doorframe.

When they arrived at the Carmichael address, there was a car in the driveway: an aging Honda that for some reason she doubted belonged to a detective. She'd expected to find the place locked, had come out here only to get a sense of where this struggling single parent, this author with a cult following, was raising his kid. But the interior door was wide open, and through the storm door window she could see most of the vacant living room and a carpeted stairway. She raised her hand to rap on the glass, but Pasco touched her sleeve and shook his head. With his other hand, he clicked the handle quietly and said, "Let's just see who's here before we announce ourselves. Shouldn't be anybody but cops, right?"

Pasco stepped inside and unsnapped the button of his holster. Drelick followed, whispering, *"It's not a crime scene."* The open door and car in the driveway were a little too bold to suggest nefarious activity in the stark light of day, but then, smart criminals knew that.

Pasco moved into the living room, treading softly on the carpet and peering around the corner into the kitchenette. He nodded toward the stairway. As Drelick climbed the first few steps, Pasco swept through the remainder of the scant first floor and then came up behind her.

At the landing, she turned to look back at him, wanting to tell him that they should either go back outside and call in the plate number on the car, or just announce themselves. She hated it when he made snap decisions and conveyed them with body language. They should have talked about their approach while they were still outside.

Hesitating on the landing where the angle of the ceiling cut the second floor from view and trying to communicate her reluctance to him using only her eyes, she heard a piercing whistle from above. It started out low and long, but then began to glide around and take on the shape of a lazy, lilting melody. Within seconds, she recognized the tune as "Take It To The Limit," by the Eagles. She exhaled, tugged her suit jacket over her hip holster and climbed the remaining stairs with less caution.

The narrow hallway at the top of the stairs ended at a man kneeling on the floor with his ass crack framed between faded dungarees and a paint spattered t-shirt. A bucket of joint compound took up most of the floor space to his right. To his left, a full-length mirror leaned in a bedroom doorway, angled to keep it from falling. She could see herself and Pasco in the mirror; black-clad lurking shapes, rising from the stairwell. But the kneeling man hadn't yet caught sight or sound of them.

"Sir?" Drelick said. The guy startled, spun around to look at her, and dropped a dollop of putty onto the carpet as he did so.

"Shit," he said, scooping it up and tossing it in the bucket. He stood up, knees popping and crackling, and wiped his hands on his jeans. "Scared the piss outta me. Who're you?" He had bushy ginger hair and densely freckled arms, a medium build, and a backward baseball cap.

"FBI." Pasco said. "Who are you?"

"I'm the landlord."

"Again, sir. Who are you?"

"Bob Haggerty. I'd shake your hand, but I'd get mud on you. What can I do you for?"

"We're here to see the scene where a weapon was found," Drelick said, pointing at the patch. "Was that the hole in the wall where they found it?"

"Yeah. Cop put his boot through it. You'd think maybe he coulda cut a clean square for me, but no."

"Do the police know that you're patching that?" Pasco asked.

"Yeah. I called and asked. They said no problem. If Desmond gets put away, I'll have to rent this out again by the end of the month."

"You mind if we take a look around?" Drelick asked.

"Why not? Cops have already poked through all his shit anyway."

Drelick approached the wall. She could see the outline of the hole modified into a rectangle by Bob Haggerty, taped and partly patched already. The room at the end of the hall where the mirror was balanced in the doorframe had to be the boy's bedroom—cluttered with toys, and children's books. The bedclothes were tangled in a hasty heap, half on the floor.

"It's a shame about Lucas," Haggerty said. "No matter how all this plays out, that poor kid's guaranteed fucked for life."

"Do you think Desmond Carmichael is guilty?" Drelick asked, searching Haggerty's ruddy face for a reaction.

"I don't know the man. He paid on time and seemed nice enough. You look around here, you get the impression he cared for his son."

"Would it *surprise* you if he was convicted of murder?"

"Yeah. But life's full of surprises."

"Did he ever go away on any trips that you were aware of?" she asked.

"Might have been gone for a week to visit his parents' around Christmas. I think he said Virginia."

"Did he ever mention California?" Pasco asked.

"Ah, I can't say I remember for sure. Maybe a sci-fi conference or something."

"Do you recall when that might have been, the conference?" Drelick flipped a pad open.

"I'm not sure about it. He might have said he was invited but couldn't afford to go."

Drelick stepped around the mirror and into Lucas's room. It was messy but also the nicest in the apartment. The rest of the little house had off-white walls, unadorned with photos or artwork, but Lucas's room was painted tangerine and dressed up with a variety of lively framed images that looked like they belonged in the room of a younger child, one not yet awakened to the comic book heroes on the bed sheets. Drelick thought the zoo animals and toddler decor had probably come from the child's previous bedroom in the house they had shared with his mother, transplanted here even as he outgrew them, intended to provide a sense of continuity, the security of familiarity.

"Did you paint this bedroom?" Drelick asked.

"No, Desmond did that himself. I do a fresh coat before a new tenant if it needs it, but if you want a fancy color, you have to buy it and apply it."

Drelick wondered if even the color had come from a can left over from the family home or if Desmond had tried to match it. "So this mirror," she said, stepping around it again, "It was on the wall you're repairing?"

"Yup."

"So it covered Desmond's own patch job after he put the sword in the wall."

"That's right."

Drelick walked through Desmond Carmichael's bedroom, but found it was as sparse as a monk's cell, and the police had obviously ransacked what little furniture and clothing he did own. She gave the usual hiding places that a non-agent might not think to check a cursory look, but found no secret cubbyholes or seams.

Pasco looked bored. "Thank you for your time, Mr. Haggerty," she said placing a business card on the lid of his joint compound bucket while he worked. "Give us a call if you remember anything more about that conference in California."

Walking to the car, Pasco gave her the look; the question he never needed to ask aloud: *whatcha got?*

"Why hide a murder weapon behind a mirror unless you identify with it?"

* * *

The best sushi in Port Mavis wasn't bad, but it wasn't L.A. either. Talking to the chef and the maître d' turned up nothing. Still, Drelick was glad she'd eaten before visiting the station because the briefing she received from Inspector Fournier over *his* lunch would have robbed her of any appetite. She knew her parents' generation had sometimes called cops "pigs," but to watch Charles Fournier take down a bag of McDonald's was to see the slur vividly illustrated.

At first Fournier seemed interested in the possibility that Carmichael might be guilty of an even higher body count, but when they found no clear points of entry into the bicoastal serial killer theory, he backed away from it. "Tell you the truth," he said, and paused to thumb a stray pickle chip back into the corner of his mouth, "I don't need to prove he flew out to Cali and whacked a complete stranger to pin these family murders on him."

"What are you saying?"

"I'm saying you're probably just gonna muddy the waters. If you can show he had a plane ticket, then I'm all ears, but without it...too many questions. Like where'd he get a sword out there? Sure didn't take one on a plane without setting off alarms. And I don't need a jury getting hung up on red herrings when I have him hiding the weapon on the same day as a kill that he had a clear motive for."

"Detective, you should understand that my investigation could uncover evidence that absolves him. It's even possible that my west coast killer came here."

"Twice?"

She shrugged. "I spoke to Carmichael on the phone yesterday a little over an hour before Phil Parsons was murdered."

Fournier froze with his mouth open, the remaining quarter of his double quarter-pounder with cheese halfway to its final destination. A slice of tomato slipped out of the bun onto his desk blotter trailing a couple of gelatin coated seeds down his hairy wrist and gold watch band on the way. He let out a shallow, incredulous laugh as he wiped his wrist with a paper napkin. "You didn't open with that?"

"My case led me to Sandy Carmichael, and I wanted to check a detail about the sword with the guy who owned it. The two murders have some traditional elements in common."

"Traditional elements."

"Samurai methods, old-fashioned sword oil. It wouldn't surprise me if you found strands of silk traceable to Japanese clothing manufacturers at one of your crime scenes."

"Well, we didn't. Listen to me: Desmond is a writer, okay? A fantasy writer. You're from L.A., so you're probably familiar with what a fantasy convention looks like? I've seen clips on *E.T.* The people who read and write that crap are obsessives. They're all about props and costumes. Role-play. And a big brain with a lot of time on his hands, like Des? He'd do the research and get those kinds of details right."

"Or a fan of his might. But I can't find any overt Japanese references in his books. You called him Des. Did you know him before his wife was murdered?"

"It's a small town. We all went to school together."

"So you knew Sandy Carmichael as well?"

"I said we went to school together. I knew her dad, too, him being a cop who coached football. Phil had an influence on me going into police work."

"So these cases are deeply personal for you."

"I wouldn't use the word *deeply*. It's a small town."

"Detective, I make a habit playing devil's advocate. Carmichael probably did kill Phil Parsons, but I am going to dot every *i* and cross every *t*. The first of those is the phone call I had with him. Did it prompt him to rush in and kill Parsons or does it give him an alibi? That's what I'm looking at."

"Whoa, wait a minute. How could your call give him an alibi?"

"I left a message on his phone while, unbeknownst to me, he was visiting Harwood. When he called me back, there was torrential rain in the background that made it hard for me to hear him. He said he was in his car. Now, I've checked the weather history, and the storm you had on Sunday moved south over Boston to the Cape. It cleared up over this area well before it did in Walpole. So even if Carmichael was driving while talking with me, the time and duration of the call might help us pin down a time range when he was south of the precipitation line."

"That sounds pretty weak. I wouldn't dream of hanging my hat on something that flimsy."

"It's just one dot to connect. A better one is—did he have an EZ pass in the car? That would give you an exact time for him going through the Tobin Bridge toll on Route 1."

"No, he didn't have one. Used to, but let it lapse when he lost his job."

"There still might be video of his car at the toll."

"You really think he didn't have enough time to get to the golf course?"

"It's tight. He'd have to drive like a demon."

"It's enough."

"I also wonder how he knew exactly where to find Phil Parsons and kill him with opportunity. Does Parsons golf every Sunday at that time? Was it a pattern that Carmichael would have been aware of?"

"*That* sounds feasible, likely even."

"But you don't know. You haven't looked into it with his wife, the club, or his golf partner who witnessed the murder?"

"It's Monday, Agent Drelick. We're just getting started building a case."

"I'd like to see Mr. Carmichael now."

"What for?"

"What do you mean, what for? I want to interview him."

"As I understand it, you're not taking over the case at this time. Isn't that what you said?"

"Yes, but I came here to investigate connections. I can't do that without questioning the suspect."

"So with you not having jurisdiction, this falls under the category of a favor? I'm doing you a favor?"

"It falls under cooperating with the FBI. I'm sure your boss wouldn't expect anything less."

Chuck Fournier sucked a sesame seed out of the gap between his canine and molar, and said, "I'll set it up."

"When?"

"We're transferring him to county later today, so soon. Sit tight."

"You have enough to transfer him to county? No chance of having to let him go when lab results come in?"

"We have everything we need, Agent. We have him with the murder weapon."

Chapter 17

"You have a visitor," Fournier said through the bars.

Desmond was sitting on the cell floor, craving a writing implement. It was a hellish joke to have nothing but time and nothing to write with. He had been scouring his memory, trying to recall every detail he could of the old man at the playground, when Fournier snapped him out of his fugue by jingling the keys. For a second Desmond looked at him uncomprehendingly; then the words took on meaning. "Who is it?"

"The FBI agent you talked to on the phone yesterday—thanks for mentioning that, by the way. She came from California to see you."

"Why?"

Fournier flashed a tight, condescending grin. "That's her hand, and she'll decide how much she wants to tip it."

"She thinks I might be innocent," Desmond said, getting to his feet. "She thinks it might be an interstate killer."

"Don't get your hopes up. Best-case scenario, from my point of view, they tie you to somebody else's sword crimes because you're already in custody with blood on your hands, and I get to watch you die by lethal injection in California, which sadly, we don't have here."

"Tell me where Lucas is." Desmond said. He wasn't going to let Fournier bait him into a fight. That would be a waste of precious time, a waste of another rare chance to get an answer out of someone who knew.

"Lucas is somewhere safe…now that you're in here."

"Is he with Karen?"

Fournier paused, puckered his mouth, and said, "No."

"Then where? He's my *son*, you have no right to keep me in the dark about who's watching him. He's my son, and until a judge—"

"You sure about that, Des? He's your son? You sure?"

The question didn't make any sense, not until Desmond read the suggestion on Fournier's face. "The fuck are you implying, Chuck?"

"Just that he doesn't look a whole lot like you. And I doubt that you can say for sure that Sandy never had a fling. You know, four years ago, that was the first time you got a little too cozy with alcohol. Maybe she sought solace in a friend."

Desmond tasted iron and noticed he had bitten the inside of his cheek.

"I know she never did that."

"But it's not like you can ask her now, can you?"

"I knew her better than you ever did." Desmond could hear the acid in his voice. He was taking the bait, couldn't help it.

"When having a kid snapped you out of your drunken stupor, you might have got to know her again, but I *always* knew her."

The sound of a truck engine amplified by the narrow corridor of buildings behind the police station thrummed through the bricks at street level, a low unsettling drone.

"Who is Lucas with? Why isn't he with Karen?"

"Karen is in shock. She's in no shape to be parenting, and she agreed that Lucas should be shielded from the loss of his grandfather for as long as possible, while everything else is unstable."

"What…is he in a foster home? I swear to God, Chuck if you had anything to do with placing him in foster care—"

"He's at my house."

"No. No, no, no."

"Don't worry, Des. My wife is good with kids. We always wanted kids of our own, but you know, we weren't blessed."

"You have no *right!*"

"Hey, calm down. I can't just bring home a kid like a confiscated bag of weed that didn't end up in the log. This is all going to go through the proper channels. For right now, I'm just doing a favor for a friend's widow. Pitching in to help a fallen vet by taking care of his grandson. That said…when the smoke clears, I may want to get a paternity test. Just so *I'll* know the truth."

"Fuck you, Fournier. I swear to God, when I get out of here…."

"What? You'll kill me like everybody else? Go on, say it, say it loud."

Hydraulic brakes hissed in the alley.

Desmond pressed his face to the bars and whispered, "You would be my first, but if I lost him because of you, I would find it in me, you fat fuck."

In a voice so low it was barely audible, Fournier said, "Tell you what, Des. My task right now is to open your cell and escort you upstairs to one of the interrogation rooms you've come to know so well. When we get to the top of the stairs, we'll be in a hallway. At the back end of that hallway, our water-delivery guy will be propping open a door that is usually locked. A door to the back-alley access road."

Fournier's eyes darted toward the ceiling. There was a sound of clattering metal. Desmond took a step back from the bars.

"If you were to try anything when we get to that point, I would have to shoot you. Understood?"

Desmond's mind was reeling. Did Fournier want him to make a break for it so he could gun him down in cold blood? Of course he would like that. Why was he telling him this? "It would be suicide," Desmond said, his mouth curling in horror.

"And it would really shame me if you got away. But if you knocked over a handcart stacked with five-gallon bottles, it's possible that a serial killer like you could actually slip out of our grasp."

"What do you want? You want me to make myself look guiltier with every move? I won't do it. I'm not playing your game."

"You know where to find Lucas, but no one knows you know. If you got out of here, most people would expect you to run *from* the law, not *to* it. And if you showed up at my house with a blade, you can bet I'd be ready to take you on like a man. Otherwise, it's nothing but lawyers from here to the end. That what *you* want?"

"No."

"Me neither. I'm gonna unlock your cell now."

Fournier slid the bars open and stepped aside, giving Desmond room to exit and walk in front of him. He didn't cuff Desmond, but his gun was easy to see on his hip. Desmond took a few uncertain steps, then glanced back over his shoulder at Fournier. Fournier tipped his chin toward the stairs, "Go on. Chop, chop."

Climbing the stairs, Desmond's legs felt like they were connected to his body by frayed strands of corroded wire, incapable of receiving the full strength of the impulses from his brain. Each step felt like an insurmountable obstacle as his body tried to shut down into whatever survival mode was the opposite of an adrenaline-charged burst. At the top of the stairs, a wedge of sunlight glided across the dirty, black-skid-marked wall of the corridor. Was that light from the back door? He heard a sloshing *thud* and imagined the water-delivery guy setting a bottle down against the metal door to hold it open. The heavy, hollow, metallic respiration of the truck idling in the alley reached his ears now with a crisp clarity that the brick walls had previously masked, and he felt himself shifting out of shut-down mode into fight-or-flight. It was true, what Fournier had told him. This move was designed to give him the opportunity to run. But it was engineered against him. Fournier, armed and trained, would be ready to gun him down, whether here or at the house where Lucas was. And maybe Lucas was safer in that house, where Fournier's wife might also be prepared to pick up a gun if she needed to.

If Lucas is even there…if the whole thing isn't a lie.

But there wouldn't be another opportunity to slip out of the snare that was closing around him. If he had a shot, however desperate, to take Lucas on the run and protect him from a threat no one else believed in, didn't he have to take it?

He did. But then Sandy's voice spoke up: *Lucas doesn't need two dead parents.*

When Desmond reached the top of the stairs, he could see a uniformed officer and a shirtsleeves detective at the end of the corridor where it opened into an office. They were staring at something he couldn't see, near the ceiling. He knew that posture from waiting in line in coffee shops and banks with wall-mounted televisions tuned to the news. They were watching TV with rapt attention, their coffee cups momentarily forgotten. And Desmond knew that this was *his* moment.

The water-delivery guy rolled past him, obstructing his view of the cops down the hall. He saw himself raising his leg, bent at the knee, and kicking out at Fournier behind him. A good kick would send him flying backward down the stairs, robbing him of the chance to draw and shoot. He saw himself rounding the corner while the delivery guy and the heavy, bottle-laden cart stood between the distracted cops and the back-alley exit.

But something about the demeanor of those cops he had glimpsed made him hesitate. He wanted to know what they were watching. Something in their body language. People had watched TV like that on

9/11. Who cares? Even if it's a terrorist attack, it's not in this *town. Use the distraction, whatever it is, to get Lucas.*

The moment passed. The water guy rounded the corner, and now a new body was striding down the hall toward Desmond and Fournier. He'd missed his chance. The loss spread through him, a sickening visceral mixture of relief and regret.

He recognized Jay Twomey, the Chief of Police coming up to him, slowing, and gazing past him at Fournier, who had now reached the top of the stairs.

"Fournier," he said, shaking out a sheet of paper in his hand like a wet dishrag, "This transfer to county is bullshit. Since when do you not run them by me?"

"I was about to, boss. I'm bringing him to talk to the agents first."

"No you're not. They're gone. Ran outta here like their asses were on fire when the news broke."

"What news?"

"There's been a massacre in Ohio. A *sword* massacre. Might have happened last night. Bodies were found this morning. We barely had enough to hold you in the first place," he said to Desmond. "At least now, I won't have to lose sleep over letting you go."

"Wait...*what?* How can you be sure?" Fournier's voice sounded weak.

"Take a look at the TV and ask me again. Whoever is out there chopping heads off is doing it across state lines, which means it's no longer our problem."

Chief Twomey made a sweeping gesture with the paper in his hand, and Desmond followed him into the lobby with Fournier still at his heels like a dog that doesn't trust his owner's judgment about a visitor, still sniffing warily and ready to bite. Desmond couldn't hear much of the TV audio over the chatter of the cops commenting on it, but the camera lingered on a shot of a yellow strip of police tape stretched between tree trunks. Beyond it, cops could be seen milling around near a small turquoise house in the woods. Sunlight on water sparkled in the distance. A tarp was draped over what had to be a body lying on the pine-needle-strewn ground.

A cell phone rang, and Desmond cocked his head as Fournier answered brusquely, "If you're calling about what's on the tube, I'm lookin' at it.... Calm down, I can't understand a word.... *No*.... How?

Jesus, Ginny, weren't you watching him?" Fournier was turning a deep, purplish-red. The hand holding the phone dropped from his ear, and Desmond could hear a thin, distant, wailing plea coming from the little speaker. Fournier stared at Desmond's chest, moving his jaw like it was dislocated and he was trying to reset it, trying to make his mouth work so he could talk, but Desmond already knew what he was going to say, and when he heard it he wouldn't be able to help himself; Chuck Fournier's jaw would indeed be dislocated very soon.

"Lucas is missing," Fournier managed to spit the words out, quick and dry.

Then Desmond was on top of him, choking him with both hands and crashing into a metal desk in a torrent of profanity, cops swarming and pulling at his shoulders and legs until the juice of a Taser lit him up and burned the fight out of his sinews.

Chapter 18

He was James Hashimoto on the flight to Ohio, but thankfully no one called him by that name. James was the name on the driver's license he carried, the name his mother had given him, but he kept it in his wallet with his currency, where it belonged. He despised his legal name almost as much as he despised the custom the younger generation had of calling their elders by first names. He had endured this at banks and stores from time to time when presenting a card. Apparently when formal dress had vanished from the workplace, so too had proper manners. But the workplace was far behind him now. What a long and humiliating game that had been—pretending to share the same ambitions as his fellows, all the while saving every dollar he could for the mission. Now he was a retiree who liked to travel. He was Mr. Hashimoto at the car rental counter and at the Pakmail location where he picked up the long, narrow box he had shipped to himself a week ago. But by the time he was driving south on U.S. 23, he was Sensei again, rolling down the windows and breathing in dusty, baked air that reminded him, almost, of Manzanar.

He had never again truly known dust like the dust of Manzanar. The closest thing was to open a bag of flour and breathe it in. The film that would cover your nose and mouth would resemble the texture of the air in that forsaken place, but the smell would be too pleasant. Manzanar dust smelled of desolation and despair, of vegetation ground to the finest granules, of human will caught like a piece of gristle in the teeth of the jagged Sierras, gnashed and spat out onto the cracked desert floor, then burned by the Mohave sun to an ash so fine it would slip through any sieve.

Sensei wanted this Ohio dust to remind him of that, but it failed.

He glanced at the package on the passenger seat beside him. The trail he was leaving would soon be picked up. After all the years of waiting and training, of reclaiming what his father had abandoned when the man boarded the boat that would carry his seed to Hawaii and then on to California in search of a new identity, a new opportunity, after a childhood spent struggling to survive in the spectacular ruins of that promise and an adulthood spent pretending to have embraced it, he had finally opened his samurai eyes and fixed them on his targets. In the course of only five years, he had found them all.

Had it already been five years since he had taken his first head? Action had flowed so quickly from research. Research had followed so easily from predatory instinct. The first had been a farmer in Arizona, heir to an estate seized by white vultures when the Japanese farmers were rounded up and bussed to the internment camps. Strawberry farmers like his father. That first kill had initiated him into the company of Spirit Warriors long dead, and for a brief moment it had quenched the thirst of the sword he had been sharpening and polishing in his secret heart since his boyhood in the dust of the Owens Valley.

The Arizona authorities were confused and unfocused in the wake of that first kill. When he took the second head, time, distance, and auspicious coincidences had shielded him from any connection to Arizona; and a blind drunk had been convicted of the murder of Sandy Carmichael. But for the third target on his kill list, Sensei succumbed to an artistic impulse and revisited Manzanar, placing the severed head in the proper context to tie a life's work together like the knot on a *hakama*.

Only the span of the continent had kept the authorities from connecting the crimes thus far, but now, with his apprentice's initiation by the execution of Phil Parsons, he could feel that uncertainty slipping into a new channel. The names he had tracked down already would have to be enough. Time was running out. When he drew steel today he would slay all of them, down to the very last soul in the Tibbets bloodline before he resheathed. After this he would no longer be able to travel as James Hashimoto. The country would be swarming with agents who carried his picture. Which was precisely why he had always known he would need an acolyte. If things went awry he could rest in the knowledge that he had trained the boy the best he could. While the master was killing the last Tibbets, the apprentice would be preparing the last Parsons. The Lamprey line had dwindled down to only one, and that one had been left gazing with crow-eaten eyes across the wastes of Manzanar.

Manzanar. He had seen pictures of the surface of Mars that were the closest thing to that barren wasteland. Returning after all these years, climbing the guard tower at dawn with Lamprey's head in a sack, and surveying the landscape from that high vantage had brought the memories flooding back. The terrain hadn't changed. Only the buildings were gone. He remembered the red squall that smeared the sun across the sky when the wind picked up, and the sound of sand pattering against the walls of the tarpapered pine shacks while the dust whistled through the knotholes in the floorboards like a roomful of boiling teakettles.

As a boy he had seen the neighbors using discarded tin can lids to cover those holes and to keep the dust out. Collecting the lids and nailing them to the floor, cutting his fingers on the ragged edges and bruising his nails with the hammer…it was one of his earliest memories — the first time he had filled his father's shoes and cared for his pregnant mother.

He didn't remember his father at all or the night when the FBI had taken him. Mama told him that he tried to kick one of the agents and she had to carry him off to bed screaming. Mama had been three months pregnant when Papa went to be interrogated at Fort Lincoln. They never saw him again.

He still wondered if the baby would have been a boy or a girl. No one told him which it was that died with his mother in the camp hospital that sweltering summer day. August 6, 1942. The day he became an orphan. He could still see Sister Mary Bernadette when he closed his eyes and thought of that time, could picture her face more clearly than his mother's. His most vivid memory of the Sister was of her sitting beside a grimy window mending a rip in his coat after a fistfight he'd had with another boy, her nimble brown fingers working the precious needle through the wool deftly and lovingly, devoid of the haste or frustration he imagined she should have felt at having to do it for the third time for this boy who couldn't hold his temper.

It seemed to him that there was a scarlet thread running through the fabric of life, one that joined events across the years, piercing human hearts and plunging underground, only to reemerge without warning, a thread connecting lives and sometimes dates. When three years later his life in the camp came abruptly to an end, he would be shocked by the date: August 6th again. The day he lost whatever distant family remained to him. The day he was cast alone into the world like a stone into a pond, and no one could have imagined the ripples he would make. On August 6th the dream he harbored in secret of one day finding his grandparents, aunts, and uncles when the war was over, the dream of crossing the ocean as a stowaway on a steamer, was blown to dust in a flash, washed away by black rain, when Hiroshima burned.

The echoes of that explosion were still rebounding.

Now, after all these years, he was going to meet the last remaining descendants of the pilot who delivered the bomb. Paul Tibbets died in 2007, and the obituary had led Sensei to Ohio. There was a camp here. Not a concentration camp, like the one he had been raised in, but a cabin on a lake where the Tibbets family was now gathering with their hamburgers and hot dogs, their soda and beer, their swimsuits and cameras, for a family reunion.

Sensei, the uninvited guest, was bringing the cutlery.

He followed the map he had purchased at a gas station. The road carried him through small towns with white clapboard churches and farm-equipment dealers. He passed corn and potato fields, and was reminded again of his time in the camp. At night the searchlights roved the grid of pine barracks from the towers where the guards kept watch with their machine guns, but in the daytime they had been allowed outside the wire to work the fields.

There was nowhere to run to. Cruel mountain ranges stood sentinel on both sides of the valley.

Toiling in the cornfield, he had befriended Mr. Kanemori, an *Issei*, who regaled him with tales of old Japan. In time, young Hashimoto learned that Kanemori-san had a family somewhere, a daughter and grandchildren in some other camp. He didn't know which; he only knew that they were not at Manzanar. The government had sent him to the wrong camp after interrogating him for months in North Dakota. A fisherman, they had accused him of running barrels of oil to Japanese submarines off the coast of San Francisco.

Young Hashimoto asked the old man if he had been at Fort Lincoln, and when Kanemori answered yes, the boy almost couldn't speak. He wanted to ask if the old man had seen his father there, but he couldn't even describe his father. All he had was a name. Kanemori didn't recognize it, but the simple fact that he had been in the same place where Papa disappeared was enough, and after that, the orphan boy went to work beside the old man every day the sisters gave him leave.

Mr. Kanemori pointed out Mt. Whitney and told him that it looked like Fujiyama. Close enough to do the job. "The sight of such an immovable mountain provides spiritual sustenance for Japanese blood. These sandstorms cannot touch it. You should meditate on this and try to be the same. Find the rock in your own heart that cannot be moved, whatever storms may come."

Kanemori told him stories of the samurai, and carved wooden *bokkens* to teach him his first *katas*. Kanemori taught him to have *yamato damashi*, to be a Spirit Warrior. And in whispered tones, told him to disregard the lessons of the Sisters and Father Steinback. Kanemori told him about the night in December of the first year when the mess hall bells rang all night and the internees rioted until a guard named Lamprey fired his Tommy gun into the crowd. Kanemori renewed his allegiance to the Emperor in his heart when those shots were fired. If he lived to see the day when they were set free, he was going back to Japan.

Kanemori didn't make it, but when years later in the 1960s, Hashimoto finally traveled to their ancestral home, he visited the village the old man was from, on his way to Hiroshima. There was a time in his thirties and forties when he had considered remaining there for the rest of his life. By then he was an accomplished martial artist, had reclaimed the culture that his *Nissei* parents had abandoned, and could have opened his own school.

But that had never been the summit of the mountain in his heart. And he knew that to fulfill his destiny, to thread the needle through the fabric of his life in a way that made an enduring knot, he would have to return to America and assume the costumes and customs of the land of his birth.

When he returned to California he brought his only true companion with him. He had not found a wife in Japan as he had hoped he might, but he had found a soul mate: the sword that now rested in the cardboard shipping box beside him. A flawless beauty, her iron furnishings were engraved with reed stalks that reminded him of the fields of Manzanar, and the blade was forged from twenty-seven inches of steel harvested from the melted girders of the Aioi Bridge at ground zero in Hiroshima, melted first by the bomb, and again by a master smith, hammered into an object of unsurpassed lethal artistry. She whispered to him when at rest, and sang to him when drawn. That song of blood and wind was a tune sweeter than any wife could ever utter. Handing the box over to the idiot clerk had been heart wrenching, almost impossible. But now, with his weapon by his side again, he could breathe deeper. Soon he would hear the song.

In the early days Sensei had gathered information at libraries, combing through newspapers and microfiche for obituaries and articles, combing through history books, and military journals, academy yearbooks and phonebooks. He was not computer savvy—Bell was better at that—but Facebook had been a revelation. It was astonishing how little some people cared for their privacy, thrilling how easy it had been to follow the thread of the family reunion, to find the dates and the place. He didn't have a GPS in the car, had even pulled into a rest stop and searched the engine compartment, trunk, and wheel wells for those tracking devices that some car rental companies now used. Nor did he carry a cell phone that could be triangulated once the authorities found the carnage. But before leaving home he had researched the lake at the library. He knew the lay of the land.

The last road was a long, winding stretch of rutted dirt, wet with mud from recent rain, little more than a trail. The car jounced and swayed, its shallow chassis scraping against the ground, making sharp screeches like birdcalls. Low-hanging branches tapped a tattoo on the windows. The family seldom came here anymore, and no one had been up in advance of the reunion to trim the trees. Clouds of midges swarmed in front of the windshield. As the road descended to the lake, it resembled a tunnel of tree limbs, then swatches of color appeared—the bright metallic paint of SUVs, the sparkling Morse code of sunlight reflecting off dark water.

Where the road widened again, Sensei slowed the vehicle and pulled into what looked like a turnaround for snowmobiles in winter. He slid the box across his lap in the little sedan, already dressed in his black *hakama* and *kimono*. He took a Swiss Army knife from the glove compartment and slit the packing tape along the seam of the box, removed the embroidered bag from within, and, reaching into the bag, closed his hand gently around the silk-wrapped hilt of the *katana*.

Sitting in the driver's seat and looking up the road for any sign of approach, any indication that he had been noticed (there was none, but he could hear delighted cries and splashes from the lake), he reached into the glove box again and flicked open a slim metal case. He pinched a clove cigarette between two fingers and put it to his lips. He lit it and, closing his eyes, took one long meditative drag. Exhaling through the cracked window, he watched the wind snatch the sweet vapor and shred it through the dripping black branches overhead.

He climbed from the little white car and, standing in the empty road, bowed to the ghost of Mr. Kanemori in the east where a haze-shrouded sun burned unseen. Holding the sword in his left hand, he slid it through his sash and straps, and then pushed his left thumb against the *tsuba*, unlocking the blade from the scabbard.

The hilt ejected into his eager right hand as smoothly as ever, and another sweet draught of clove scent wafted up into his sinuses. Soon he would smell the iron of freshly spilled blood. The joyful shrieks echoing through the lake air would change color through a spectrum of anguish like the foliage of this place in autumn.

He tossed the glowing cigarette into a wheel rut. Then, with all ceremony attended to, he commenced to walk toward the enemy.

It was not a walk like any in the western lexicon of foot travel. It was a crouching, sliding step, executed with slow, gliding grace. The walk was a meditation unto itself. With his legs and feet concealed in the black pleated folds of the *hakama*, any observers would have thought they were watching a man float over the ground on a carpet of winds.

The first thing he saw as he cleared the trees flanking the dirt lot was a cold fire pit. The blackened concrete brought to mind the buildings of Hiroshima, forever blackened with the photographic shadows of human bodies vaporized in the blast and blown on a breeze of carbon dust at the cusp of the rolling shock wave. Trimmed branches leaned against the concrete, their tips sticky with marshmallow residue. This fire pit was cool, but the smell of charred flesh tinged the air, and a film of smoke from a nearby coal fire smudged the sky above the grassy yard where it sloped down toward the lake around the corner of the cottage.

A gunshot punctured the air, close and loud, then rolled across the water.

Sensei did not flinch or alter his stride.

He crept close to the pale turquoise wall of the cottage where the propane and water tanks covered him from view of anyone in the yard. From this vantage point he could see a portly, middle-aged man with gray hair, dressed in cargo shorts and a polo shirt, scraping a spatula across a portable grill. In his left hand he held a .22-caliber rifle by the barrel. A girl in a bathing-suit top and cut-off jeans reached impatiently for the gun while the man flipped the hamburgers.

"My turn," she said.

But the man didn't give up the gun when the girl, who appeared to be about twelve years old, tugged gently at his wrist.

"Hang on a minute, Annie Oakley," he said. "I'm gonna show you something."

The pair stood in a clearing, on the edge of evening, the indigo sky fading to deeper purple between the trees. Soon the children in the lake would notice the air getting colder and would quit their water games, climb back up the rocky lawn toward the smell of dinner. A dollop of hamburger grease dripped onto the coals with a sizzle, and orange light flared up, illuminating the man's face for a second.

Sensei recognized him as Bill Tibbets. Bill was slightly more scrupulous than some of his relatives about what information he shared online, but even a single profile picture was enough for a positive identification. Bill was a Tibbets, and that put him on the kill list.

Bill Tibbets waved a hand at his face, swatting away a mosquito, then slapped at another on his forearm, leaving a smear of his own blood. He brushed his hand on his shorts and told the girl, "Light those citronella candles, would you, honey?" He put the spatula down and took a swig from a beer bottle, seeming to relish making the girl wait for permission to take the rifle.

There was a paper target stapled to an oak tree some fifteen yards away where the lawn met the woods, its inner rings untouched, the perimeter pockmarked to reveal the golden flesh of punctured wood through the holes in the paper.

Sensei looked at the rifle and followed the line of it up the man's arm to the little blossom of blood. Soon the Spirit Warrior would taste what the mosquito had. While studying martial arts in Japan, he'd heard accounts of the Rape of China. Thousands of Chinese heads had lined the roads on bamboo poles to demonstrate the ferocity of the Rising Sun, thousands of bodies stripped of flesh and fed to dogs at first...later to men. Then the war against the Australians in New Guinea when food shortages in the bomb-scorched Pacific islands almost starved the Emperor's army. But for the true Spirit Warrior, there was never a food shortage as long as there was an enemy. Soldiers were ordered not to eat fallen comrades, but the flesh of foreign foes was known to increase one's spiritual vitality.

Sensei wondered if he would have time to consume the spirit of Bill Tibbets. It would depend upon how quickly he could work. And where was Bill's brother, Tim? Approaching the house, Sensei had seen a woman through a window, setting paper plates and plastic ware around a picnic table. They would eat indoors to avoid the mosquitoes. It was a small gathering for a reunion, but there were still spouses and children present who were not on the kill list. He had come here to sever a thread, to end a bloodline, to slice a name from a scroll. But events were moving quickly now, and it was possible that the cutting would not be as clean and precise as he had intended. The flyboys who dropped bombs on cities didn't care for such things, but a samurai was different. Anyone could kill indiscriminately, but the sword was a symbol of pristine discrimination. In the hands of the Bodhisattva Fudo Myoto, the flaming sword was an emblem of the wisdom to separate this from that.

Sensei watched the girl as she leveled the rifle with her eye and placed the wooden stock in the hollow of her shoulder. Whoever she was...she was not on his scroll. He took a deep breath and felt it flowing into his sinews and the subtle channels that carried the *Qi* throughout his body. Speed would be of the essence.

There was a rustle in the branches overhead, and the cawing of an angry crow. A flutter of black wings. Looking up, he saw that a hawk had alighted on the tallest branch of a dead, lightning-split oak, scattering a black cloud of scavengers. Sensei smiled. This was an auspicious omen.

The girl had been startled, but she had not fired. Tibbets was instructing her, adjusting the set of her shoulders. Then she squeezed the trigger, and the sound set the hawk to flight as a new hole exploded from the gray skin of the target tree across the field. The paper was unharmed. Tibbets reclaimed the gun from the disappointed child and told her to run along and tell the others that dinner was ready. She trotted toward the water, sandals flapping, ponytail swishing.

Time to strike. Sensei called out, "Bill! Check this out."

Bill Tibbets cocked his head, scrunched the worry lines on his balding pate, and squinted at the corner of the cottage where the evening shadows had grown long and deep. He stepped out of the circle of light cast by the bug candles, holding the rifle loosely, as if only half aware which was in his hand at the moment—gun or spatula. It was like leading an animal to slaughter. You spoke its name, gave it a command, and it came to the blade.

When Tibbets was in range and out of sight of the lower lawn, Sensei stepped forward, drawing steel, and lopped the man's head off in a single fluid motion, sending it flying onto the grass near the tree line, trailing a ribbon of blood. There was no sound from the victim but a gurgling of air escaping the severed windpipe, a bubbling in the arterial flow for a moment, and then the dull impact of the heavy body hitting the dirt. Sensei swung the *katana* around in a spinning arc, ending with a short stop that sent a curtain of blood and tissue flying from the edge of the blade to patter on the leaves of a nearby fern.

He drew the spine of the blade across the webbing between the thumb and forefinger of his left hand where they gripped the mouth of the scabbard, and in a graceful flash that slowed toward the end of the motion, resheathed with another long, low, audible exhalation. His eyes remained fixed on the eyes of his victim as they ceased to blink.

Now he reached between his knees and slapped the pleats of his *hakama* out to the sides so that he could kneel in *seiza*. He drew the short blade, the *tanto*, and with the casual confidence of a surgeon cut the blood soaked polo shirt away and sliced into the corpse's pasty flesh, removing the liver with flawless efficiency. No motion of the knife was superfluous. All was executed with ceremonial concentration, unhurried grace, and cool equanimity. He felt no rage and no fear as he rose from the ground and tossed the liver onto the grill among the charring hamburgers. The fire flared again as the dripping blood sizzled and smoked on the coals.

Sensei thought of the profile pictures. Even at the advanced age of seventy-five, his memory was diamond sharp. While his meat cooked, he walked down the lawn to the dock in search of familiar faces.

Chapter 19

The haunted house where Shaun Bell had spent an October chopping the heads off of wax dummies was deserted now. Approaching the familiar building, he felt an ache of nostalgia for simpler days, and wondered—not for the first time—how it was that the police had never come looking for him after Sandy Parsons was beheaded. After all, how many locals had watched him do the deed, sending a wax head flying on the crest of a wave of theatrical blood without so much as clipping an errant lock of hair from the mannequin's wig?

But those days were gone. The owners of the Palace of Pain had packed up and moved south, leaving the abandoned shell of the attraction to finally settle into the business of the authentic neglect and decay that it had for so long artfully imitated.

Bell drove his secondhand Saturn up the long dusty road to the barn behind the Palace. The boy lay sleeping on the back seat with his hands cable-tied. They'd been on the highway for a while, and Bell figured the stress must have knocked the kid out. Either that or he was only pretending to sleep to get his kidnapper's guard down, planning to kick him when he opened the door. But the kid was only four. Was he really capable of that kind of plotting?

Kidnapper.

Bell had been thinking about that word for a while now. He was already a killer, so he couldn't say why it felt uncomfortable adding this to his list of felonies. If his role in the boy's life remained kidnapper only and didn't progress to killer, then it would be a step back from the precipice. Yes, he had killed, but he had not yet killed a child. Sensei was now hundreds of miles away, but Bell could still feel the momentum of his master's wishes like a gale-force wind at his back, pushing him forward, at times lifting his feet off the ground.

He got out of the car and watched the kid through the window. The boy didn't stir when Bell closed the door. He stood silently for a moment, staring through the film of brown dust they had picked up on the back roads, and when the boy still appeared to be sleeping, he had a momentary flash of panic. Was the kid still breathing? Had he suffocated under the duct-tape gag? A peculiar mixture of fear and relief welled up in his chest as he wiped the dust from the window and narrowed his gaze to the boy's torso, looking for the rhythm of respiration.

The boy's shirt was rising and falling. Bell let himself breathe in again.

At this very moment Sensei might be wiping the blood from his blade, confident that Bell had already cut this final, low hanging fruit from the Parsons' family tree.

Would Sensei feel confident that his apprentice had completed the task he had been trained for? Or did the old man doubt his *yamato damashi?* The last thing the old man had said to him on his way out the door with his suitcase in hand was the same old farewell they had established years ago, a teasing refrain: "Don't start watching TV."

Bell vividly remembered the first time they had sat down in front of one to watch a program together, one of the only times, back in California. Mr. Hashimoto didn't have a TV in his apartment, but he had asked Shaun, while his parents were at work, if they had a VCR connected to theirs. Of course they did. The old man had fetched a tape from a mailing envelope, and together they watched a documentary about the atomic bomb in rapt silence. Shaun had learned that the tens of thousands vaporized in the flash were the lucky ones. The effects of the radiation made the Nazi showers and ovens look like amateur hour. In quiet moments, the stories of the survivors still echoed in his mind: the mother too weak to lift the wreckage from her burning children as they pleaded and screamed in agony; the farmer who bred mutant animals after the black rain fell; the smiling bomber who told the camera, "The target was there just as pretty as a picture.... I made the run, let the bomb go. That was my greatest thrill."

There was a dusty television in the house he and Sensei shared in Port Mavis now, but it was seldom on, and when it was, always tuned to the news. Watching reports of drone strikes in Afghanistan, Shaun wondered if American flyboys still got a thrill when firing at a wedding party with a joystick from a trailer in the Nevada desert. The mathematics of war enraged him. There was no honor in it. Two countries invaded for two towers, and two atomic bombs for Pearl Harbor. *Two*. Fat Man and Little Boy.

But recently Shaun had begun to wonder if Sensei also killed more for the thrill than for the mission.

He walked through the dust to the barn door, put his shoulder to the wood, and slid it along the stubborn track. Inside the barn, moldy hay lay in mounds left over from the days before the Jensen family had turned a farm into a Halloween attraction. Wedges of sunlight sliced through the darkness from the window seams and traced an angular geometry of gold dust across the dark green hull of a well-maintained tractor. Bell hesitated and then looked back at the car where the boy slept. He scanned the stark landscape for other vehicles tucked into the shelter of the house, anything he might have overlooked while driving in, any sign of occupants. He had planned to park his car in the empty barn to hide it. But if the tractor was here...had Jensen really abandoned the place? Wouldn't he have sold the machine? The thing was in top shape, relatively new. Jensen had used it to cut the corn maze each year, and while he probably wouldn't have trailered it to Georgia, he certainly wouldn't have just left it to rot. You might not be able to sell off a bunch of homemade animatronic ghouls, but you damn sure could sell a tractor in New Hampshire.

Bell stepped back out of the gloomy barn into the full blaze of day and rolled the door closed again. He would have to find somewhere else to conceal the car.

If I don't find someone home.

He ran to the cover of the cornfield and crept along its edge to the rambling farmhouse that had been converted into the Palace of

Pain. The Jensen family home was an outbuilding across the road, little more than an apartment atop a garage. The residence wasn't visible from the gravel road he had followed to the customer parking lot (a muddy field cordoned off with ropes and barrels each October) but when he came to the end of the corn maze, he could see that the driveway beside the apartment was vacant. The place had an uninhabited look to it, the composite result of too many subtle details for him to put his finger on.

There was no one here. He ran back to the car, only now realizing that he hadn't locked it. One of the rear doors was open and the boy was wriggling onto the ground like a fish flopping on the deck of a boat. His eyes were wild and red. At the sight of Bell, a muted scream trumpeted through the duct tape and mostly back-drafted through the kid's snot-clogged nose.

Bell slowed to a jog, then to a walk. Even if his quarry could manage to get to his feet right now, there was nowhere to run to. He reached the car and bent to pick the boy up but had to shuffle backward to avoid a flurry of flailing kicks. He should have cable-tied the kid's ankles too, should have at least done it while the kid was sleeping in the car, but now it would be impossible. Somehow he'd assumed that the boy would walk on his own two feet when they got here, but why should he? Bell would have to carry him like a sack of potatoes—an impossibility if the kicking continued.

Bell stood back and gave the boy time to kick himself out, to exhaust the urge. *The Boy. The Kid.* He'd been avoiding thinking of him by name. By thinking of him only as *the boy*, or *the kid*, he'd been dehumanizing him in preparation for the slaughter. He forced himself now to embrace that ugly word. *Slaughter*. It tasted rancid in his mind. Was he going to slaughter Lucas like a pig at what used to be a farm and was now a house of horrors? The tape over Lucas's mouth changed the look of his face, robbed it of almost enough personality to help Bell gain some distance. But the boy's eyes were so big that it was little help. *I'm doing it again*, he thought. *Lucas has big, expressive eyes*, he thought. *And right now they are expressing pure hatred*.

Lucas had managed to stand up, but now he toppled into the dust again from kicking out too far. His head bounced off the car door on the way down, and he became still except for a steady shudder that would have been a crying fit if not for the tape.

Bell stepped forward and touched the back of Lucas's head. The unwashed hair felt coarse, yet delicate against his palm. Lucas didn't recoil immediately at the touch, not in a way that would indicate a pain reflex. He turned his head and looked at his captor's face with a darkly furrowed brow that surprised Bell with its maturity. It was amazing how quickly children learned to imitate the expressions of their parents. Did Desmond Carmichael wear that serious, dark expression so often that his son had picked it up like a regional accent?

Bell lifted Lucas by the shoulders and set him on his feet.

Lucas broke into a run, cutting across the field for the tree line. Bell watched him run while reaching into a duffel bag on the passenger seat for a few extra-large cable ties. Then he gave chase with long strides and swept the boy up in his arms. He flipped him sideways and fell to his knees, trying to hold the small body still while absorbing kicks to the gut as he fumbled to get the cable ties threaded and locked. He should have taken the kid's sneakers off in the car and made it harder for him to run, harder for him to land a kick with impact. The *kid*. Maybe that was best.

It took most of Bell's strength to subdue the boy and bind his legs. Even then, the flailing continued for a moment, rippling out from the child's midsection, and making him look like an undulating eel. Finally, the squirming stopped, the futility of it sinking in, until the only sound was the rapid, ragged intake of breath through the nose. It sounded like it could be hyperventilation.

Bell didn't like the look or the sound of it, so he braced himself for the screaming, and ripped off the tape.

But the screaming didn't come. The boy just dragged in deep, panicky draughts of air, his eyes closed, tears cutting trails across his dirty cheeks. Eventually the gasping slowed to a deep heaving, which soon took on a tone, a slow rising whine that grew into a fit of crying. The tension in the little body had dissolved into helplessness. Bell slung the boy over his shoulder and carried him with both arms wrapped around the bound legs, half expecting to feel tiny teeth biting into his back.

They passed the entrance of the corn maze and continued along the wall of rustling stalks. The only sounds were the sporadic chatter of birds and insects and the coarse botanical gossip of the stalks as they swayed in a gentle breeze. Bell remembered how he had cut his fingers trying to pull one of the stalks from the ground in an idle moment one day, paying for the attempt when the edge of a husk surprised him with its sharpness. It was a lesson to him that a sharp enough blade didn't need to be made of steel to cut cleanly. At the right angle and speed, even paper could cut. As he trudged past the rows of corn with the boy over his shoulder, he reflected that he would need to be careful with this one. Sometimes it was the smallness of things that made them dangerous.

Bell remembered last year's corn maze. Every year Jensen chose a theme for the maze, a design that could be seen from the air and, after cutting it, had a crop duster photograph it for the website and brochures. Last year it was a spider web, but a peculiar one: an intricate labyrinth of dead ends with only one true path leading out. It took most patrons most of an hour to find their way back to the Palace of Pain after being led to the giant spider topiary in the middle. More than a few people had to raise the red poles they'd been given upon entry to signal that they were hopelessly lost and giving up the game.

It looked like the web maze was still mostly intact. The winter had roughed up the corn with freeze and thaw, but the field hadn't been razed.

Lucas was snuffling now, his respiration almost normal. Bell hurried his pace to get into the building before a second wind of kicking or screaming started up. Hurrying, but not breaking into a run (that might jar the kid into resistance), he jammed his hand into his jeans pocket and fished out the key he'd retrieved from under a whiskey barrel beside the barn. Thank God the key had still been there. It nagged at him that this was one more sign that maybe the place wasn't abandoned for good, that maybe Jensen would be back, but there was no time to worry about that now. Better to take it as an auspicious omen: if the key hadn't been under the barrel,

Bell would have had to break a window or kick in a door, all while handling the boy.

The entrance hall was claustrophobic by design. The decorations hadn't been removed. Long strands of dusty, theatrical Spanish moss hung from the ceiling and crawled across the sculpted foam walls, which had been spray-painted in motley shades of gray-fade to create the appearance in low light of a stone crypt. At the end of the hall a ninety-degree turn, invisible until one reached it, led to an arch, usually lit with a black light to make the neon-green inscription glow but now dark. Bell had passed under it countless times and knew that it established the theme of the attraction. Beneath an inverted pentagram were the words: IN MY HOUSE THERE ARE MANY MANSIONS.

The Palace of Pain had been designed with a sweeping global ambition in mind. Dreamed up by a hick with a gift for machines, a man who had toured his home country extensively with a carnival but had never left the continent, it nonetheless presented a tour of the horrors of cultures far flung across history and geography and did so with painstaking attention to detail, beginning with scenes from European folklore—elements of the Brothers Grimm set in the woods and cottages of Germany's Black Forest—and extending to the headhunters of the South Pacific.

Lucas went limp and silent as Bell carried his bound body into the first exhibit between transported tree trunks. Even without dry ice to provide a heavy ground mist or theatrical lighting to cast eerie shadows, the scene still suggested a haunted forest to young eyes adjusting to darkness.

Bell expected the power to be out, but he carried Lucas to the sidewall anyway and parted a curtain of silk leaves to feel for the switch. When he flipped it, there was a familiar heavy *clack* and *hum*, and the ceiling lit up with constellations of pinprick stars, while the pale shadow play of wolf and crow silhouettes embarked on their circular climb across the dusk-painted walls, rising and falling, round and around the room.

Bell felt the boy gasp at the scene—out of fear or awe he didn't know, but he wished he'd shoved the flashlight from his duffel bag into his jeans pocket before bringing him in. It was a minor miracle for the place to have power at all, but he would need to be careful about which lights he turned on. The farmhouse was an electrician's nightmare, each room on its own circuit to keep fuses from blowing when the animatronics were running all day. Most rooms had triggers on door hinges or motion sensors to choreograph the action and pace the progress of visitors through the exhibits. He didn't need Lucas freaking out at the sights of the mummified aliens in the Egyptian room or the African cannibal masks in the Congo room.

The Hindu charnel ground was innocuous enough without Pete Gruen, who used to spend his days crouching in there wearing only a loincloth and a coating of ashes, gnawing on bones like a Saddhu on the banks of the river Ganges. The horrible climax of the tour, the Mayan sacrificial chamber, was at the far end of the building where the tour reached the Americas. The room they were headed for, the room Bell knew best, came before that.

Moving deeper into the interior, Bell flipped on the plain white house lights selectively, which meant stumbling through several rooms in total darkness, clamoring through sets revealed only partially by touch: fur, silicone, and the sticky residue of theatrical blood.

When they reached the Japan room, Bell left the lights off and set Lucas down on a straw mat in the center of the floor.

Before the frightened child could get his bearings, Bell ran back through the Palace and out into the dazzling sunlight. He parked the car behind the barn, then took the duffel bag with the food and bottled water in one hand and the silk-wrapped sword in the other. Left hand. Right hand. Divergent paths, and he had yet to choose.

Back in the Japan room he turned on the lights and saw that Lucas had rolled across the dusty floor and kicked through one of the paper screens. At least he hadn't hurt himself by tangling with the kimono clad automaton—the half-wax, half-machine mannequin that knelt in the center of the room waiting for spectators to trigger the floor tile that would initiate the *seppuku* sequence: mechanical arms plunging the dagger into the abdomen until the moment when Bell would step forward and cut the head off, severing a dowel and clearing the way for a blood tube to spray red sucrose across the floor.

When the lights came on, Lucas craned his head around, his eyes darting, trying to take in the whole scene at once. "What is it?" The boy's voice was hoarse.

"It's an amusement park. It's supposed to be scary. For older kids."

"Why?"

"Why what?"

"Why do they want to be scared?"

"For a thrill, I guess."

"What's that?"

"A thrill?"

"No, *that*. The guy."

"Oh. I call him Bob. He's fake. Part of the scene."

"What are those?"

Bell followed the direction of Lucas's gaze to the trio of giant *taiko* drums suspended from the ceiling. "Those are drums. There's a machine that hits them with big sticks to make a beat. They're loud."

"Oh. Don't turn them on."

"I won't."

"I don't like it here. I want to go home."

"Just rest, okay? Here, have some water."

Lucas shook his head. "Are you a bad guy?"

Bell considered the question…. "I don't know."

"My Daddy says bad guys usually think they're the good guys."

"Huh."

The boy's smooth forehead furrowed. "Where's my Daddy? I want him."

Bell went to a low table against the wall where he kept a few personal items that blended in with the scene while lending it veracity: a brush calligraphy set and a few loose sheets of rice paper. He had sometimes practiced his *kanji* when business was slow. Now he picked up the inkbottle and unscrewed the cap—

stubborn at first, it had been closed for so long. The brush was in poor shape, but he smoothed out the strands, licked his fingers, and gave it a little twist.

"Did you kill my mother?" Lucas said, sounding too much like an adult.

Bell dipped the brush in the ink and stared at the clean square of paper. No reason to wear gloves now, he thought. This would all be coming to an end soon. If there were prints, so be it, they could be part of the message. He held the paper straight with the thumb and forefinger of his left hand, and stroked a line. He thought about the trigger under the floor tile, about how the execution scene played over and over, hour after hour, day after day, with only a pause for cleanup and resetting. He thought of how he too, even with all of his art, was still an automaton like the one on the mat. Someone stepped on a spring and the sequence was set in motion. He merely watched, waited for his cue, and cut.

"What are you doing?" Lucas said.

Bell didn't answer the question until the last stroke was drawn. He blew on the ink to speed the drying, then took another sheet of rice paper and squared it under his left hand. Before drawing the same character again, he looked at the boy and said, "I'm writing to your father...and to mine. You should pray that yours finds us first."

Chapter 20

Drelick and Pasco gave Desmond a ride home. They parked behind his car in the driveway and followed him into the house they had visited uninvited just hours earlier. Desmond put a pot of coffee on, told them to have a seat, then went upstairs to brush his teeth and put on a clean shirt. Pasco followed far enough to listen to the man's movements, but Drelick waved him back to the kitchen table. They both looked at the ceiling and listened to the progress of his footsteps and the pause at the top of the stairs where they imagined him looking in the mirror that the landlord had just remounted over the patched hole in the wall. When Carmichael had been on the second floor for longer than it should have taken, Pasco started to get antsy. He drummed his fingers on the table and said, "Think I'll check on him."

Drelick shook her head. "He'll be back."

"You clear him already? You think there's no chance he killed either of them?"

"It would be a hell of a coincidence," she said. "I know he didn't abduct his own son because he was in custody when it happened. And I know he didn't kill anyone in Ohio last night."

"Maybe he has a partner, someone who grabbed the kid for him. Maybe he did read about the Lamprey case and decided to use it as a cover, an opportune time to kill his father-in-law. Just because he's not part of a larger pattern of sword murders doesn't mean he didn't do a couple of his own. You know that, right?"

"Yes. Look, it doesn't help that the police botched this as badly as they did, but from what I gather since we've been here, there's more evidence pointing away from Carmichael than toward him. Let's hear him out."

Desmond's footsteps creaked heavily on the stairs. The two agents stopped talking as he entered the kitchen and placed a manila envelope amid some toast crumbs and spilled salt on the table. The envelope was soon joined by mismatched mugs from the cupboard and a carton of milk from the fridge. Desmond poured the coffee, waved at the milk, and said, "I'm afraid I'm out of sugar."

Pasco raised his mug toward Desmond. "Why ruin perfectly good coffee with milk and sugar?"

Drelick reached into the manila envelope and removed a creased white paper square with bold black calligraphy on it. She looked at Desmond. He looked haggard, his eyes rimmed pink in a way that suggested something more than water splashed on his face while he was upstairs.

"Lucas found that paper in a friend's tree house the other day. It was folded into an origami butterfly."

"Have you had it translated?" Drelick asked.

"It says *Fly.* I think it was a warning, someone telling me to get Lucas away from here. But then Phil took him…and was killed the following day."

"Do you think this was written by Phil Parsons' killer?" Drelick again.

"Who else?"

Pasco leaned forward. "Why would someone intent on killing members of your family, someone planning to abduct Lucas, warn you to flee with him?"

"I don't know. They're going out of their way to give me messages, but the messages are enigmatic, even contradictory. Did Fournier tell you about the haiku someone wrote on my laptop?"

Drelick felt Pasco looking at her and avoided meeting his eyes. She knew he thought Carmichael might have written the poem himself. "Yes, I saw it," she said. "The police thought you wrote it yourself, whether you knew it or not." She sensed Pasco shifting in his chair, unhappy with her candor.

"Do they think different now that Lucas has been taken?" Desmond's fingers were wrapped around each other like claws, each hand squeezing the other bloodless where they made contact.

"I don't know what they're thinking after you jumped on Fournier. It's a wonder we're not having this talk back in your cell."

"Well, Chuck didn't press charges because he knows he's guilty of practically kidnapping my son."

"That aside...they let you go, so it seems that their focus is more in line with ours now."

"And that is?"

"I'm looking for a cross-country serial killer."

Desmond looked down at the dirty tabletop and drew a ragged breath like a man buckled over from a punch.

Drelick said, "This can't be news to you after your wife and father-in-law were killed, after the messages you've received. You must have been thinking the same."

Desmond was nodding his head. "It's just kind of fucked up to hear the words *serial killer* from an FBI agent when your son is missing. Has this person you've been tracking ever killed a child?" His voice broke on the words. He looked up at her desperately, his arms wrapped tight around his abdomen. He looked cold, as if he were on the other side of a glass door where the temperature was not the same that she felt in the stale kitchen.

Drelick looked at Pasco, using her eyes to keep him from talking while she chose her words. Some details of the Ohio massacre were still being kept from the media, but not for long. If he dared turn on a TV, Desmond would know everything before she had even boarded her flight to Cincinnati in two hours. "There were two children killed in Ohio," she said. "Girls, older."

"Christ."

"But Lucas going missing doesn't necessarily mean he was taken by Phil's killer. It may have no connection to what happened in Ohio."

"How could it not?"

"There's no way that the killer in Ohio could have been in both places within that time span. You used the word *they* earlier. Do you have reason to believe there's more than one person stalking your family?"

Desmond sighed. "Maybe. When I visited Harwood in prison, I asked him about his memories of the night Sandy was killed. He didn't have much because he was a blind drunk at the time, but he said that two angels in black robes handed him the sword and told him he needed to confess what he'd done."

Pasco snorted. "Two angels? He give you anything more descriptive than that?"

"No. But you might have better luck. You could spend more time with him."

"Okay," Drelick said to Pasco, "That's two meetings for you while I'm in Ohio. First priority is Mrs. Fournier. Then follow up with Harwood. See if he has enough for a sketch."

"He might start making shit up if he thinks there's a chance of being acquitted," Pasco said.

Drelick shrugged.

Desmond said, "The police used a sketch artist with Lucas to get a picture of the man who almost abducted him at the playground. Have you seen it?"

Drelick felt a quick thrill of hope that things might start moving faster. "No. I'll have them scan it and send it to me en route. What can you tell me about it?"

"It turned out he didn't see the man's face, just a mask, a faceplate from a samurai suit of armor. I won't be surprised if Harwood describes something similar."

"I'll be asking him different kinds of questions than what you would have." Pasco said. "We might get height, shoes, voice type, et cetera. He probably remembers more than he knows."

Drelick read the sick look on Desmond's face, a face weathered with grief, now preparing itself to erode to deeper strata. A face aged beyond its years. She reached across the table and placed her hand over his forearm. "I don't want to give you false hope," she said, "but if Lucas *was* taken by the same people, if he didn't simply run away...then it doesn't fit their pattern to take a victim to a different location. That's a small thing, but it's good, I think."

"Because they usually kill their victims where they find them," Desmond murmured.

She nodded.

"What could it mean? What if they took Lucas somewhere just because it was too risky to do it at a cop's house in broad daylight?"

"It's harder to take a live person with you. Even a child."

"I think Lucas would struggle. I think he'd make noise. That's what I've taught him anyway, if he remembers. But scared, I don't know, maybe he would go along."

"I'm speculating here, mind you," Drelick said against her better judgment, but the man needed *something* for the despair. "If we have *two* killers working together, then this abduction while one of them is out of state…to me it suggests hesitation, possibly a lack of conviction."

"You think the one capable of killing children is the one in Ohio?"

"He's probably not in Ohio any more, but I still need to go out there and investigate. The police are setting up roadblocks on all of the main roads and some of the smaller ones. We're looking at flight records for the past few days. We will likely catch him before he can return to this area."

"How do you know he won't just go south, go in some random direction and leave the country?"

"I don't."

"Lucas is his unfinished business," Desmond said.

"Let's hope so, or we lose the fucker," Pasco said. Drelick flinched. She would be talking to him later about his bedside manner. To Desmond she said, "The victims in Ohio were a family named Tibbets. Does the name mean anything to you? Have you heard it before?"

Desmond's eyes flicked back and forth over the tabletop as he searched his memory. "No."

"Maybe Phil Parsons mentioned the name to you? Think."

"No. Sorry."

"Well, please give it more thought while we search for your son."

Desmond took his pen from his jeans pocket and wrote the name down on the manila envelope. Drelick nodded at the paper square with the calligraphy. "Can I take this with me? I'd like to have the paper and ink analyzed."

"Please."

She took an evidence bag from her briefcase, and dropped the paper into it. "Thank you, Mr. Carmichael. You have our numbers, and Agent Pasco will be nearby. I have a plane to catch."

"Don't," Desmond said, standing up. "Don't go to Ohio. You're the first person who believes that we're being stalked, and you won't find Lucas in Ohio. *Please*. I can't lose him. Not him too. I just...please. I don't know how much time we have." His voice thickened as he begged. He gripped the chair for support.

Drelick looked at Pasco. He looked as uncomfortable as she felt. "We're going to do everything we can to find your son, Mr. Carmichael," she said, and to her own ears the words sounded like the reheated assurances of a doctor who has seen too many terminal cases. She needed to get out of here and do what she was good at.

Chapter 21

Erin Drelick stared for a long time at the sketch of the samurai mask. The fact that a little boy, a boy now missing, had described this face made her shudder. It was a hot summer day, and sitting beside the wall-length airport window, dressed in her black slacks and shirtsleeves, she should have felt hot. But the thought of Lucas Carmichael looking at this mask right now in some basement or barn, the thought of the boy she had never met wetting his pants and waiting for the masked man to do to him whatever gray and indistinct abominable thing he imagined had been done to his mother chilled her in a way that seemed to glow cold and blue from her core, as if her vertebrae were a string of ice cubes.

Was she doing the right thing, flying to Ohio? Flying away from the zone in which Lucas was likely to be found, alive or dead, within the next forty-eight hours? She had seen the crime-scene photos on her tablet computer; those grim images were sleeping in the memory chip in her lap right now. What was there that she needed to see in person? The photos were bad—especially the ones of the blonde girls—but they didn't chill her the same way the mask did because in Ohio the deed was done. It was past. The threat foretold by the mask was worse because she could still do something about it if she caught the right scent.

But going to the crime scene was what you did. There could be some detail, some bit of information that might not emerge if she wasn't there reading the scene and the people, developing a rapport, and using her intuitive sense to ask the locals the right questions.

Possible intuitive connections. Was that enough to fly away from Lucas Carmichael for?

"He could be anywhere," she said aloud, looking now at a photo of the boy on her screen.

Anywhere...but probably not Ohio.

Why Ohio? Why this family, Tibbets? Why Massachusetts for that matter, and Parsons?

The hours in flight would feel like being in a holding cell. Unable to connect to the web, her hands would be tied. If she was going to dig in and try to connect the dots, she had better do it here at the airport terminal before they boarded her. She drummed her fingers, tapping her nails across the glass touch-screen. She had to prioritize. An intuitive search process could take too long.

The inflamed corner of her toe was broadcasting infuriating low-level pain again, pain that thrummed below her consciousness most of the time, straddling the threshold between actual hurt and a kind of itching sensation. She wanted it to either go away or really hurt, not just flirt with hurt. She opened a search engine, typed "Tibbets + Parsons," and ground the toe of her shoe into the dark blue carpet, reveling in the bright flare of actual pain, a sensation with conviction.

* * *

Chuck Fournier was trailing Agent Pasco through his own house, trying to interject himself into the conversation, but Pasco was only interested in talking to Ginny. Fournier had never seen his wife talk to an officer before. Well, not within the framework of an interrogation, anyway, and he was horrified by the spectacle. She wasn't guilty of anything, but she still managed to answer every question in a way that felt *way* too direct and incriminating to Chuck. She was a wreck, and all she had to offer was the bald, guilty, nauseating fact that she had let Lucas out into the backyard to play while she washed dishes, and when she looked up he was gone.

"Was the yard secure?" Pasco asked.

When Ginny looked confused by the question, Chuck said, "There's only the one gate, and the latch is too high for Lucas to reach."

"Detective, you were not at home. I'm asking *Mrs.* Fournier about something only she was in a position to observe."

"I just thought that seeing as it's my house and I'm the only one who uses that gate when I mow the lawn—"

"Don't worry, I'll have plenty of questions for you soon. I want to hear all about what made you think you could take the child home in the first place."

Fournier squeezed his chin and cheeks with the fingers of his right hand like he was trying to wring a rag soaked with enraged anxiety dry and, managing to keep his mouth shut, turned to face the fridge. He wondered if making a sandwich would constitute some kind of *faux pas*. He was, after all, in his own kitchen, and it wasn't entirely clear to him at the moment if he was here as a cop or as a suspect.

* * *

Erin Drelick found an immediate connection between the names Parsons and Tibbets, but not Lamprey. She knew she should turn off the tablet and put it back in her briefcase, knew she should get in the boarding line that was now moving, but she was staring at a black-and-white photo taken in August of 1945 on the island of Tinian.

A group of young men from the 509th Composite Group are standing in front of the riveted aluminum hull of an aircraft, a huge beast of a plane judging by the small section that can be seen in the photo. Behind them, one of the wheels and a segment of hydraulic landing gear are visible. They are dressed in what look like plain, beige Boy Scout uniforms devoid of any insignia. Only their hats vary in style. One looks like the visor cap of a Marine or an airman, another is some kind of wool skullcap, and the tall, serious man, second in from the left is wearing what she thinks of as a folded newspaper boat hat — the hat of a Navy man, and sure enough, the caption identifies the tall man who might be older than the flyboys surrounding him as Navy Captain William (Deak) Parsons.

In the center of the photo, a baby-faced young man, shorter than the others, with a thick head of black hair to match his black eyebrows, stands with hands clasped behind his back, looking like a man who would belong at the center of every photo that ever captured him. The afterimage of a smile plays across his face as if someone — probably him — has just cracked wise. Erin Drelick knows his type from the Academy. Different eras may come and go, different styles of clothing and music, different presidents and different wars, but if there is one thing that America produces with consistency, it is cocky young men. The caption identifies him as Col. Paul Tibbets.

Drelick felt a sensation of groundlessness, as if she were already on her flight, rising against a headwind. She had to work fast now, had to open as many browser windows as possible and load them with information she could read in flight when she would be unable to connect. She had found the photo of Tibbets and Parsons by searching for images only, knowing that it could save time to find two people with those names in the same photo for starters. Now she would need to copy the full names into Wikipedia, but first another image search for "Carmichael + Parsons."

There it was. A tingle passed through her stomach, a sensation that told her she had just connected enough dots to see the big picture when she widened her field of view. Here was a photo from a science fiction and fantasy magazine called *Teletrope*. She clicked on it and found that it was from an interview the magazine had done with Desmond Carmichael in 2006 at his home. The caption read, "Desmond Carmichael in his home office with wife Sandy Parsons, whose photography illustrates their forthcoming children's book, *The Forest Queen*."

Desmond was seated at his desk, his swivel chair angled toward a slim, pretty woman who sat at the end of a couch with her legs crossed and her hands folded in her lap. Two objects were mounted on the wall behind the couple: a large framed print of a mushroom encircled by what looked like an aura of wispy fairies, and a Japanese *katana*.

The frisson of pattern recognition flushed through Erin Drelick's synapses—an infusion of truth riding a wave of neuropeptides. It was a tenuous connection, she knew. It was anything but legally admissible evidence, but she recognized the familiar, if rare, sensation for what it was: the conjunction of disparate elements into a form that would be absolutely concrete when the waters of intuition receded—the solution to a puzzle.

The killer had seen this photograph. Maybe he had stumbled upon it by chance or maybe he had been searching like she had for the name *Parsons*, but when the killer saw the sword and recognized it as a Japanese infantry blade, a puzzle had been solved for him as well. Something had slotted into place like a detonation cap into a bomb.

She looked up. The line for boarding had run down to its end, and the uniformed lady behind the microphone was looking at her with a raised eyebrow that said, *Do I really need to turn this thing on just to tell you it's last call?* Drelick stood up to show that she was coming and took a tentative step toward the gate, toward the portable corridor through which she would soon walk with the noise of aircraft machinery rushing in through the gaps, toward the flight crew that would greet her at the end and look at her boarding pass.

Flight crew. She tapped a tab on the screen in her hand as she walked.

The plane that Tibbets and Parsons and the others were standing in front of was the *Enola Gay*, a B-29 Superfortress. And not just any B-29. This was the plane that had dropped the first atomic bomb over Hiroshima on August 6, 1945. Tibbets, the pilot, had named the plane after his mother. The bomb had a name too: Little Boy. Drelick imagined that bomb dropping out of the behemoth aircraft like a baby out of a mother's womb.

The birth of an apocalypse.

She clicked again. If there was a midwife for that birth it was Deak Parsons of the Manhattan Project, he who had spent a sleepless night on August 5th in the cramped munitions bay of the bomber, practicing the maneuver he would execute in flight the following day: loading the mammoth shell with powder charges and arming the mechanism that would drive the uranium slugs together with divine velocity like the sound of one hand clapping.

She could read the rest on the plane. She raised a finger to turn the tablet off, and froze. Looking at the corner of the screen to check the time and confirm that she wasn't getting her ass in gear quite as late as the woman at the desk was implying with that expression, she saw the date: August 6th.

* * *

Chuck Fournier decided that making a sandwich while watching his wife get interrogated by the FBI would be in poor taste. Instead, he grabbed a jar of peanuts from the cabinet, screwed the lid off, and tossed a handful into his mouth, dropping a few on the kitchen tiles. He bent over and plucked the runaways from under the bottom cabinets; he didn't want Pasco to think he was a slob or something. His knees popped on the way back up, and he had an embarrassing moment when he thought he might not be able to get fully upright again.

Pasco was looking at him with a funny expression on his face. What did you call that, *bemused?* More like fascination. What was with this guy? Pasco slowly swiveled his attention back to Ginny. Chuck tossed the dropped nuts into the trash under the sink and brushed his hands together over the steel basin to knock the crumbs off. He wasn't really tuned in to the line of questioning. He was thinking that the nuts he'd just tossed weren't really dirty; Ginny kept the place spotless. He wondered if Pasco was a two-second-rule kind of guy. Would the fact that Chuck had tossed the nuts in the trash instead of tossing them back make Pasco think the floor *was* dirty? Who would know the cleanliness of the floor better than the man who lived here? Chuck was deciding to get a fucking grip and forget about the nuts, it wasn't like Pasco was from Child Services or something. *Get a fucking grip, Chuck, and start acting like a man because this is your turf, your territory. And not just the house but the whole goddamn town.*

Running his foul mental-mouth off was already helping him feel more like himself. He'd tried to clean the language up a bit while Lucas was in the house, but it put a strain on the brain. Maybe censoring himself was what had knocked him out of his groove so that somewhere along the line he'd let this Mexican desk jockey, this *cocksucker*—there you go, feelin' better already—get the upper hand.

Having a little something for the ol' blood sugar was also helping. Maybe he could focus now and stop feeling like everything was sliding into the shitter off a table with a broken leg. One mistake was all it took sometimes. One good mistake, and like a broken table leg or a blown-out tire, the three good ones didn't matter anymore.

Pasco was yammering about the "child's disposition." Ginny was making noncommittal vocalizations that weren't even words, but maybe that was good. Maybe she was thinking right after all. If he had a nickel for every time he'd told her about a dumbass who could have got away with something if the dumbass had enough sense to keep his trap shut, he could buy a decent cigar. So maybe she knew that. Hell, she watched enough TV she ought to know it by heart.

"Did Lucas seem anxious about being here? Was he withdrawn? Did he have an appetite? You were watching him, weren't you?"

"I...I don't know, that was like five different questions. He um, he seemed okay."

"Do you think he might have run away? Was he afraid of you and your husband?"

"That was two again."

Hot damn, she was doing all right.

Pasco's phone rang. Saved by the bell.

"Pasco," he said and listened. Fournier watched him take a ballpoint and a flip pad from his breast pocket. "Yup. Go." Pasco jotted two names in an impeccable, feminine cursive that filled Fournier with contempt: *Paul Tibbets* and *William Parsons*. The last names Fournier already knew, but the first names were unfamiliar.

"Both are dead?" Pasco asked.

So these are new vics? Fournier wondered.

"What am I looking for in the obits?"

Fournier strained to hear the faint metallic chatter emanating from Pasco's phone. The guy's hair was too shaggy to let it through.

"Okay, that it...? What else...? Could be a lot of convenience stores and gas stations. It could take a while. You don't sound like we have that kind of time."

Pasco listened with a frown. "What anniversary?"

An unnerving silence passed in the kitchen while Chuck Fournier longed for a louder phone, better ears, a sandwich.

"Alright, I'm on it." Pasco pressed END. His next question for Ginny was, "Can I borrow your yellow pages?"

"Of course," Ginny said, opening the drawer below their wall-mounted landline. She produced the floppy, seldom-used volume—so much thinner than the one Chuck had grown up with in this same town—and placed it in his hands.

"What are we looking for?" Fournier ventured, glancing over the agent's shoulder at the Cs, and wondering when Pasco would make it explicit that he was being cut out of the loop.

"Convenience stores," Pasco said, flipping his spiral notepad closed and tucking it back in his pocket. In Fournier's experience, if you were hunting through a phone book, you usually kept your pad out, and he figured Pasco had stowed it just to keep it from prying eyes.

"Why convenience stores?"

"And tobacco shops. You want to stay involved in this case?"

"Which case?" Fournier asked with trepidation.

"Let's say the kidnapping case. Wanna stay on the investigating side for a little while longer, maybe redeem your ass?"

"Hell, yeah."

"Good, because I have other research to do and I'm short a partner. I want you to call every shop in town that sells smokes and ask if they sell clove cigarettes. Make a list of the ones that do and tell them you're looking for a suspect who smokes them, a Japanese man. Ask if they know who you're talking about. Let me know if you get a hit."

"So we have a suspect?"

"Not really. It's a long shot. Something Carmichael asked Agent Drelick to look into. But you can let the shop clerks think you have more to go on so it doesn't come off as ethnic profiling."

Fournier smiled. Maybe, just maybe, he could get to like this Pasco, if the wind started to change direction. "What does this have to do with those names you wrote down?"

Pasco looked out the window at the back yard. "It's just a theory."

Fournier nodded and tried to suck a piece of peanut skin from under his gum line. It wouldn't come.

"You sure Lucas couldn't reach that latch?" Pasco asked, turning to look him in the eye.

Fournier sighed. "Pretty sure. You think he ran away?"

"No. But I hope he did." Pasco headed for the door. "I want to hear from you soon, Chuck," he said, swinging it shut behind him.

Fournier seized the marker from the magnetic dry erase board on the fridge. Below where Ginny had written LIGHT BULBS, and EXT 237, he scrawled: PAUL T. / WILLIAM P. He would Google them later, find out what Pasco had his nose in.

Then he looked at Ginny, and solemnly shook his head. "Babe. How the hell did you lose him?"

She was shaking her head too, and he saw that tears were spilling out of her eyes. "I don't know. I was right here at the window, I swear, Chuck, I didn't look away for more than a minute. He just...he was gone...so fast. *So fast.*" He knew he should embrace her. He knew, but he chose not to. Let that be enough. He wasn't going to rip her a new one. He didn't have time for that, and what would be the point? *He* had put this on her. She hadn't asked for it, not exactly. He'd wanted to make her happy. She had always wanted kids, but he'd never been able to give her any. Her shoulders collapsed inward like the support beams of a burning house, and she lifted her folded hands as if in the gesture of prayer, covered her nose and mouth with them, and breathed into her folded palms, looking at him as if over a mask.

He closed the phone book and tapped his pocket to make sure his car keys were still there. He didn't need a damn book to figure out where to start asking questions in this town. Sherry down at Tradewinds would have clove cigs, and she'd be able to tell him every other shop in town that carried them. Sherry wouldn't be shy about gossiping on customers, either. Tradewinds was right across the street from the station, and Chuck stopped in most mornings to grab a ham-and-egg sandwich before hitting his desk. He decided to leave the 'vette at the house and take Ginny's car. Pasco might head to the station, and Fournier wouldn't mind if that guy didn't know his exact whereabouts just yet.

"Chuck?" Ginny said, looking a lot older than she had yesterday, when having a boy in the house, even a boy who looked like he wanted to pee in a corner like a frightened puppy, had flushed her with vigor. In time she would have coaxed Lucas out of his shell, would have nurtured him and made him smile. He knew she would have been good for him, and he for her. Now she was a frail bird of a woman, clutching her teacup in both hands like she needed to draw every unit of warmth it could offer, even in the middle of a hot summer day. "What that agent said about a suspect, someone who smokes the cigarettes you're supposed to be looking for..." —she shot a glance at the names on the whiteboard—"does that mean that Desmond isn't crazy, that he didn't kill Phil?"

He almost said something noncommittal about not having all of the facts yet, the kind of bullshit he could reel off without thinking when someone from WBZ put a microphone in his face. Instead, he found that it felt better to just tell her. "Yeah. Probably. Des tried to tell me about the cigarette thing before, and I thought it was a red herring. I fucked up, babe." He sucked on his teeth, and the peanut skin came free. "But I'm gonna fix it."

She absorbed this, staring into her teacup as if it were an oracle.

* * *

Sherry sold cloves but didn't know of any Asians who bought them. She sent him to two other vendors she thought might have them: a cigar shop in nearby Sayville and a gas station/convenience store at the western edge of Port Mavis. He knew the second place—it used to be an auto-repair shop run by one of his old high-school football buddies. The minimart had been added when Mike sold it to a Pakistani guy and moved to Connecticut. It was off the beaten path, out by the firehouse and the big playground with the wooden castles.

He aimed the car west and readied himself for the unhappy prospect of squeezing a Pakistani shopkeeper for information about his customers based on ethnicity. As it turned out, that wasn't a problem.

"I special order them for him," Mr. Sharif said. "His name is Hashimoto, he live in the neighborhood. This old man is criminal suspect?"

"I'm afraid so. You know where he lives?"

Now Sharif looked slightly uncomfortable, but it had still been a big win, and in the first five minutes. "I couldn't tell you his address, but it must be nearby because he walks. No car."

"What direction does he come from when he walks?"

Sharif waved his hand at the road. "That way."

"Alrighty, thank you, Mr. Sharif. You've been very helpful."

Fournier took a couple of steps toward the door, then turned back to face the counter. "That's a nice American flag you have out front. Big one. You buy that before or after 9/11?"

Sharif suddenly appeared to take a keen interest in examining the scratches in his glass countertop. "What does that have to do with your case?" Sharif said in a quiet but steady voice.

"I only ask because I saw some small business owners like yourself having to deal with unfortunate acts of vandalism after 9/11. Just because some ignorant townies questioned your loyalty. So I can see why a man in your shoes might buy a big flag. Biggest one you could find, right? Profiting off the high price of a barrel of oil...you want people to know which team you're on. Am I right?"

Sharif nodded.

Fournier approached Sharif again and, in a conspiratorial tone, said, "Now this Hashimoto, he's a person of interest in what may turn out to be a terrorism case."

Sharif looked up from the counter. "Does this have anything to do with the murder of the policeman whose daughter was killed last year?"

"I'm not at liberty to say."

"Because the papers are talking about a serial killer."

"Let's stay focused here, Mr. Sharif. I need you to think carefully before you answer my question. Did Mr. Hashimoto ever pay you with a credit card? Maybe sometimes he bought more than cigarettes, maybe he gassed up his car one day. Think about it."

Sharif looked Fournier in the eye and said, "No. Cash only."

Fournier tapped his meaty palm two times on the counter and said, "Thank you for your time."

He left Ginny's car in the gas-station lot and headed down the sidewalk on foot. He knew he could use a walk, both for the exercise and to get his brain working on a different wavelength. On foot he'd be more apt to notice details in the neighborhood. Since he didn't know exactly what he was looking for—other than an old Japanese man or an unlikely mailbox with the name on it—he wanted to just take it all in, see what caught his eye. If Hashimoto really was an old man, he probably wasn't walking more than a mile. But if this cigarette thing was leading him to an old-timer, Japanese or not, what were the chances he had successfully murdered all of those people with a sword? A gun, maybe, but swinging steel and butchering people without getting caught? That was a young man's work.

The day was hot and humid, with gathering curtains of black clouds threatening in the north. Maybe evening thundershowers would break the stifling heat. His shirt was already wet with perspiration by the time he reached the first stop sign…and the first decision: keep going straight on the main route or branch off into the residential streets? He was regretting not taking the car and considered going back for it. In the car he would have air conditioning and shelter if the sky decided to open up. In the car he could also have a bag of Fritos and a Coke.

Too many distractions and too much speed. Yes, he could cover more streets in less time, but he might miss something. And the car felt like more comfort than he deserved. If Lucas was being held bound and gagged by the madman who had killed Sandy, then he owed it to her to make his best effort. Back in high school before Desmond had sealed the deal, Sandy had wounded Chuck with the f-word: *friend*. He'd never wanted to be her friend, but if ever there was a day when she needed him to be one...today was that day.

"Don't kid yourself, Chuck," he said aloud. Redemption might be the main dish on the menu here, but if he was going to be honest with himself, there was also a side of glory. If he found the killer before the FBI did, if he single-handedly rescued Lucas, then it wouldn't matter what missteps he'd made before, he'd come out of this a hero.

Mulling over the potential effects of success—in the department, in the papers, hell fuck the local papers, **COP SAVES BOY FROM KATANA KILLER** was one for the cable news tickers, interview at eleven—he looked up from the pavement...and providence smiled on him. There, in front of a little pale yellow cape cod, tucked between two rows of neatly trimmed shrubs, was one of those raked white gravel gardens with a squat, black Asian lantern stained green with oxidation from the rain.

Chapter 22

Shaun Bell set the paper crane in the center of the kitchen table like a folded linen napkin, then abruptly knocked it over when an assertive triple knock thundered from the front door. There was a doorbell, but whoever was on the step had decided that a chime wouldn't convey the urgency of their needs. He looked at the clock in the den. Sensei would be home in less than an hour, would find the crane in less than an hour, and would come for Lucas soon after. There was no time for diversion.

He crept to the door as quietly as he could, sliding his feet on the wood floor in the way that he had been trained to do for stealth and stability. He crouched low when he reached the bay window, and peered out through the slit in the white curtain without touching it.

The street was easy to see from this vantage point. There were no cars parked in front of the house. No police cruisers, no vans marked or unmarked. The body at the door was a man in a polo shirt and khakis, heavyset with big arms. It was impossible to see his face. Bell considered moving to the window in the master bedroom to get a wider view, but moving would burn time he didn't have.

He had already given Desmond a head start by setting the first bird to fly in the back pocket of a teen on a bike. For a twenty dollar bill the kid had promised to deliver the crane to Desmond's beach house mailbox, and had ridden like the wind, at least for as long as Bell could see him. Carmichael was a free man now. He might be at home or he might not. He might decipher the message quickly, or not. That was as it should be. Bell felt he owed the boy a chance, but only a chance. He wanted to see if Desmond Carmichael would do what his own father had never done: act with the urgency of love, be in the right place at the right time. The man lived in a fog of selfish fantasy. Bell had hoped that the steel breeze blowing through his life would wake him. So far it hadn't, but people could change.

Sensei was a more reliable force. He would arrive with the gravity of a guillotine blade. Sensei carried no cell phone because the police could track the GPS chips, so his every move had been planned in advance, from here to Ohio and back. Flying back to Massachusetts wasn't an option after yesterday's massacre, and the drive was fourteen hours without roadblocks. Very soon he would be back. He would expect to find Lucas Carmichael, the last name on the scroll, waiting in the basement for him.

Things would be a little different, however. Instead of the boy, he would find a message—mysterious to the police but quite clear to him—telling him where to find his prey. If the cops were onto their scent, the change of scene for the execution would make sense. If this was a cop at the door, then it could be an auspicious turn of events, a broom across the tracks of the betrayal Bell was flirting with.

The man on the front stoop shielded his eyes with his hand and tried to peer into the house through the curtains. It was Fournier, the detective from whose house Bell had seized Lucas. How could the cop have found him so fast? He had been practically invisible during the abduction, had spent less than a minute on the property, and had used stolen plates on the car. Fournier must have found the house by other means. Was the cop alone? Did others know where he was? Bell felt the urge to run out the back door and disappear, race back to the corn maze and kill the boy before the cruisers and SWAT vans swarmed the place, before Sensei even found the note. But he knew that flight would guarantee pursuit. Better to confront the threat here, to sever this loose thread and pray to Fudo Myoto that it wasn't tied to a larger net.

The face withdrew from the window and the knock came again, followed by the door chime. Shaun Bell looked down at his clothes. His black jeans were dusty from the Palace of Pain, but there was no theatrical blood from the exhibits on his knees or shoes.

He inhaled, opened the door, and presented a puzzled expression with raised brow.

Fournier held up a leather wallet, flipped it open and displayed a badge. "Detective Charles Fournier," he said, looking first at Bell's hands and hip pockets, then past him at the room beyond. "I'm looking for Mr. Hashimoto. Is he here?"

"He's out of town visiting relatives. Should be home tomorrow. Is there anything I can help you with?"

"Who are you?"

"I'm house sitting and looking after his cat. I'm actually on my way out."

"I didn't ask what you're doing. I asked who you are. Name."

"Shaun Bell."

"You mind if I come in for a minute, Shaun? I'd like to ask you a few questions about Mr. Hashimoto. He may be in trouble, and it's important that I reach him."

"Okay," Bell said, taking a step backward, and attenuating his posture and body language in countless small ways to create the illusion of a scrawny, graceless teen with no training whatsoever in martial arts. He almost tripped over a footstool as he made way for Fournier, who seemed satisfied with his own intimidating presence as he stepped into the room and gestured for Bell to sit on the couch while he picked up a wooden rocking chair, spun it around to face both the couch and the door, and sat down with his back to a wall.

"Just a sec," Bell said. "Let me just close the cellar door, so the cat doesn't get out. I was scooping the box when I heard you knocking."

"I thought you said you were leaving."

"Almost. I'll be right back."

"He keeps his cat locked in the basement?"

"Only when he's away. She acts out, scratches the furniture. Let me just make sure she didn't follow me up, shut that door," Bell said, already walking toward the back of the house without waiting for permission. As he passed through the dining room, he brushed his hand across the table and swept the origami crane up. He could hear Fournier following, the big man's heavy footsteps creaking on the wood floor, then squeaking on the linoleum, but by then Bell had reached the cellar stairs and descended the first few steps into darkness.

Fournier stood in the doorframe, a silhouette, drawing his weapon. "Hey! Get back here!" he yelled. "Back the fuck up the stairs with your hands on your head."

Bell stood in the shadows just below the last stair that the light from the kitchen windows could reach. Silent and motionless except for his left hand, now taking a *katana* from the stairwell wall where it hung beside a calligraphy scroll—a sword that could pass for decor if the house was ever searched or could serve the purpose at hand.

Fournier took cover around the corner of the doorframe, pointed his sidearm low in both hands, and shouted, "Now! I want to hear you stomping up these stairs right now, or I will start shooting into the dark."

The light switch was inside the stairwell, close enough to the top that Bell knew Fournier could see it. Was the detective brave enough to reach for it? Bell hoped so, because the other cop move to make right now was to call in help. It was the smarter move and the one that he might not be fast enough to prevent against a man with a gun on higher ground.

Bell centered himself with three cleansing breaths. He slid the scabbard through his belt and unlocked the sword with his thumb. If Fournier shot into the darkness...was the man really that impulsive?

Bell resisted the urge to scurry down the stairs or to flatten his body against the wall. Impulsive moves driven by fear, they would commit him to a path based on actions his opponent had not yet taken. Far better to remain alert yet empty, ready to allow his body to move spontaneously in the living moment.

He heard Sensei's voice: *You must accept your death, embrace it, get it out of your way, and then make every cut with such conviction that it is your final move, your only move. The true warrior ends the conflict before he has even drawn the sword because he has killed his fear. Everything that follows is merely writing a poem you have already composed in your mind. The verse arises in the moment, and the blade, like a brush, merely paints the strokes in your opponent's blood. Every cut is the killing cut.*

Fournier was looking around for something he could flip the light switch with—a broom handle or any kind of pole that would keep his hand out of range of that terminus of shadow beyond which razored steel might lie in wait. For a man with a firearm, he looked nervous. Was he crazy enough, reckless enough, scared enough to discharge his weapon at someone who might be a mere cat-sitter?

The question was answered with barking fire. Three shots, deafening in the narrow stairwell. Before the first was fired, Bell saw the trajectory of the cop's arms rising and committing to a direction as if in slow motion, saw the wrists twisting inward as the hands tightened their grip on the gun's handle, and saw the predictable pattern emerging, left, center, right, the shots sweeping across the shadowy void. Somehow Bell had intuited the mind of his enemy, and without thinking, rolled his body into the first shot, moving toward the flash of orange light, toward the cloud of plaster dust felt like mist from a waterfall on his cheek. He ducked under the first shot, and was clear of the second and third when they followed fast in its wake.

Fournier stepped into the stairwell and fumbled for the light switch. Bell rose on his haunches and squeezed the silk braid of the sword hilt gently, his wrist limber, ready to draw and cut Fournier's hand clean off before the light could come on. But before Fournier could find the switch plate there was an explosion of splintering wood followed by the thunderclap of the front door rebounding off of the wall in the foyer. Fournier swung around and pointed his gun at the den.

"Jesus!" He said, and then knowing he had lost the advantage unless his shots had wounded or killed (and there had been no cry, although Bell now thought maybe he should have faked a yelp of pain to lure Fournier forward), he threw his bulk around the outside of the doorframe again, pointing his gun at the floor.

Bell doubted that the new body on the scene really was Jesus. Had to be another cop alerted by the shots. Sensei certainly wouldn't enter his own house by kicking the door in. If Sensei had come home to the sound of shots fired, Fournier would already be in pieces on the kitchen floor.

"Suspect fled to the basement," Fournier said.

"Just one?" A low, calm voice that did little to put Bell at ease.

"Yeah."

"Armed?"

"I don't know. Have you been *following* me?"

"Thought you might pull a dumb stunt like this. You don't know if he's armed, but you shot at him?"

"He fled questioning."

"Did he threaten you?"

Fournier shook his head.

"You're gonna take me down with you," the other cop said in wonder. "The only cause I have for busting in here is your shots. You trying to kill a man for his brand of cigarettes or did you find something?"

"We can discuss it later, Pasco. Are you gonna help me catch this shifty fucker or not?"

Pasco said, "I circled the house and there's no basement door, just small windows. Is he thin enough?"

"Might be."

Pasco reached for his belt, but what he drew wasn't a gun or a radio. It was a flashlight.

Bell danced down the stairs, light-footed and silent, careful not to knock the scabbard against the wall. At the bottom he slipped out of range of the searching beam but lingered near enough to hear their voices.

"You see that statue in the front room?" Fournier asked. Pasco must have indicated "no" because Fournier said, "Some kind of Buddhist demon with a flaming sword and a chain. This be the place, Mac. This is our guy."

"Call in backup." Pasco said, then in a loud, clear voice, "Sir, we just want to talk with you. I'm going to turn on the light, and I want you to come forward with your hands up."

When the light came on, Bell was already in the far corner of the basement. He pivoted on his heel to face the wall, and then lowered himself into *seiza* position on one of the *tatami* mats, kneeling with his buttocks on his heels. He heard only one set of footsteps, first on the stairs behind him, and then on the concrete floor. The other cop would be hanging back until the first one got a read on the room.

"Put your hands on your head," Fournier said, sounding more confident now that he had a partner and a clear shot on a well-lit target. If, that was, he decided to shoot a kneeling man in the back. "Forget the windows, I've got him covered!" Fournier shouted at the stairs, and Bell could tell from the way the voice bounced around the room that Fournier had turned his head about 45 degrees to the right to call for Pasco. "Hands on your head, motherfucker!" Fournier yelled, now facing forward again.

Bell remained as still as a statue but for the deep focusing breaths. His shoulders did not move with those cycles, only his stomach, his center of gravity where he gathered the *Qi*. His hands rested on the insides of his thighs, and he gave not the slightest sign that he had heard the command. Not a word, not a move, not a tick of the head. But he listened so very closely to the texture of Fournier's footsteps as they moved across the concrete and the grass mats. The room became an acoustic chessboard as he stared at the blank wall tracking Fournier's unseen progress across the grid of mats. If he did nothing he would soon feel the cold muzzle of the gun between his shoulder blades. He imagined how hard it must be for a man as impulsive as Fournier to resist shooting someone who had a sword strapped on after all those victims of the blade. But Bell was presenting an indefensible opportunity for a kill shot. Forensics would show that he had been shot from behind while kneeling. It was impossible to make a threatening gesture in such a position. And yet, Shaun Bell knew that in his Zen silence, immovable as a rock, he was broadcasting an air of menace as thick as a curtain of incense.

There was only one more thing he needed to hear, and there it was, the sound of Pasco jogging down the stairs and coming up behind Fournier. These lighter footsteps veered off to the left behind him. Pasco sounded a little winded when he said, "I know your motive, but what you don't know is you've been killing the wrong people. I have proof." Bell let these syllables wash over him like birdsong, or the barking of a dog. The sounds arose, vibrated the air molecules in the room, and vanished into emptiness. There was nothing in them that could lure him off balance, no wind in them that could stir the deep waters of his mindfulness.

There were *katas* for every configuration of opponents, forms that began from sitting, from kneeling, from standing, with opponents front and back, or at angles, but all of the traditional forms were designed for use against opponents who were themselves swordsmen, who would need to come in close to strike. Now Bell was drawing two gunmen in close, and he expected that within less than a minute he would be dead. There was a temptation to surrender to this knowledge. If he died here now, he would not have to kill the boy.

But expecting death and reconciling himself to death did not mean that he was willing to *give* them his death. They would pay dearly for it because he was a Spirit Warrior, and a samurai.

Bell felt the latest inhalation reach the root of his central channel, then, rising on the winged heels of its release, he spun around—a motion he had practiced thousands of times in the days since he'd been a gangly teen in California: the opening of the *kata Ushiro*. In one fluid motion the orientation of his body changed, pivoting on the anchor point of his right knee, his left coming up at a right angle to the floor as he stomped his foot forward, his blade flashing through a high horizontal arc that sliced Fournier's eyeball open like a grape, then bisected the bridge of his nose where a ribbon of blood streamed out in its wake. Accelerating again once freed from the minor resistance of cartilage, the blade swung out to the uttermost limit of Bell's reach where it nicked Pasco's wrist as he recoiled in a reflexive shielding gesture. It was a fatal mistake for the second cop, who should have stepped back and fired, but he'd been thrown off by the sudden need to dodge steel where less than a second ago there had been only a kneeling man facing a wall.

Fournier dropped his gun and staggered backward, half blind and howling, pressing his hands against the gushing laceration on his face. Bell came up into a standing pose, swinging the sword around in a whirling motion that in the *kata* would have been a blood throw, but now became a kind of rechambering, bringing the blade overhead for a downward killing stroke.

Pasco regained his balance and dropped into a stable shooting stance. Bell spun on the ball of his anchored left foot and launched a side kick into Pasco's gut, causing him to buckle forward. The gun went off, punching a hole clean through Bell's still airborne calf, the bullet ricocheting off of the concrete floor with a spark.

The wound was painless at first, but Bell soon felt a scorching sensation spreading through his leg as he brought the blade down. The kick that had caused Pasco to buckle at the waist had also presented the back of his neck like a gift. Bell brought his foot and blade down in synch, and sliced through it.

Pasco's head hit the floor before the rest of him. Twin jets of blood sprayed from the severed neck as the body collapsed.

Fournier was screaming. He had witnessed the decapitation with his good eye and was now scrambling across the floor, trying to retrieve his gun with the hand that wasn't holding his sliced eyeball. Blood burbled over his trembling lip, spattering out ahead of him onto the floor, propelled by his ragged shrieks. The crawling man was an even easier target, and Bell took the second head off with a leisurely sweep, sending it tumbling across the slick crimson floor, the hair and mustache picking up thick arterial blood.

The samurai surveyed the carnage and listened for the sound of sirens. The street was quiet for now, but he knew he would soon hear them. Casting his gaze over the blood trail, he made eye contact with Pasco's lifeless head where it had rolled up against the wall and now stared into eternity. What had the man said about killing the wrong people? Weren't *all* victims the wrong people from a cop's point of view? There was no time to linger here. If one of them had called for backup, or if other police knew that they had been heading to this address, the place would be swarming soon.

He had to leave the house, had to get back to his car, back to the boy.

The paper crane.

He couldn't just leave it here now for Sensei to find. The *kanji* would mean nothing to the police at first, but it wouldn't take long for that to change. It was a coin toss now, who would arrive at this house first: Sensei or more police.

Bell limped to the workbench and popped the latch on the little metal first-aid kit. He splashed some Betadine on the bullet hole in his calf and then pressed a square of gauze against it. Blood poured down his leg, but it didn't look like Pasco had hit an artery or shattered the bone, and fortunately the slug had gone straight through. He doused a second gauze pad with the disinfectant, pressed it to the exit wound, where it adhered to his bloody skin. Forgoing medical tape, he rummaged through a cardboard box of rags for a flannel shirtsleeve to bind the dressing. The wound didn't hurt as much as he thought it should until he tied the rag tight.

He walked to Fournier's body, rolled it over, checked the pockets, and found a cell phone in the fat man's khakis. A quick scroll through the Recent Calls list showed nothing within the past hour. Little reassurance, when the shots might have been heard by a neighbor. Bell popped the battery out of the phone, aware that he was leaving fingerprints but too hurried to care. His prints were all over this house, and the game would soon be over. Moving to Pasco, he found a notepad, another phone, and a folded sheet of printer paper in the inside breast pocket of the man's sport coat, along with an FBI card in a slim wallet. In this phone's memory, Bell found a more recent call to someone named Drelick. Recent enough to have been made after Fournier fired the shots in the stairwell? He didn't know. This was a more expensive phone and the battery wasn't accessible, so he walked it over to the tidy little workbench in the corner where two blows from a ball-peen hammer rendered it untrackable.

He left the sword where it lay on the mat, stuffed the folded paper from Pasco's coat into his back pocket with the origami crane—the thing that had brought him here in the first place and that he could no longer risk leaving behind—and climbed the stairs.

There was no sign of police on the street, and Bell didn't think it would be subtle when they arrived; they would come in howling and blazing.

I have proof, Pasco had said.

Bell couldn't wait. He needed to know. He tugged the paper square from his pocket and unfolded it. It was a printout of an obituary from a newspaper archive dated December 6, 1953. Rear Admiral William Sterling "Deak" Parsons. Bell skimmed over what he already knew: Parsons' tenure in the Manhattan Project and his role in the flight of the *Enola Gay* over Hiroshima on August 6, 1942. His eye shot down to the last line of the article, which had been underlined in wavering blue ink: "He is survived by his father, brother, half-brother and sister, his wife Martha, and daughters Peggy and Clare."

Daughters. Only daughters. No son, no direct descendant to carry on the family name, no connection to Phil Parsons, or Sandy or Lucas. The daughters, and any children they may have borne, were the last branches of the Admiral's family tree.

He and Sensei had been pruning some *other* Parsons tree.

Sensei had boasted about the years of research he had done, but for all Bell knew he had selected his targets by flipping through the nearest phone book.

And how carefully were the victims at Hiroshima chosen? The women and children who were grateful to drink the radioactive black rain to quench the thirst in their roasted bodies. Hiroshima had been chosen over another city at the last minute because the weather there was clearer. Better for the cameras. But the United States *had* warned the local population, had urged them to evacuate one of the last cities that hadn't already been immolated in jellified gasoline by a relentless flock of B-29s. Yes, he had studied the history, but maybe he hadn't read enough, and now he was out of time.

I killed the wrong man. Phil Parsons. He could see the man's intestines spilling out in a coil of bloody rope on the freshly cut grass, the look of terror in his eyes like an animal cornered in a slaughterhouse. His own guts twisted at the memory, but the fasting of recent days had left him with nothing to vomit. He put his hand against a support pipe for balance, folded the paper in his hand, and shoved it back into his pocket. He climbed the stairs, hurried out the front door, and limped down the sidewalk to his waiting car, his mind reeling, his breath accelerating. Was the Tibbets family that Sensei had butchered in Ohio even related to the pilot, the man who, in naming the bomber after his mother and in naming the bomb Little Boy, had once and forever identified himself with the murder of eighty-thousand people? There was nothing a Spirit Warrior could do to rival that act. No number of innocents slain by the sword would ever stir the needle on that black scale.

Bell pressed the button on the key fob and heard the mechanism in the door of the black Saturn sedan turnover as he approached. Maybe it had been fate that led the detective and the FBI agent to him and prevented him from leaving the crane. He could still free Lucas Carmichael.

He scanned the street, north and south. Nothing stirred. The warm air was silent, the neighbors all at work or school. Listening for sirens, he could hear the faint purr of an engine approaching; and taking cover behind a tree, looking at the crest of the hill where a mirage of liquid vapors pooled on the pavement, he saw a white car rising into view with a HERTZ frame around the license plate. It slowed to make the turn into the driveway. Bell ducked into his own car and slid down low, his head concealed by the seatback. He put the key in the ignition, but wouldn't dare start the engine until Sensei was inside the house.

Only, Sensei didn't make the turn into the driveway. Watching the car in the side mirror, Bell imagined the old master sniffing blood on the air, sensing some wrongness in the scene. The white rental car crawled forward, leaving the house and driveway behind. Without pausing to think, Bell cranked the key, revved his engine, and gunned it out into the street ahead of the other car before it could block him in.

Chapter 23

"Mr. Masahiro, it's Desmond Carmichael. Thank you for helping me again. Forgive me for being brusque, but have you seen the image yet?"

"Yes. I heard about your son on the news. Do you think this *kanji* was sent by his kidnapper?"

"I do. Please don't talk to anyone about it. It could be my only chance of finding him."

"Of course. There are two words this time. *Castle* and *Maze.*"

"*Castle* and *maze.* What's that supposed to mean?"

"I'm afraid I don't know."

"Okay. Thank you. I have to go."

"Good luck finding your son."

Desmond paced the kitchen. He wanted to run out the door, wanted to get in his car and burn rubber, wanted to punch something, anything, and break it. The restless need to move, to overcome this ignorant impotence was too much for him. He had to focus, had to think. *Castle.* He and Lucas called the playground "the castle playground," but that wasn't the name on the sign. Still, their stalker might know what they called it. Lucas might have even told him about the place. If so, that was maybe a sign that Lucas was still alive. But what was the maze? There was no maze at the playground.

"Where is there a castle and a maze?" he said to the ceiling.

And then a little miracle happened right there in the apartment kitchen, in the deepest ditch of despair. His associative mind kicked in and started flashing connections at him, the way it did when he was solving a problem in a book: *maze, maize, corn, corn maze.* And a shadowy corner of memory was illuminated. He had taken Lucas to a corn maze last year. They had almost gotten lost in it. It had been around Halloween, at that old farm with the apple orchard and the haunted house that Lucas was too young for. *Palace*. Pain Palace, or something. And wasn't *palace* another word for a *castle?* Now he did start to run. He swept up his keys from the kitchen counter and bolted for the front door but stopped short when he saw the sheathed *katana* poking out of the old milk can that held their umbrella. An officer had returned the sword to him shortly after the FBI agents had left. Now he stared at the cursed thing. He had never cut so much as a watermelon with a sword. But this was the only weapon in his possession. He would call the cops on his way to the farm, but he needed to leave now.

He wrapped his hand around the hilt. These people who had Lucas were trained, and he was an overweight desk jockey who got winded when he mowed grass. But he took the sword anyway because it was all he had, and he hoped that desperation might trump skill when it mattered most.

He was locking the door behind him with the sword nestled between his elbow and torso when he heard the slow gravel crunch of a car rolling to a stop. He looked up but didn't recognize the vehicle: a little silver Scion. Then he saw the veil of reddish-brown hair swinging around as the driver climbed out, and there, striding briskly across his lawn, her white shirtsleeves rolled up to the elbows and her gun at her hip, was Erin Drelick, taut determination in her eyes. Desmond was surprised by the slight sexual charge he felt when she stepped up close to him and her sapphire eyes pierced him. Maybe his ruminations on vengeance had sparked an infusion of testosterone.

"Hey, Joe," she said, "Where you goin' with that sword in your hand?" And Desmond could hear the next line of that modified Hendrix song: *goin a kill my old lady*. But he hadn't killed his old lady with this sword, and she knew it.

"You came back," he said.

"I changed my mind at the last minute."

"Why?"

"I think today is a significant date for the killers."

"Killers...plural?"

"The more I think about it, the more it makes sense that there are two of them. I think one got everyone he was after in Ohio, but today is important to them, and Lucas needs me here."

"Follow me," Desmond said, unlocking his car.

"Seriously, Desmond, where were you going with the sword?"

He hesitated for a couple of heartbeats, but she was quicker than that. "They sent you another message, didn't they? Was it haiku, or calligraphy?"

"Calligraphy. A clue about where Lucas is."

"Where? Where is he?"

"I won't let anyone tell me to let other people handle it. Not the cops, not you."

She looked at the sword. "We can ride together, but I can't let you bring that."

"Then you'll have to follow me, because I'm bringing it."

She sighed. "Desmond, you'll get yourself killed. Have you ever cut anything with a sword, like *ever*?"

"No, but I'm not going unarmed."

She patted the sidearm at her hip. "Consider yourself armed."

"Not good enough."

She laughed. "Read much history? The gun beat the sword a while back."

"I'm going with a weapon. You can follow or not."

She squeezed his shoulder as he tried to step past her and looked him in the eye. "There is no time for this," she said. "I have information about what's motivating these people, and there's a chance I can divide them against each other because even by their own sick logic, they've made horrible mistakes. Now you can waste precious time and risk Lucas's life by keeping me at a distance, or we can ride together and I'll fill you in so you understand what you're walking into. But you have to leave the sword behind."

Desmond looked at the wretched thing. How many people had it killed in the war before it came into his life? Now he wanted to kill the men who had taken Sandy with it. Sandy, who had used the breath in her lungs and the blood in her veins to do good, to nurture her child and support her dysfunctional husband and help perfect strangers. Those men had taken her breath and blood and spilled them out irretrievably into fathomless darkness for nothing. Desmond wanted more than anything to kill them, and if they had taken Lucas from him too, *God forbid the glimmer of that possibility,* if they had taken his son…then he wanted them to take him too, and he didn't need to be a samurai to charge into death, he just needed to make them bleed before he followed his family over the horizon.

"You're not a character in one of your books," Drelick said. "This isn't some hero's quest."

She was right. He wasn't a hero. He was a sad, middle-aged man who had squandered precious years with a family who loved him because he was off chasing windmills in his imagination, and maybe he deserved to die for that. And maybe he'd get to see Drelick pop one of the bastards before it happened. She pinched her left pants leg and pulled it up to reveal another small gun strapped to her calf. "If we're in a firefight, I'll arm you, but anything less than that I will handle myself."

Desmond trotted up the steps, opened the door again and dropped the *katana* back in the milk pail.

* * *

Shaun Bell knew how easy it would be to get lost on the back roads where a dead end could trap him. The low speed limits in this sleepy, hilly neighborhood where small farms and schools were the only things to break up the long stretches of wooded suburbia would draw attention to him if he sped through, and the last thing he needed was a series of calls to the police with descriptions of his car and partial plate numbers. With this in mind, he made his boldest maneuvers right at the outset, hoping to lose the old man and then blend in on the longer stretches of road. He raced through the first few empty residential blocks, blowing the stop signs and pushing the pedal to stretch the distance between his car and Sensei's. Then, with a cut across a baseball field, he veered onto the route that would take him east to a juncture where he would have to choose between the Palace of Pain and the highway.

He glanced at his eyes in the mirror: they were feral, electric. At least he had an American face and no sword in the car. His sword was hidden in the corn stalks, waiting. He felt sweat prickling in his armpits, and he marveled at how none of these fight-or-flight reactions had plagued him while dispatching the two cops. It was the presence of his master bearing down on him. The old man wasn't much of a driver, but he had more than enough reckless bravado to make up for it. Bell could see him now, roaring out of the baseball field, dragging a cloud of brown dust onto the pavement.

He remembered that his driver's license showed Sensei's address. He fished his wallet out of his jeans pocket, arching his back and pushing the accelerator down in a burst of speed, then tossed the entire wallet out the window into the trees. He crested a hill and, throwing caution to the wind, gunned the engine into the trough, flying forward on a surge of gravity and gasoline.

The juncture in the road was coming up at the yellow blinker a half-mile ahead, in front of the fire station. Left to the old country road that would take him over the river and out to the Jensen farm, or straight for another mile to the I-95 entrance ramp. Was there any chance that he could make it all the way into the back roads of rural Maine before the police discovered the bodies and barricaded the interstates? He punched the radio on and scanned for news channels. With a gas-station map and a little luck, he could burrow into the woods two states away, break into a vacant cabin, and wait for things to settle down while he plotted a course for the Canadian border.

The radio was finding only music and letting the controls and the noise scatter his attention wasn't worth the trouble. He spun the dial down, slowed just a little at the blinking light in case a cop with radar was hidden in the brush—slow but not slow enough for Sensei to think he might be turning—and cruised straight through the intersection, past the road to Lucas Carmichael, and on toward the highway.

His hands were shaking on the steering wheel. Sensei had been close enough to see that the boy wasn't in the car, unless bound in the trunk. Bell watched the mirror and almost ran off the road into the ferns and the litter-strewn gravel gutter when he saw Sensei slow at the blinker and turn onto 110 toward the bridge over the river, toward Heather Road, toward the maze where Lucas was bound and waiting.

He knew! Just as he knew every feint, every strike and parry when they sparred, he knew his apprentice and could anticipate Bell's moves. "Don't look at my blade," Sensei had taught him. "Look at my eyes and you will know where the blade is going." Bell gunned the gas and launched the little car forward, scanning the trees for a turnaround.

* * *

The morning humidity had gathered high in the darkening sky above the cornfield, the thick, cloying air prescient of a storm. Ash-gray tatters of cloud trailed down to touch the horizon in the north where it was already raining. When the storm rolled in it would be driven by the lash of summer lightning, but for now there was only a distant rumble of thunder like the rolling of *taiko* drums droning under the sawing of cicadas in the sun-bleached stalks. No wind stirred the corn until the two cars came roaring to the edge of the field, trailing dust and startling the crows to flight.

Shaun Bell sped past the maze entrance where his *katana* lay concealed in the cornstalks. He hit the brakes; the car slewed sideways in the dirt and almost crashed into the rickety porch where a neglected ticket-taker's podium stood wrapped in cobwebs both real and theatrical. Sensei's car screeched to a halt a few feet behind him. Within a heartbeat, the old man was out the driver's door and advancing with his sword drawn, the pale blade glowing in the diffuse evening light.

Bell stepped backwards toward the wooden arch that invited patrons to TOUR A WORLD OF TERRORS. His other sword, not as good as the one in the corn, not as sharp and maintained, was deep inside the building, in the Japan room where he'd used it for his act. He might reach that sword before Sensei cut him down. It was a slim chance but at least he would be drawing the old Spirit Warrior away from the maze. Bell took a step backward onto the creaking boards of the farmhouse porch. Sensei stepped forward slowly, matching him step for step, stalking with the trance-inducing eye lock of a predatory beast. Neither man was dressed in the traditional garb—no belts and skirts to hold scabbards. As Sensei approached, he lowered his sword to waist level, the hilt pointed at his target, the blade held at an oblique angle that made the killing edge difficult for Bell to see. It could flash out at any angle, at any second.

"We've been killing the wrong people," Bell said.

Sensei's face—etched bronze framed by a curtain of silver and black hair—was impassive yet menacing.

"Deak Parsons never had a son," Bell went on. "If he has a grandson somewhere, it's not from the man I killed on the green. All they have in common is a name."

The rotting boards groaned under Sensei's advance, and Bell, still walking backwards, put a hand behind him to feel for the doorframe. At some point soon he would have to turn and run. "And Tibbets, the one you wanted most, I looked him up too before I left the house. When he died in 2007, he had a grandson in the Navy, but no granddaughters. So those girls you killed in Ohio…. Who were they?"

"Where is the boy?" Sensei whispered.

"Just because Tibbets was living in Ohio when he died, you think everyone in the state with the same name is related to him?" Bell felt the doorframe under his fingers, and the curtain.

"The boy."

"And I took your word for it. All of it. We could have been killing anyone. Random strangers. All that bullshit about karma, about the sins of the fathers…bloodlines…."

"Give me the boy, and you can go. I will spare you."

"No."

Bell saw a glimmer of silver, as if Sensei were holding a flashlight instead of a sword hilt. He felt the muscles in his legs and torso twisting reflexively, heard the zip of the *katana's* blood groove and felt the breath of sword-wind on his left cheek, followed by a scattering of wood splinters as the blade cleaved into the doorframe. Sensei could afford such a bold move against an unarmed opponent, and while the old man worked his blade free of the rotted wood that had greedily embraced it, Bell chanced a backward glance at the door, gripped the knob in his sweaty palm, and pushed through into the dark interior of the Palace. He could lose Sensei in here, could take a route as convoluted as a path through the corn maze inside this building where he knew how to find the hidden doors, the staff passageways that ran behind and between the exhibit rooms. But he'd barely taken one step into the darkness when two sounds stopped him in his tracks: the labored whine of an underpowered car coming up the dirt road, and the high, thin cry of a child floating over the corn, calling out, *"Dadday!"*

Sensei pivoted, a swift, graceful rotation, hips following eyes following ears toward the cry of his prey. Holding his sword low, gripping the hilt with both hands, the blade trailing behind him, the old Spirit Warrior ran across the road and vanished into the corn just fractions of a second before Desmond Carmichael's SUV bounded into the space he had just occupied.

* * *

Desmond saw a black-clad figure cut in front of the car. There was too much dust on the windshield for him to make out more than a silhouette, but it was the size of a man and moving fast. By the time he hit the brakes, it had already disappeared into the corn, and his first thought was that he should have accelerated and hit the fucker. Drelick was drawing her gun while jumping out of the lurching car as it rebounded from the sudden stop. Desmond felt his heart thud in his chest, mimicking the car, startled by the impact of a second dark figure sliding across the hood. This one knocked Drelick sideways. She slipped and fell to the ground but kept her hands locked on the grip of her weapon, which she trained on the second man, now following the first into the maze.

"FBI! Stop or I'll shoot!" she bellowed. But he didn't stop, and from a half-kneeling position in a mud puddle beside the car, she fired two shots. They crackled across the sky, but only tickled the corn stalks.

Desmond got out of the car and ran to help her up, but she was already on her feet when he got there. She held up a raised palm and pushed the air with it, signaling him to stay back, and then sprinted down the aisle of corn. Desmond had only caught a glimpse of the first man, but was pretty sure he'd seen a sword in his hands. The second man appeared to be empty-handed. The pair had been running from the building and into the maze before the car arrived. Desmond took a few steps in the direction of the porch with its wooden demon masks, threatening signs, and peeling paint. If the men were leaving Lucas behind in there, could he possibly still be alive? It was like walking through water. Desmond didn't know if he had the strength to step inside and search among the fake horrors for a real one. Then he heard the siren of Lucas's voice, a sound he would recognize even among a chorus of children all calling out the same word, a word that gave him back the only identity he wanted in the world: *Daddy.*

Desmond ran into the maze, his sneakers slipping on fallen husks. He could hear the mechanical beating of angel wings off in the distance—a helicopter coming in response to Drelick's call. He trotted behind her, watching her move with both hands on the gun, holding it low, aimed at the ground but coiled and ready to spring up. He guessed she had good form, prayed she was good enough to save Lucas. There was a slight stagger in her step, as if she were favoring one foot. He would have felt better if her partner were with them, or if she'd let him carry her ankle piece. He felt helpless, merely a witness, and he touched the silver fountain pen in the front pocket of his jeans; a talisman, a piece of Sandy that he had tucked in before leaving the house with some inarticulate notion that it would bring him luck and strength. The pointed tip slid under his thumbnail and sent a flare of pain through his hand. Maybe he deserved something worse for being here as an impotent bystander at what might be their son's murder. The shot of pain roused him from his creeping fugue and grounded him in the moment.

He could hear a clanging of steel on steel now. Lucas's crying went silent. Had he realized that yelling would only help the bad men to find him? But weren't they the ones who put him in the maze in the first place? It didn't make sense, and neither did the sound of sword on sword, but he was pretty sure that was what he was hearing.

He jogged along behind Drelick, huffing to keep up. She stopped at the end of a row and flattened her body against the corn, somehow slimming her profile without rustling the stalks. She glared at him, but he refused to stay back more than a few paces. The noise of the duel around the bend was unsettling. There were long moments of charged silence, followed by rapid flurries, clangs, and grunts. He could see Drelick's chest rising and falling in a slow, deep rhythm. She seemed to be gearing up for action, preparing herself for it while the swordsmen were engaged with each other. When she looked at Desmond again, her eyes were wide and somehow brighter, kindled with the fierce energy of being alive in a moment when death was circling the perimeter of the campfire, looking for an in.

Sotto voce, she said, "You stay put. I don't need another victim."

Desmond shook his head.

"You need to let me do my job and save your son. I can't be worrying about you."

"He's my responsibility, and I'm coming."

She looked away from him and took one last deep breath, her breasts pushing her stiff white cotton shirt at the lapels of her black blazer. Rain began pattering on the pale green husks, blooming in dark gray spots. Drelick rounded the corner, bringing her gun up level with her eyes as she moved beyond Desmond's line of sight. He slipped into the position she had just occupied and peered around the end of the row. He couldn't see Lucas, and for a second he thought he might pass out as his body floated on a swelling wave of relief, the tension he had been holding onto so tightly now momentarily unwinding.

He saw the fighters—one, a young American man with long dirty-blonde hair in a ponytail, the other a short, sturdy, Japanese man with silvered black hair and bronzed skin, his eye sockets deeply wrinkled at the corners but his body exuding the limber vitality of a much younger man, as if his old face were only a mask. Their swords were locked together in a block, low down near the hilts. Their faces were close, like lovers reading the prospect of a kiss in each other's eyes, when the old man somehow swiveled his sword around, breaking the lock and thrusting the butt of his hilt into the young man's face, breaking his nose with a crunch that Desmond could hear from all the way at the end of the row.

Drelick took the opportunity to close in, but the motion of her approach caught the old man's eye, and he brought his blade around with a twirl as he spun to face her. The gun was clearly trained on him, and it prevented him from finishing his opponent. The younger man— his lips, chin, and shirt drenched with blood from his nose—darted through an opening in the corn row while the old warrior turned to face the oncoming threat. It looked like a point-blank shot when Drelick finally took it after a wildly unnerving pause in which Desmond felt simultaneously terrified that she was taking too long to aim, and impressed by the cool control she was exercising. The shot boomed out, crackling across the sky. It seemed incredible that such a loud sound could come from such a small gun. The sword flashed out in a silver streak from the old man's left hip to his right shoulder, faster than a shooting star, but with a white spark and a sound like the ringing of a bell at the center point of the arc. Drelick uttered a weak, frightened sound that could have been a laugh, but sounded more like a trembling sigh of awe. Her reaction cost her the chance to fire a second round before the samurai could recover his balance. He saw it in her face and disappeared through the opening in the corn.

Desmond's legs felt numb, anchored to the ground. Had he really just seen a man whose eyesight should be failing cut a bullet in half in midflight?

Lucas's shrill voice rose from the center of the maze again, calling for him. Desmond wobbled on his heels a couple of times, overrode the inertia of his terrified body by sheer force of will, and followed Drelick deeper in.

Around the next bend they came to three openings. The rain was picking up, turning into a thin gray curtain, hissing in the stalks. On the ground, brown puddles danced with droplets. Drelick was running along a dead-end aisle, listening to the corn, trying to rule out the leftmost of the three paths. She didn't give it much time, and Desmond didn't know if she had a reason to choose the middle path or if it was just a coin toss she made in her head to save time, but that was the one she ran into without so much as a glimmer of eye contact toward him.

Desmond scanned the mud at the threshold of the right-hand path and, finding no footprints, followed Drelick.

He caught up with her before the next set of openings. She was stepping through a roughly reaped gap in the corn, making crunching sounds as she stepped on the freshly felled stalks. There was nothing stealthy about following this trail chopped by one of the swordsmen. It looked to Desmond like whoever had blazed it was desperate for the quickest, most direct exit possible. Then he saw the drops of blood on the fallen husks and his heartbeat doubled in his chest at the thought of Lucas before he recalled that the younger man had been dripping blood from his nose after the hilt strike. But his heart didn't have a second to settle back into its regular terrified register before he heard Lucas shrieking, "*No!* Lemme *go!* Let goame.... *Daddy! Help!*"

Desmond knocked Drelick aside and charged through the curtain of rain and broken stalks, the razor edges of husks swatting and slicing at his face and fingers as he stumbled and fumbled and raked his hands through them.

Then he could see Lucas's face above a collar of twisted duct tape that had left a sticky gray film on his lips, wet hair clinging like strands of kelp to his forehead, the water on his face a mixture of rain and tears. His small body was draped over the left shoulder of the man carrying him; the younger man, it had to be. A rag tied around the man's right leg dripped blood as he staggered on, limping under the weight of his hostage and swinging the sword in long strokes to clear the way ahead. Lucas's eyes found Desmond and widened, his face suddenly infused with a desperate feral energy. He kicked, flailed, and cried, "Daddy!"

The swordsman heard the change in the boy's voice and rotated toward Desmond, swinging Lucas to face behind him. The rain had thinned the blood on the man's face, but there was enough of it smeared across his mouth to make him appear grotesque when he smiled at Desmond. There was something strange and unexpected in that smile, something genuine that seemed to say, *So you made it.* He stood there smiling, the sword in one hand, rain sparking off the blade, and the boy in the other, with no direction open to him.

"Put him down," Drelick said.

The young man's eyes had a faraway cast when he spoke. "You can't save him."

Desmond felt Drelick's bullet whiz past his face. It opened a blossom of blood in the middle of the man's chest, and brought him down.

Lucas was running toward Desmond now, shrieking in the aftermath of the deafening shot, but Desmond turned his head to look in the direction the bullet had come from. Drelick was in a shooting stance, legs shoulder-width apart, her Glock gripped in both hands. Beyond her, the old man swept into view, raised the sword above her shoulder, above his head, and when it reached the apex, brought it down in a fluid stroke like water gliding over a stone shelf, sluicing through her long hair and cleaving into her body at the juncture of shoulder and neck. Blood sprayed Desmond's cheek before he could scream.

Drelick fell forward, squeezing off another shot reflexively as her fingers curled inward. The bullet missed Lucas, burrowing in beside the first round in the young man's kneeling body. Then she was face down in the cloddy mud, the old man's foot already in the small of her back, giving him the leverage to yank his embedded blade from between her shoulders. There was a sickening sound of suction as it came free. The samurai stepped over the body, bent down, and twisted the gun from her clawed hand, then cast it high over the corn.

Lucas crashed into the back of Desmond's knees as he had so many times in the days when life seemed long and sweet, days when getting bowled over by a hyper toddler had tested his patience. Now the collision felt like a bittersweet gift from heaven because he knew that they would be going there together soon. They were in a dead end, surrounded by corn that the younger swordsman had failed to cut through to an adjacent path. All that mattered to Desmond now was that death came quick and that he not be spared, God help him. He wanted to go first. It was selfish and wrong, he knew, but he wanted the old man to take him first so he didn't have to live with a dead son for even a minute.

But the old man rushed right past him and bent beside the fallen young man whose breath was coming in lurching, ragged gulps. The old samurai knelt and laid his sword down on the ground beside him in a way that seemed ceremonial. Then, laying his left hand on the ground first, followed by his right he bowed low to the young man, touching his forehead to the ground. "My son," he said.

The samurai would take up his sword again in a moment to finish them, but for now Desmond and Lucas were insignificant. Both swords were within the old man's reach in the wreckage of fallen stalks, and although the helicopter was getting closer now, the sound of its beating blades inspired no urgency in him. He would strike when he was ready; he would pay his respects and not be rushed. The child and his father posed no threat.

Desmond held his hand over Lucas's mouth lightly, but firmly enough to communicate the message: *Don't make a sound, don't wake the dragon.* He put his mouth to Lucas's ear, felt the fine hair brushing against his nose and lips, and whispered, "Close your eyes, Lucas. Just close your eyes and keep them closed." He kissed his son's temple.

Lucas turned and stared at him, eyes wide and white. Then he shut them, squeezing tears from the corners.

Desmond looked down at Drelick's body. Her hair was turning darker in the rain, her blood thinning in the water. Her ankle holster was still concealed by her black rayon slacks, but there was no way to reach it through the narrow channel of corn without crawling over the body and even then, no fast way, no silent way. She was close to him, but the old man was even closer.

And which leg had he seen it on?

He thought it had been on the left, but he wasn't sure. He stretched across her body, her blood soaking through his shirt, and clawed at the black fabric of her pants but couldn't expose her calf.

Greg Harwood's hollow voice echoed in Desmond's mind. He could see the haggard patsy in his prison smock, clutching the phone receiver, mumbling something about *"Reapers…. Death angels in black skirts. Two of them."* These two men had approached Harwood with the bloody sword that night, the night Sandy was murdered. And the younger one, the one dying in the corn, the one Desmond was already thinking of as The Apprentice, was wearing an indigo hoodie. This was the one who had tried to warn him of what was coming: The Dragon, The Master, the one who had cut Sandy down in the dark, just as he had cut Erin Drelick down right before Desmond's eyes.

A hot spark of vengeance flared like a magnesium torch in Desmond's solar plexus. He came up on his knees and slid his hand into his pocket, withdrew the fountain pen with rain-slicked fingers, and folded it tight in his palm. He cocked his arm back, got his feet under him and lunged forward, bringing his fist down like a hammer, plunging the silver nib into the side of the old man's neck at an angle to avoid the spinal vertebrae and increase his chances of hitting the carotid artery. The pen speared through flesh with shockingly little resistance, and he felt his fist connect with the man's neck in a flash, the force of the blow knocking the aged body sideways.

Desmond leaned forward and whispered, "Mightier than the sword, motherfucker."

At first there was no blood: the barrel of the fountain pen plugged the hole. The samurai lurched forward and let out a guttural howl that morphed into a cry of rage. Tendons sprang into taut ropes along the man's neck as his right hand shot out and seized the sword hilt.

Desmond pivoted on one knee, swept Lucas up in his arms, and tossed the boy over Drelick's body, sending him crashing into the corn. Lucas shrieked in midair, landed roughly, and rolled. Desmond yelled, "Run, Lucas! *Run!*"

Lucas looked back in horror, must have seen the old man staggering forward with the pen poking out of his neck, but Desmond guessed it was the hideous sounds the man was making more than the sight of him that spurred Lucas to flee.

Desmond staggered backward over Drelick's body. He almost tripped but then used the momentum of what could have become a sideways tumble to launch himself into the wider path that the younger swordsman had been trying to cut his way out of. The old man's eyes were losing vitality, losing even the bright spark of rage, and his breath now made a labored whistling like a cheap wooden flute. He looked as if he wanted to say something to Desmond before cutting him down but could no longer make his voice work.

The samurai raised the blade. Desmond's trembling hands had found the holster on Drelick's left calf, and he scrambled to work the gun free. Too slow. It was snapped in. His fingers, dumb and numb, cold and clumsy, were going to cost him his life, cost Lucas another parent after all.

Then a mechanical beating sound that had previously been absorbed and attenuated by the corn suddenly rose to deafening volume, and the angle of the falling rain shifted. The stalks were blown flat, and Desmond hit the ground with them. The helicopter thundered overhead, bullets whistling along the trajectory of the raindrops. It was gone as fast as it had come, and the old samurai fell back into the corn stalks beside his apprentice, his sword still clenched in his dying hand.

Desmond turned and ran, screaming Lucas's name over the wind and the rain and the receding roar of the chopper, now circling to land.

NINE YEARS LATER

Epilogue

Lucas wakes to the smell of bacon and eggs. It prompts him to roll out of bed a little earlier than he otherwise would. At thirteen, he isn't an early riser, and a brisk jog to the bus is a regular part of his day, but today is his birthday, and the smell of his father's cooking arouses anticipation in his belly that affects him like caffeine. Maybe Kirsten will remember his birthday, too, and shoot him a card on his phone. He wonders if she'll sign it with the L-word.

Twenty minutes later he is showered, dressed, and lumbering down the stairs in his sneakers, jeans, and t-shirt; the device on his hip is already hitting the third song on his playlist. He takes the hardwood stairs two at a time, past his Mom's framed photos on the mustard-colored walls that always look more yellow in the morning when the light floods in through the high cathedral windows. When he reaches the landing, he glances through the sliding glass doors out of habit. The deck chair where his father usually spends his mornings this time of year, banging out the daily word quota on his laptop, is vacant today.

In the kitchen he finds his old man in chef mode, complete with ridiculous apron. Lucas taps the pause button, pulls the headphones down around his neck and leans on the marble-topped island where cracked eggshells lay scattered on a folded paper towel. In the dining room, a cluster of blue and white helium balloons strain toward the ceiling on strings tied to the back of a chair.

"Smells good," Lucas says.

His dad lifts a pot lid from a steaming plate of eggs and bacon and passes it to him. "Toast already popped, but you might want to warm it up."

"Thanks," Lucas says, taking his plate to the table and sitting down beside a rectangular package, clumsily wrapped in colorful paper. Whatever it is, it looks too big to be the video game he asked for. He shakes some salt onto his eggs and begins shoveling them in, eyeing the package with disappointment and deciding it must be a shirt.

"No mad dash for the bus today?" his dad asks, sitting across from him with his own plate. "I figured I'd drive you to school, anyway. Give you time to eat a proper breakfast for a change."

"My nose woke up before the rest of me. This's good," he says around a mouthful of scrambled eggs.

His dad smiles in that goofy way of his, like he always does when watching Lucas enjoy something. "You can open your present, you know. You don't have to wait."

Lucas takes another bite, then sets the fork down, picks up the box, and gives it a slow shake. It is heavier than he expected. He tears the paper off and opens the box to find a hardcover book nestled in a bed of tissue paper. Gold letters stamped on the spine read:

ORPHEUS

DESMOND CARMICHAEL

"Wow, one of your books. You pull it off the shelf this morning and wrap it before I woke up?"

"Have you ever seen this one on our shelves?"

Lucas turns it over and looks at the spine again. He shrugs his shoulders.

"Don't worry, I have something else for you later, when we have cake with Nana."

"If you want me to read one of your books, you can send it to my handheld, you know. Easier to carry around."

"This one was never published. And it's not a fantasy, like the others."

"No? Isn't the name from one of the myths?"

"That's right. Who was Orpheus?"

"Um…a musician who visited Hades to rescue his dead wife?" Lucas hears the lightness evaporating from his voice as the sense of this recited trivia sinks in.

Desmond nods. "This book is sort of a memoir, and it's about your mother."

Lucas lays the book down on top of the shredded paper in a way that reminds him of his dad placing a dead bird in a shoebox last summer after it hit one of the tall windows. Now there are butterfly stickers on those windows.

"The year after she died, around the time when the bad men came back, I was writing a book with that title, and it *was* a fantasy—a hero's quest with a dragon and a maiden and everything. A real piece of crap, but I was trying to write her into it, trying to save her in my imagination because I couldn't save her in real life." He sighs and takes off his glasses. Lucas has noticed that sometimes his dad takes them off not to see something nearby better but to remove a layer of separation between his eyes and those of the person he's talking to.

"She took a lot of photos, you know," he says with a vague wave of his hand at the walls around them. "And you can think of this book as my photos of *her*, and of us, from a time you were too young to remember." Desmond looks down at the glossy tabletop, picks up a napkin and wipes a teardrop from the surface. After a deep breath, his voice grows stronger. "I've waited until now to share it with you because it's honest. It shows my faults and hers. Which isn't to say that it's not biased—of course it is, in the way that anyone's memory would be. But if there are places where it *seems* like fantasy, remember that it's not. That's just love, as best I can recall and describe it. As true as I can tell it."

"Thanks, Dad."

Desmond rolls the napkin into a ball in his fist, and nods. "Happy birthday, son," he says. He smiles his weary smile, and gazes beyond the butterfly stickers at the sky.

Acknowledgements

First and foremost I'd like to thank my wife Jen for supporting my writing in countless ways. She was the first reader of this book, and her enthusiasm for it gave me the confidence to see it through. Considering what I did to her fictional counterpart, I think that's true love. Thanks also to my crack team of beta readers for improving the story with insightful critiques: Jeff Aach, Chuck Killorin, Jeff Miller, Jill Sweeney-Bosa, and again, Jen Salt. You guys rock.

Brian and Cathy Cuffe, Esq. were very helpful in answering my questions about the legal details of guardianship cases in Massachusetts. Any errors or liberties in that area fall squarely on me. I'm also indebted to Howard and Diana Salt for being the kind of in-laws who make life better in every way. *Domo arigato* to Sensei Alex Markauskas, Sensei John Dore, and Jamey Proctor. Anything I got right about *Iaido* is thanks to them, and any misrepresentations are my own. Thanks to Christopher C. Payne, Dr. Michael R. Collings, and everyone at JournalStone for working hard to make good books, and to Jeff Miller for another amazing cover.

Credit where it's due goes to a couple of non-fiction books that were instrumental in my research: *Farewell to Manzanar* by Jeanne Wakatsuki and James D. Houston, and *Flyboys* by James Bradley. The former breathes life into a chapter of American history that we are in danger of forgetting, and the latter depicts the horrors of the war in the Pacific with a depth and complexity that my novel can only hint at.

Douglas Wynne is the author of the rock n roll horror novel *The Devil of Echo Lake*, which was a first place winner of JournalStone's 2012 Horror Fiction contest.

He lives in Massachusetts with his wife and son and spends most of his time hanging out with a pack of dogs when he isn't writing, playing guitar, or swinging a sword. You can follow him on Facebook and Twitter and at www.dougwynne.com

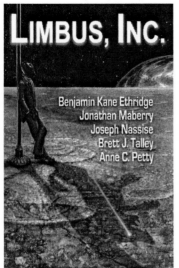

LIMBUS, INC.

Benjamin Kane Ethridge
Jonathan Maberry
Joseph Nassise
Brett J. Talley
Anne C. Petty

Publishers Weekly -
"This shared-world anthology about a mysterious metaphysical employment agency is pleasingly consistent in tone. The execution and intriguing theme leave

Are you laid off, downsized, undersized? Call us. We employ. 1-800-555-0606 *How lucky do you feel?*

So reads the business card from Limbus, Inc., a shadowy employment agency that operates at the edge of the normal world. Limbus's employees are just as suspicious and ephemeral as the motives of the company, if indeed it could be called a company in the ordinary sense of the word.

In this shared-world anthology, five heavy hitters from the dark worlds of horror, fantasy, and scifi pool their warped takes on the shadow organization that offers employment of the most unusual kind to those on the fringes of society. One thing's for sure—you'll never think the same way again about the fine print on your next employment application!

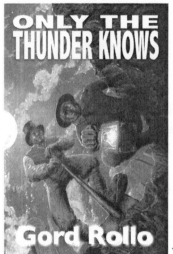

Rena Mason proves she is a rising new voice in horror." —**JG Faherty**, author of *The Burning Time, Cemetery Club, Carnival of Fear,* and the Bram Stoker Award® nominated *Ghosts of Coronado Bay.*

William (Billy) Burke and William Hare were two real-life, beer-swilling, fist-fighting lowlifes who managed to stumble their way into infamy in Edinburgh, Scotland in the late 1820s. Step by step, they graduated from the unemployment line to petty thievery, to grave robbing, and then on to cold bloody murder – ultimately becoming Britain's first documented serial killers.

What history doesn't know about, or consider, is the possibility that Burke and Hare may not have been acting on their own; and the blame for those heinous crimes might not entirely be theirs. Two mysterious strangers have arrived in the city–an old sculptor and a stunningly beautiful actress–both of which use their money and influence to manipulate the young Irishmen into searching for an ancient artifact rumored to have the awesome power of Heaven and Hell combined.

Seized by the vicious killings of Jack the Ripper, Victorian London's, East End is on the brink of ruin. Elizabeth Covington, desperate and failing to follow in her beloved father's footsteps, risks practicing medicine in the dangerous and neglected Whitechapel District to improve her studies. News of a second brutal murder spreads. Elizabeth crosses paths with a man she believes is the villain, triggering a personal downward spiral taking her to a depth of evil she never knew existed. Only she knows the truth that drives the madness of a murderer.

CPSIA information can be obtained at www.ICGtesting.com
Printed in the USA
LVOW131535080713

341885LV00006B/709/P